HERE'S TO ADVENTURES

She saw their plan. They hoped to circle around and duck behind the kegs again as the two barkeeps came back out.

Faia was going to be right in the line of sight of those self-same barkeeps—and unlike the kids, those two would be looking for someone, and so would probably catch her as she hid. She tried frantically to think of some diversion—

And then one of the kids stepped hard on one of the boards she'd loosened in her escape from the basement. One end of it flew up, then the board fell back into place with a slam. The sound seemed as loud as an explosion. One barkeep came flying around the edge of the kegs in front of her, but looking toward the noise, while the other doubled back and charged straight into them. The girl shrieked, "He tricked me!" The boy yelled, "I never!"

And the innkeep thundered into the kegroom and roared, "Where in the sixteen blue hells of Fargorn is my bedamned beer?!" before he saw what his barkeeps had caught—his naked daughter and her equally naked swain.

The innkeep bellowed. Both kids howled.

Faia muttered, "Seize the moment," and slipped through the door, through the line of drunks that began trickling back to find out what all the excitement was about, and out into the cool, smoke-filled air.

She found herself on a narrow, dark, nearly empty street—barefoot, without her pack or her weapons, lost, broke, weary, hurting and hungry . . . though she did still have the other potato and the rest of the bottle of wine. She sighed, looked up the road, looked down the road, and saw nothing she recognized in either direction.

"Well, then." She lifted the wine to the sky. "Here's to adventures—may they happen only to other people from this day forward." She swigged the d_____lt, and started off in a direc_____n the second raw potato.

As she passed an alley

10666784

MIND OF THE MAGIC

HOLLY LISLE

MIND OF THE MAGIC

A Baen Books Original

Baen Publishing Enterprises
P.O. Box 1403
Riverdale, NY 10471

ISBN: 0-671-87654-6

Cover art by Clyde Caldwell

First printing, May 1995

Distributed by Simon & Schuster
1230 Avenue of the Americas
New York, NY 10020

Printed in the United States of America

Dedication

This book is dedicated to Dave and Becky,
who had the courage to tell.

And to Becky Kimbrell and all the employees
of the Scotland County DSS, and Det. Mike
Kimbrell and all the officers of the Laurinburg
Police Department—with my thanks for your
compassion, your dedication, and your
integrity. You set a standard for public service
few equal and none exceed.

And to my colleagues and friends in SFWA and
on GEnie, who have pulled us through our
darkest night—with all my love and gratitude.
Because of you, we persevere: strength through
adversity (with a lot of help from our friends).

And to Chris, who is my love and my sanity.

Acknowledgments

Special thanks:

To Michael Calligaro, Geo Rule, and Ron Jarrell, for willingly suffering the slings and arrows of outrageous fortune

And to Jim Baen and Toni Weisskopf, for comments gently offered which made the book better

And to Russell Galen, and Jim and Toni again, for having faith that I would finish this book in spite of everything

Author's note: I had intended to dedicate this book to my cat Fafhrd, who died half an hour after the first draft of it was written. Fafhrd was a wonderful cat and is a sorely missed friend and companion . . . and someday I hope he will get a book of his own.

SOUTHEAST TRILLING

WEN TRIBES
1 Allwater   4 Blackstone
2 Pennifish   5 Firemountain
3 Smoke

ARHEL

DELMUIRIE'S BARRIER

PENNAR CHAIN

AMOTIC ISLE

BÓSÉLEIGH BAY

Wennish Jungles

SAG SEA

PENNAR

PUNDAK OCEAN

CUMBLEY SEA

2

Klaue Ruins

3

Wen Tribes Line

5

3

4

Omwimmee Trade

Treaty

Bonton

Hak

Forest Province

Dumforst

Little Tam

Big Tam

Cunnit

Cumbley Bay

ARISS

Maisee Cliffs

FEY PLATEAU

Bright

Willowlake

BOOR MTS.

Otwoch

Swom

Fey Province

Sainte

Belldote

Bonwite

Fisher Province

Branch River

Punce

Caille

Chak Pass

Chak River

KÉLE SEA

Braxtile

Fey

Chak

Huong

Hoós Domain

LITTLE SOUTH SEA

Stone Teeth

DELMUIRIE'S BARRIER

Chapter 1

The old sign on the massive, carved wooden gate read:

Qualified, Certified-Safe Magics—
Guarding, ~~Transporting~~ and Livestock Our Specialties
~~Also Historical Research~~
~~We Buy Books!~~
Private and Group Lessons Watterdaes
NO LOVE SPELLS!!!

Faia Rissedote finished nailing up the new sign beneath it.

Rede-Flute Lessons Fueredaes and Wuendaes
Hiller-Crafted Weaving, Inquire Within
Herbals and Healing Extracts
Reasonable Rates

She might as well have put up a sign that said, "Give me something to keep me busy . . . please." She made a face and stepped back from her handiwork to get a better look at it—and saw Matron Magdar Netweaver strolling up the walkway from the marketplace, her acquisitions floating in front of her. Magdar nodded politely. "Pleasant daymeet, Faia."

"And to you, Magdar."

Faia's neighbor stopped to study the sign. Faia watched

1

one eyebrow slide upward. "Rede-flute lessons and *weaving*?"

Faia nodded.

"I suppose the new magic is cutting into your other business, eh?"

"You could say that."

Magdar gave her a purse-lipped little smile. "Thought I did." She smiled again, and said, "You really ought to see the new tower Gammitch Leech is for magicking up— over to the corner of Warren and Fancy, it is. Thin as a needle and tall as the heavens, eyah—sparkles in the daylight like a big block of southern ice. He plans to go hunting another missus soon as he finishes it. Reckon he'll be for stopping at your doorstep, same as the rest, eyah?"

Faia ignored the last remark. She looked southwest and discovered that she *could* see Gammitch's magic-built tower rising over Omwimmee Trade—a thin green line that stretched skyward like a thread stiffened and stood on end. "Doesn't look very stable," she offered at last.

"Don't reckon it needs to be, do you? Plenty of magic to go round nowadays—not just for you big-city magickers like it used to be."

Faia didn't argue with her neighbor, although she disagreed vehemently with what Magdar had said. She'd been the most vocal naysayer in the town meetings that followed the sudden, inexplicable rise in the accessibility of magic four months ago, and no one in town had forgotten that fact. Or forgiven, either. Her neighbors figured that she was jealous of their sudden good luck, or worse, that she was trying to take advantage of them by preventing them from using the mysterious magical power they suddenly all had.

That wasn't the case at all, of course. Faia knew what power without knowledge could do—she had argued from the standpoint of a woman who had once accidentally melted a town; they argued from the standpoints of people who not only had not melted any towns, but who had never seen it done either, and who figured it could not have been as bad as it sounded. They were determined that they were going to do things magically, whether they knew what they were doing or not—and when that fact became apparent, Faia shut up. She had the chore of putting back together two of the three idiot-wizards who blew themselves up, and she had given the widow of the third a nice jar for his ashes. Meanwhile, she kept her opinions to herself.

"Speaking of men looking for a missus," Magdar said, interrupting Faia's gloomy ruminations, "I heard you turned away Geltie's son Ludd when he came asking for you to wed him."

Faia sighed. She'd *known* that story would get around. "You heard true."

Magdar shook her head and put her hands on her hips. "So what's that now? . . . Ludd, and Wicker's boy Nait, and the other butcher's youngest . . . I can't rightly recall his name. . . ."

"Stord." Faia supplied the name. Magdar would have remembered it sooner or later anyway.

Magdar snapped her fingers. "Stord. Exactly." The older woman frowned. "A girl like you shouldn't be so picky. They won't keep coming forever, you know. Once you lose your looks, there's not a one of them will give you good daymeet."

"That's hardly a recommendation to marry them now," Faia murmured dryly.

Magdar seemed not to have heard her. "You having that child and all, you're lucky there's any who come courting anyway. When I was young, the men of Omwimmee Trade would never have looked twice at a girl who'd been . . ." Magdar glanced up and down the street and her voice dropped to a loud whisper. ". . . *with* men." Her neighbor nodded at Faia's five-year-old daughter, Kirtha, who was at that moment sprawled on her stomach on the raised walkway, studying the bugs that crawled along the cracks. "The proof that you have done *that* is sitting over there for all to see. She's hardly something that you can flaunt— bit of an embarrassment to your character, truth be known. You really ought to get another man while one is still willing to look at you, eyah."

Faia looked at Kirtha, who was kicking her feet in the air, and giving every impression of being engrossed by the insect world below her—but Faia would have bet her house her daughter hadn't missed a word. "She's no embarrassment to me."

Magdar sniffed. "No. You wouldn't be ashamed of yourself. But then, you're outlander, and citified, too. Not a one of us in Omwimmee Trade doesn't know about city morals—you could find more morals in a tomcat than a city girl." She shook her head and gave Faia a pitying smile, as if what she'd said was not an insult, but simply a fact of life. Faia was used to both the assumptions and the expression. "By anysuch, you'd get invited to events if you were respectably married, you know. Everyone wants to be polite, but, Faia . . . the town has to have some standards."

They were stupid standards, Faia thought, but they were standards . . . and the town had them. By the bucketload.

She sighed and imagined marrying dull Ludd, who had never been beyond Omwimmee Trade and had no desire to see anyplace else, who had spent his whole life cleaning and gutting and drying fish, and who had no other interests. She couldn't imagine marrying him just so she could get invited to the exciting social events of Omwimmee Trade. The weaving-gathers, the house-raisings, the sitting-ins for births and deaths—and for all of that, she would only have to put up for the rest of her life—or his—with the sullen company of a man who talked almost not at all, and who, when he did deign to speak, spoke of fish.

"When I find someone I want to take public bond with, I will," Faia said. "But I have never been in love, and I won't choose a bondmate until I am."

Magdar shrugged. "I wouldn't waste love on a husband, girl. I couldn't stand either of mine—the one I have now is a loathsome toad. Husbands are to give you a place in society. If you want love, that's what backlight lads are for. Get married, get some respectability, and you can have all the love you want then, can't you?"

Faia bit her lip and nodded, not saying a word. The town had its standards, all right.

Magdar looked at the sign again. "Rede-flute, eh? Maybe my youngest three would be interested in lessons. Would get them off my hearth for a bit, any case." She snorted. "Eyah. You think about what I said." Then she sauntered away, her groceries once again floating in front of her. Magdar was nearly to her own front door when Faia realized the back of her neighbor's long, full skirt was smoking. Faia stared down at her daughter, who was glaring after the departing busybody; she looked back up just in time to see the first flames lick along the hem of the fabric.

"Kirtha!" Faia sent a fire-smothering spell racing after Magdar. The neighbor's skirt sizzled and the flames died. Magdar appeared not to have noticed at all. But if she hadn't yet, she would soon, and would come back with another lecture—the one about children who didn't feel the switch often enough. Faia picked up her daughter and dragged her into the house, "Kirtha, you can't *do* things like that!"

"I don't like her, Mama." Kirtha looked unrepentant.

Faia understood exactly how her daughter felt. She wasn't fond of Magdar Netweaver either. That didn't change anything. "The Lady's Gift of magic is something you never misuse, Kirtha. You never make a spell in anger, or out of greed, or for frivolous or wasteful reasons."

"Hmp!" Kirtha was unimpressed.

Faia put her down in the walled courtyard to play. "We are going to discuss this again later—but I want you to think about what you did. If I hadn't seen Matron's skirt catch fire, she could have been hurt. That would have been very bad, Kirtha. Very, very bad."

Bad to a five-year-old was a meaningless term, and Faia knew it. And teaching a five-year-old with too much power and not enough self-control the ethics of magic was nearly impossible. But *I'll manage,* Faia promised herself. *Somehow, I'll make her understand.*

Just then, a castle sailed into view over the west roof of the house, chasing clouds eastward; gaudy pennants flew from its graceful whitestone turrets, and its roofs flashed silver in the sunlight. The sound of music and laughter drifted down to Faia and Kirtha. Faia stared upward while the castle floated overhead, and listened to the happy sounds that came from it.

The world was full of the insane, she thought. Those people in the castle were proof of it. True, magic in inconceivable amounts had recently become available to almost everyone in Arhel. And true, there now seemed to be almost no limits to what some people could do magically. But a sudden unexplained jump in the availability of strong ley lines seemed to her to be a reason for caution, *not* for building castles in the air, of all things.

A fair-haired woman leaned over the parapet and fluttered a gaudy silk flag in greeting. Faia gave her only polite acknowledgment, the sort of greeting that seemed appropriate for an insane stranger one couldn't simply ignore. Kirtha, however, waved her arms wildly and shouted, "Bye, castle," until it drifted over the east roof and vanished from sight.

When it was gone, Kirtha quit waving, and her back stiffened.

Now it comes, Faia thought.

Kirtha turned to face her, with brows furrowed and lower lip stuck out. "I want a flyin' castle," she demanded, her voice pitched shrill and loud.

Insanity was to be the order of the day, then, Faia reflected. She missed the world of four months ago, when life and its occurrences still made some sense. She told her daughter, "No," keeping her voice calm and reasonable.

Kirtha tossed her red hair and stamped her foot. "I *want* a flyin' *castle!*"

Faia rubbed her fingertips against her forehead. They'd had this argument several times a day since the first such castle had appeared, perhaps two months earlier—and Kirtha never, ever listened to reason. "Those castles are dangerous," she said at last. "And no matter how much you want one, you cannot have one!"

"You're mean! You could make me one, but you're jus' mean! I want to fly in the sky an' live on a cloud. An' *you* won't let me!" Kirtha closed her eyes and held her breath, and her pale, freckled face turned as red as her hair. She pulled in threads of magic from the earth and air and in an instant built thunderclouds that appeared suddenly, filling the tiny patch of sky just above the garden; the clouds crackled with energy and rumbled as they bumped against each other. Little bolts of lightning shot from cloud to cloud.

"That's enough!" Faia banished the clouds before the lightning could catch the thatching of the roof on fire. Lady give me strength, she thought.

A sudden incredible clamor came from the front of the house. "Stay right there," she told her daughter. Faia frowned and started toward the gate. Whoever stood out there was not politely knocking, but slamming the metal knocker down onto the plate over and over again. The booming reverberated in the breezeway and filled the garden—she was suddenly certain it was Magdar, back to complain about the damage to her skirt. She took a deep breath and got ready to make her apologies. She lifted the heavy bar and flung open the inner door in the gate. No one at all stood there, however, and quick glances in both directions proved the entire street to be empty.

Children, she thought—though Kirtha's little friends were usually polite and well behaved when they came over to play, and most of them couldn't even reach the knocker. They were so invariably good, Faia suspected, because their parents had warned them about her . . . Omwimmee Trade's own outlander magic lady, who would turn them into wingless hovies if they were naughty. Perhaps some new child had moved into the neighborhood.

Faia sighed. Whoever the prankster had been, he was gone. She began to pull the door shut, but as she did, a faint breeze stirred something on the ground, something someone had shoved up against the sheltered overhang of her gate. She stopped and looked over the mess. Why, she wondered, would anyone dump their old rags by my gate, then make such a racket to get me out here to find them? Puzzled, she propped the door open, and went out to investigate.

The rags weren't simply rags. They were the filthy, tattered clothes of the person who still wore them. It was a tiny person, too—she thought at first that someone had abandoned a small child, but when she knelt and brushed back some of the shredded clothing and matted hair to get a better look, she realized the huddled figure was a man—dwarfed, misshapen, and very near death. He was bruised and bloody, hardly breathing; his skin clung to his bones so tightly she could make out the shapes of his teeth beneath his lips. His eye sockets and cheekbones stood out in ridges so sharp Faia could almost have believed he had no flesh at all. Looking at him, she could not imagine how he still lived.

"Oh," she whispered. "Oh, poor man."

She couldn't imagine who had left him there—the villagers, when they brought one of their sick to her, hovered over her and worried aloud about their loved ones while she worked. They always brought some pay for her, too—if not silver or copper, then a piglet or a fat duckling or a half-measure of dried, smoked fish.

Whoever had brought this man obviously didn't intend to pay her anything. She sighed and scooped both the little man and his pack into her arms. "Which isn't *your* fault, though, is it?"

He weighed almost nothing. "Poor man." She looked down the street again; it remained empty. In Omwimmee Trade's tropical climate, that was normal; midday was the time when business shut down and everyone went home to nap through the worst of the heat. Still, she wished she knew who had brought the little man to her. Knowing something—anything—about him would have helped her a great deal.

She was almost glad to find him there. Until only months ago, she had taught preliminary magic classes to students who hoped to one day be accepted into the great universities of Ariss or Bonton or distant, mysterious Dumforst. She performed warding spells and healing, hired out her services to break the spells of local hedgewizards who were forever renting themselves as cursemongers for the peevish masses, and in other ways made herself useful and needed in the little trading and fishing town. None of her students had seen fit to continue their studies when the magic changed, however, and her services in Omwimmee Trade became redundant. She had always had plenty of free time before—now she and Kirtha had nothing but free time.

She didn't want to take pleasure in the misfortune of another . . . but caring for the sick man would make her feel needed again, for however long he might survive.

I'll put him in the guest room—he'll be there only a day or two, most likely, and then he'll die and I'll have to notify the Omwimmee Trade council and get a permit to bury him.

She sighed. Death remained the one thing magic could not postpone forever, or reverse when it came. She might not be able to save him. She would do whatever she could for him, though; if he died, at least he would not die friendless and alone, huddled in some street corner.

The stranger's eyes flickered open just before Faia carried him into her home. They stared directly into hers—bright, crafty, and incredibly alert. She paused, foot lifted above her threshold but not yet over, subject to a sudden wave of vague uneasiness. The man was completely helpless— but the look in his eyes sent tingles down her spine.

Almost immediately, though, he closed them again— and once again was as obviously helpless and near death as he had been a second before.

Faia shifted, disquieted.

Maybe I should leave him where I found him. Maybe I ought to just put him back and pretend I never saw him.

Then she shook her head. Oh, Lady, I should be ashamed of myself, considering a thing like that. He's dying, he has no one—and I get the chills because he manages to open his eyes for an instant to look at me.

She felt terrible. Mortified by her momentary callousness, she carried him through the gate and inside, down the long breezeway to her large guest room, really the main bedroom of the house, which had once belonged to Medwind Song, barbarian mage and ex-headhunter, and her tenth husband, Nokar Feldosonne, one-time librarian of Faulea University and a powerful old saje.

Faia wiggled the door latch awkwardly with the tips of her fingers, trying to keep from hitting her guest's head on the wall, and shoved the door open with a hip. Musty, dust-laden air blew into the breezeway, and she stifled a sneeze. She hurriedly placed her guest on the bed, and threw open the windows; light streamed into the dark room and illuminated the dust motes that swirled and spiraled upward with every step she took. The bookshelves were cobwebbed and grey with dust, the corners of the round rug she'd made while she was pregnant with Kirtha appeared to have been gnawed by rodents, and spider-silk hung in long trails from the beams overhead.

She winced. The room had been long vacant and long neglected.

She closed her eyes for an instant, picturing everything as it should have been—fresh sheets on the bed, fresh flowers at the bedside, the room clean, the air sweet-smelling. The task took her no time and little energy. She opened her eyes to a bright, welcoming room.

"Better," she said to herself as she began undressing the little man. "It's a start, at least." She needed cool water and wet towels to bring his fever down quickly; she needed to start a healing broth simmering over the fire and to pick some fresh herbs for restorative simples. She would have to put thought into remembering the training her mother had given her for focusing wellness into the sick.

Perhaps Kirtha can gather the vigonia for me, she thought. She needs some tasks that must be done by hand, and with care. A little responsibility will be good for her.

Suddenly finding herself with much to do, Faia covered her guest with a sheet and hurried out of the room and down the breezeway. Not until much later did she realize she was singing as she worked.

Chapter 2

Much to her amazement, her guest lived. First he managed to open his eyes and watch as Faia and Kirtha worked in his room, then to sip broth through a reed; and one morning he rolled over on his own while they were bathing him. He gained weight at a prodigious rate, never as fat, but as muscle; that was a trick Faia pondered over in her off hours.

The little man's presence was as good for Kirtha as it was for Faia, too. Kirtha proved attentive, and each day delighted in pointing out "her" patient's improvement. Faia, once again honestly tired from hard work when nights came, felt happier than she had since Arhel's magic changed. Her careful spell-working was the best she had ever managed.

And at last the day arrived that the little man spoke.

Faia and Kirtha were tucking fresh bedclothes over him, thinking he was asleep, when suddenly his eyes opened and he smiled at both of them.

"You are too kind, fair ladies," he whispered, "too kind indeed, to come to the rescue of a helpless wretch like me."

"Mama!" Kirtha squealed. "He can *talk*!"

Faia grinned, as delighted as her daughter. "Indeed he can."

He struggled to sit up, then swung his legs over the side of the bed and stood, with the sheet wrapped around him. He gave a shaky bow. "I'm Witte," he told them both. "Witte A'Winde. Sometimes known as Witte the Mocker." He staggered a little, and his next bow nearly landed him facedown on the floor. "At your service."

Faia and Kirtha steadied him and helped him back into bed, while Faia noticed for the first time how very much he'd changed since she'd found him on her doorstep. Though he was still no taller than Kirtha, he'd become as wide as he was tall, and muscled like a bull. Thick cords of veins ran over the backs of his huge hands, and broad, flat muscles made his neck thicker than most men's thighs. His eyes, no longer sunken-in and hollow, were the bright and impossible green of spring leaves; his hair, that had been so dirty and matted, was the pale yellow of butter. It stood out from his head in a wild, shrubby mass at the front, though the back—which Kirtha had braided with great delight—reached nearly to the ground.

"You're going to hurt yourself," Kirtha scolded, perfectly mimicking what her mother had said to her on more than one occasion. Faia, looking at her daughter, realized Kirtha even had her hands on her hips, the way Faia invariably did when saying the same thing.

The two of them helped Witte back into the bed and Faia nodded. "Kirtha's right. You aren't ready to get up yet."

"Kirtha. What a pretty name." He flopped back, weak and obviously worn out from his few moments of standing. "For a lovely little girl."

Kirtha preened.

"And, lovely lady, who are you?"

"Faia. Rissedote."

"Faia, you are as beautiful as you are kind." He closed his eyes. "But you are, I think, correct. This has been too much for me."

After that first day up, he recovered even more quickly. Less than a week later, Faia came into her guest's room to find Witte up and sitting on the side of the bed, dressed except for one boot, which he was polishing. He tugged on the boot and jumped to the floor as she came in, and again bowed, this time with a quick, bobbing, almost birdlike motion. He wore an odd, short-skirted robe of gorgeous red silk with the front of the skirts tucked up into his sword-belt—and his sword, she thought, would have made her a serviceable carving knife. His red silk pantaloons, piped in gold along the seams, bloused over the tops of black boots that reflected the room around them like twin mirrors.

He looked hilarious—and Faia could just imagine her daughter's response as soon as she saw Witte's outfit. Kirtha was going to want one just like it.

Faia managed to keep a straight face in spite of her amusement, and bowed back.

"I think I am ready to be up and on my way," he told her. "I was on important business when I was taken ill, and now I must conclude it. Did I get as far as Omwimmee Trade, or have I still a distance to go?"

"This is Omwimmee Trade."

He smiled. "Ah. How wonderful. Then, perhaps you could tell me how I can repay you. Whatever I can do, dear lady, I will do."

"I've enjoyed . . . feeling useful again," she told him. "You owe me nothing."

"Nonsense—but I can see in your eyes you're stubborn as well as beautiful. I'll repay you in my own way if you won't tell me what you'd like."

Faia smiled. He was looking up at her, so sincere. "I have my repayment. You're well."

He smiled. "You are kindness personified. Then if you can do me one further good turn, I'll be on my way. Do you by chance know how I would get to the home of Nokar

Feldosonne, the saje master? I've come far to see him, and with important news."

"You're a friend of Nokar's—" Oh, no, she thought. This is too cruel.

"I am an *old* friend—come to see him from the other end of the land, all the way from the cold and the dark of South Point Bay, and come to meet his lovely wife."

Faia took a deep breath. She felt sick. "This . . . well, you found the right house. . . . Ah—when was the last time you and Nokar visited?"

"This is Nokar's house? Then you must *be* his wife—and beautiful as he described. When did I visit him last?" He looked at his feet, and sighed. "He was still Librarian at Faulea—it's been that long. Sad, isn't it, how old friends lose touch? However, I got a letter from him, oh, I guess almost two years ago—he was working on something fascinating. I haven't heard from him since. I've had a breakthrough in my own research that may give him some of the pieces to his First Folk puzzle, so I thought I'd take time off and visit him." Witte looked around. "Is he out?"

Faia shook her head slowly. "I'm not his wife. Her name is Medwind Song. And . . . maybe you should sit down. This *was* his house. His and Medwind's."

The little man frowned and hopped back up onto the bed. "Was?"

Faia breathed out slowly. "Oh, I am so sorry to have to tell you this. He died—just more than a year ago."

Witte's face fell. "Died? Oh, no!" His eyes filled with tears, and one ran down his cheek. "How terrible. And I've come so far to see him and his wife—and with such important news, too." He looked up at Faia, his expression suddenly thoughtful. The tears stopped as if his eyes were pump-wells and he'd just stopped pumping. "Now that I think about it, he mentioned a Faia in his letter as well as his wife—though I simply did not connect the names.

You're the young woman who made such a mess in Ariss, aren't you?"

Faia felt herself blush. "Well—"

Witte waved a hand as if to brush away his remark. "You shouldn't be embarrassed, dear girl. At least it was an interesting mess." He hopped down and paced, thumbs hooked into his belt. "Oh, dear. Nokar dead. That is terrible—simply terrible, and for more than one reason. The last letter I got from him indicated that he'd discovered an interesting First Folk artifact, and had a lead on more. Do you know if that came to anything?"

Faia leaned against the door and raised an eyebrow. "Yes. It came to quite a bit, in fact. I'm surprised you haven't heard."

Witte tipped his head. "Oh? Why is that?"

"Scholars have been studying the First Folk ruins Nokar discovered for about a year now—I would have thought everyone had at least gotten news that they'd been discovered."

Witte stopped pacing, and his eyes went wide. "First Folk ruins? Someone found First Folk ruins? Really?" His excited smile lit up his face.

Faia remembered Nokar wearing the same expression when he arrived, at last and after great hardship, in the ancient ruins that had once been an enormous First Folk city. He'd lived to explore them briefly, and to find the great library of stone tablets that he felt sure would give him the identities and history of the elusive Arhelan First Folk, but he had not lived long enough to discover the real wonders hidden deep within the catacombs beneath the library.

"You hadn't heard?"

"Dear child, I haven't heard *anything* since that last letter from Nokar. I've been doing research in the Fisher Province—there is no news there. The Fishers have only barely discovered fire—and they haven't got the hang of that yet." The disgusted face he made was so comical Faia couldn't help but laugh.

He resumed pacing. "A First Folk ruin. I wonder . . ." He looked up at her. "Have the scholars found anything, ah . . . *interesting* in the ruins?"

The most interesting thing Faia could think that they'd discovered was that the First Folk weren't human—or anything like human. She told him this.

He looked stunned. He sat himself back on the bed and leaned forward. "Not human?"

Faia nodded. "They were huge fliers. They looked a lot like giant, winged kellinks."

"Oh, no. Everyone has always believed the First Folk were our ancestors." Witte shook his head woefully. "You say this is not true? You've been to these ruins? You saw the First Folk, perhaps? You know this to be fact?"

"I saw the mummified remains of First Folk scholars. And the statues they made of themselves. They were huge and hideous, with scaly skin and sharp claws; they had enormous teeth. And wings," she added. "I'm absolutely certain they weren't human."

"Then the information I got is impossible, and my trip was in vain." He covered his face with his hands and groaned.

"What's wrong?" Faia asked. She felt so sorry for him. He could not have looked more depressed if she'd told him the world was ending.

"I thought I'd found proof that the First Folk and the Delmuirie Barrier were related, and I just located what I would have thought was absolute confirmation of that; however, if the First Folk weren't even human—"

"Delmuirie is *in* the First Folk city," Faia blurted. Then she amended that. "At least, there was a Delmuirie scholar with us who found a man inside a pillar of magical light, and was certain that man was Edrouss Delmuirie. The rest of us couldn't figure out who else he might be, so we assume the scholar was correct."

The little man bounced to his feet, grinning. "That's *him*! That's *him*! That *must* be him. The records all point to Delmuirie being trapped in a 'cage of light, bright as morning sun'! How tremendous! How exciting! And you say you know where he is? You've seen him?"

Faia shivered, remembering past terror—recalling the Delmuirie scholar, Thirk Huddsonne. He hadn't simply found Edrouss Delmuirie. Once he'd found his idol's trapped body, he'd assumed that the wizard from the past was still alive. He had attempted to sacrifice Kirtha to raise the magic he needed to break open the "cage of light" and free his hero. Only the intervention of his assistant, Roba Morgasdotte, had saved Kirtha's life . . . and in saving Roba from the consequences of her heroism, Nokar Feldosonne died.

Faia turned her back on Witte A'Wind and closed her eyes. She could still see Thirk slicing into Kirtha's tiny arms with his knife—and she could still see the bedamned worshipful expression on the madman's face when he looked at the trapped Delmuirie.

"I saw Delmuirie," she said at last; her voice grated harshly in her own ears. "A man almost killed my daughter because of him."

Witte said, "I'm so very glad the madman failed. Kirtha is a wonderful child. It would be—have been, I mean—a shame for anything to happen to her." The little man shook his head thoughtfully, then began to pace again. His braid bobbed when he did, so that to Faia he looked very much like a plump little perryfowl strutting. "You *have* seen Edrouss Delmuirie, though? You know he really exists?"

Faia nodded warily. "Yes."

"Then you could take me to the ruins?"

"I won't go back there."

Witte's expression became woeful. "You . . . you *won't*?" He looked at her with eyes full of hope. "Dear lady, I pray that you don't really mean that—"

"I do."

"I—I see." He hung his head. "Ah. Well." He turned away from her and leaned against the windowsill; he stared out into the busy street. Faia, across the room, only barely managed to hear his next, whispered, words. "Alas, my old friend, Nokar—that which I could have done in your memory must now remain forever undone."

Guilt settled on Faia's shoulders. It wrenched at her heart and knotted her stomach. This was Nokar's friend she had just turned down—Nokar's friend, who had nearly died traveling to bring news he thought Nokar needed to hear, who had already been devastated . . . *somewhat* devastated, she amended . . . on discovering his beloved friend's death.

"I will be on my way, then," the little man said. He picked up his little pack, and sighed.

Faia's mouth opened, and words poured out. "How would you get there?" she heard herself asking, even as her mind screamed, *Don't volunteer!*

Witte looked up at her—the expression he wore at that instant was the same one her dogs had worn when they thought she might be coming to give them something, but were afraid she wasn't. "I'd transport us," he said. "You are, perhaps, familiar with traveling by saje transport—the blink of an eye, a puff of smoke, and you stand where you wish to be?"

Faia nodded slowly.

"If you—having once been there—would only take an hour; if you could just picture the place and lead me there the first time, that would be all I'd ask of you. I promise it would be no inconvenience."

Faia stood in the old room, considering Witte's offer. It was a good offer. Overland travel through the jungle had been deadly before, and by all accounts had become worse. Survivors staggering into Omwimmee Trade from the East Road told of giant trees that now lurked along

the edge of the Wen Tribes Treaty Line and lumbered
out when human prey moved within reach; the grasping,
deadly trees devoured people and worked magic. Faia
knew the travelers spoke of the Keyu, the Wen tree-
gods. And the thought that the Keyu had come to control
enough magic to pull their roots out of the ground and
walk terrified her. Nor were the Keyu the only dangers
of overland travel. Venomous flying snakes, the deadly
six-legged kellinks that hunted in packs, poisonous plants
that set traps and wrapped their tendrils around hapless
victims drawn too near by the sweet scent of their flowers;
all lurked in wait for even the wariest sojourner.

Air travel in the Arissonese airboxes offered other but
equally deadly threats. The magic that kept them airborne
in the civilized lands vanished in the airspaces over the
jungle—so that passengers on a seemingly safe flight found
themselves dragged into the villages of the bloodthirsty
Wen, the north's reclusive human inhabitants.

But to simply transport—that would eliminate all risk.
Faia had returned from the First Folk city via the saje
transport magic, blinking out of existence in one location
and into existence in less than an instant.

She would have the chance to see her friends again,
friends who were diligently studying the ruins and who
had been out of touch for months. She would be able to
let Kirtha visit with her father, Kirgen. She would get a
chance to visit with her mentor, Medwind Song.

And she would get out of the house for a bit. She smiled
at that last thought. Omwimmee Trade was becoming too
confining for her. She yearned for distant places and new
faces, for adventure—even if it was only adventure of a
very small and not particularly noteworthy sort. Travel
by saje transport would remove all the danger from the
trip, but still end her up in an interesting location.

She smiled slowly. "I'll take you."

"Wondrous! Wondrous! Ah, how can I repay you,

dear lady? How at all?" He bounded back into the garden, his face almost glowing with happiness. "Come, then, and—"

"Not now," Faia said. "Not today. *When* I go, I'll have to stay and visit with friends. I have to pack, and to get gifts ready, and find someone to watch my house for me while I'm gone—I'll have to prepare supplies for an extended stay, and check my gear again. . . ." Her smile grew broader. It would be good to be back in the mountains again, to smell the cold, crisp air and feel the tingle of excitement that seemed to be a very part of mountain air.

Witte nodded. "Of course. Then perhaps tomorrow."

Faia chuckled. "Impatient man. I cannot possibly have everything ready by tomorrow. But soon—certainly in the next week. No more than two. Meanwhile, you're welcome to stay here—keep us company. You can rest and rebuild your strength. Kirtha and I will be delighted to have you as a guest."

At that moment a large grey tabby cat bounded onto the open windowsill, clutching something that gleamed dully of gold in one stubby, furry fist. He looked from Faia to Witte, clutched his booty tighter, and darted for the open door behind Faia, running three-legged so he would not drop his prize.

"Hrogner!" Faia yelled, and slammed the door in the cat's face. Both man and cat jumped.

"Close the shutters," Faia yelled as she dove for the cat.

Witte managed to pull them to before Hrogner escaped. Faia cornered him under the bed and dragged him out, protesting.

"Give," she snarled.

He growled.

She pried the golden thing from his fingers while he yowled and glared at her, then held it up to show Witte— a gaudy gold ring, set with stones. "Belongs to one of the neighbors, of course—though I'll have a time figuring out which one." She dropped the cat to the floor and grumbled, "He steals things."

"He has *hands*," Witte murmured.

Faia opened the shutters and shooed the cat back outside. "Yes. He does. The Mottemage at the university I attended thought it would be useful if her cat could open doors for himself, so she gave him hands." Faia watched Hrogner sulk through the tall grass, and turned back to her guest. "It was an incredibly stupid thing to do. The characteristic bred true—and the little monsters have all the bad characteristics of normal cats, and a few nasty quirks all their own. They strike quicklights they find lying around, and catch things on fire. They pick simple locks, and take things apart . . . but they never put them back together, of course. . . ." She shook her head. "And they steal. Hrogner is a brilliant thief. My neighbors loathe him."

"And you named him *Hrogner*." The little man chuckled, and his eyes twinkled.

"Hrogner is the saje god of mischief. I thought the name appropriate."

"No doubt it is. But have you never considered that if you run about calling that name aloud, more than the cat might answer?" He winked at her.

Faia snorted. "No worry about that. Hrogner never comes when called. He's a cat, after all."

"Nevertheless, you need equal measures of kindness and paranoia, dear girl. Otherwise, there's no telling *what* might show up at your house someday."

Chapter 3

Preparing *nondes* that evening, Faia found herself even more excited than she had been about getting away from Omwimmee Trade for a while. She ran over a list of all the gifts she would have to buy—it was extensive.

She pounded her fists into the bread dough and thought, while she listened with only the smallest part of her attention to Witte entertaining Kirtha in the garden. They both laughed merrily at intervals. She couldn't make out the words they said, for both of them talked at full speed and at the same time.

Faia smiled. Witte was such a nice man—he'd told some wonderful stories about Nokar in the years before she knew him. She had never known that Nokar had once climbed into the tower room of his university's chief administrator and replaced all of his grand robes with the simple robes of a first-year student, yet when she heard the story, she had no trouble imagining it. Nokar had been very much the sort of person who would delight in such a prank. The new stories brought him back to her, and made her miss him afresh.

Kirtha's giggles drifted in from the garden. She was ordering Witte around again—giving orders was one of the things Kirtha did best. She considered the little man a cross between her patient and her slave; for his part, he'd been her willing and good-humored servant.

It was pleasant having Witte as healthy, happy company—and Faia realized, listening to him talking and laughing with Kirtha out in the garden, how she longed for the sound of a man's voice in the house. Witte's presence was comforting after her solitary year in Omwimmee Trade.

Rejected suitors notwithstanding, I've been alone too long. I need to find someone I can care about.

She slid the bread in the oven and began cleaning the fish, enjoying the simple physical pleasures of cooking and preparing a meal without magic. Lost in her own thoughts, she didn't realize the garden had grown quiet until Kirtha's screams shattered the silence—screams of pure terror.

Faia charged out of the kitchen, her heart in her throat, to find Kirtha crouched behind the *b'dabba*, the Hoos plains hut that Medwind Song had left behind when she moved away, while in front of her, Witte fended off a tiny grey swallow that belched spurts of fire at him. The little man beat the air with his arms, but the bird refused to break off its attack. Already Witte's hair and eyebrows were singed.

By the Lady! Faia thought. She had never seen such a bird.

Then Hrogner launched himself out of the garden tree to chase the swallow, sporting a brand-new pair of very functional wings.

The swallow saw its attacker, made a tight loop in the air, and took off over the roof. Then it curved back and caught the pursuing cat full in the face with a tiny, bright blue stream of flame. The cat yowled and veered away; the swallow darted after him, singed his tail, and simultaneously caught the thatching of the roof on fire.

Faia suffered only an instant's hesitation. Then she pulled

the energy of sun and earth around her and created a raincloud above the little tongues of flame that licked along the thatch. She no longer needed to search for ley lines—in the last few months, they had come to overlie everything in Omwimmee Trade. She merely willed water out of the air and there it was. Rain poured onto the roof and put the fire out, leaving the thatch smoking and hissing.

She stopped the swallow in midflight, magically looked inside of it, and discovered the changes that had allowed the bird to breathe fire; they were clumsy, childish changes that would have proven quickly fatal to the tiny creature. Faia returned the swallow to its normal state, and with a peremptory mental suggestion, sent it on its way before the cat realized the bird was once again harmless.

Then she turned her attention to the cat. "Hrogner," she said, "come here."

Hrogner, no longer pursued by the vicious swallow, had landed on the roof, where he sat licking his singed fur. He wore the air of one who has taken an unfair and totally unwarranted blow from life.

"Hrogner!" Faia called again. "Come here. Here, kitty, kitty. Come here, cat!"

Witte came to stand beside her and said, "You brought me back to health and drew rain from the sky; you are not unskilled at magic. Why do you not make the cat come?"

Faia said, "You haven't had much experience with cats, have you? No one can make them do anything. They are immune to magic." She turned to Kirtha and said, "Bring me a handful of chud jerky from the pantry. I want to get Hrogner off the roof."

Kirtha, wide-eyed, nodded and ran into the house.

Witte stared at the cat, puzzled. "Immune to magic? Then how do you explain the creature's hands . . . or its wings?"

"I did not say that well." Faia turned to Witte. "Cats are not immune to *all* magic—they only ignore the magic that doesn't interest them or, in their self-interested little minds, offer some benefit for them. The only reason my little monster still has hands is because I can do nothing to change them back to paws."

Kirtha returned, carrying a handful of very smelly dried brown flakes. "Here, Mama. For Hrogner-cat."

Faia took them and held her hand up. "Here, kitty, kitty. Come here. Come get the tasty fish."

Hrogner gave his burned fur another lick, then flew down and landed, clumsily and with claws out, on Faia's arm.

"Ow!" she yelped. She grabbed up a handful of fur at the scruff of his neck and dragged the hissing, snarling Hrogner into the house.

Inside, she stopped and frowned. She turned back. "Come with me, Kirtha." She eyed Witte, who noted her expression and followed, too. "I want to know what happened."

Faia studied the cat once everyone was inside. The changes in him were altogether more subtle and clever than the changes in the bird had been. The wings looked clumsy enough, and the feathers were the sort of silly detail she would expect from a five-year-old, but there was an underlying soundness of structure and form that implied knowledge of flighted creatures—a knowledge Faia did not think Kirtha had. She narrowed her eyes in concentration and magically probed deeper. The musculature was very finely done, while the boning and changes made in the cat's spine to accommodate the addition of wings were as elegant as anything Faia had ever seen from the Mottemage during her time at Daane University.

She arched an eyebrow at Witte. He grinned sheepishly.

Hrogner, having acquired wings, was not willing to part with them.

"You cannot keep them," she muttered at the cat, who gave her a disdainful look. "The neighbors would execute both of us." She couldn't force him to give them up, however, and she knew Hrogner knew it.

Nothing she tried would get him to let her remove them, either—until he passed a mirror and saw his own reflection. He hissed and arched his back, and the clumsy feathered wings splayed out, gangling and awkward-looking.

Hrogner seemed terrified of his appearance—he who usually loved to admire himself.

Faia used his reaction to her advantage; she laughed at him. All cats hated to be laughed at, and vain Hrogner was no exception. He glared at her, stalked away, and snagged a wing on a chair dowel when he tried to walk under it.

Then and only then did the cat permit his wings to be removed. Dewinged, he skulked down the breezeway. Not until Faia heard a crash from the kitchen did she remember the fish she'd been cleaning on the tray.

"*Nondes!*" she yelled, and ran after the cat into the kitchen. But it was too late. The tray and two of the seabrouk were on the floor; the third Hrogner had apparently dragged off to eat in peace.

Faia turned on her daughter and Witte. "So much for a nice meal," she said. She crossed her arms over her chest and studied both of them. "I want to know what happened."

Kirtha looked at their guest, her eyes accusing. Witte said nothing.

"Witte told me a story," Kirtha said at last.

Faia tilted her head and looked at him, eyebrows raised.

"I merely recounted the old Forst fable about why cats climb," Witte said quickly. "You know the one, perhaps?"

"No." Faia settled into a chair and crossed her arms over her chest. "Why don't you tell it to me."

"Well—" Witte cleared his throat. "Well. When Fetupad created cats—"

"Fetupad?"

Witte hopped up into a chair across from her. He sat, his feet dangling more than a handsbreadth above the floor, looking at that instant very like a guilty child. "In Forst Province, the people worship Fetupad as the god of beasts. In any case, when she made cats, she created them with wings. For a time, all was well. But cats, with their great pride, flew to the sky home of Fetupad—the Forsters believe all their gods live in the clouds, you see—and moved right in. They bothered Fetupad's sacred hounds, and ate Fetupad's sacred birds, and they sang and carried on all night on Fetupad's sacred roof."

"Her *roof* is sacred?" Faia asked.

"All things which touch the gods are sacred," Witte said stiffly.

"Of course."

"So, in a fit of anger, she ripped off the cats' wings and threw the beasts to the earth. Cats, of course, are so well made that they were not harmed by their fall from the sky. They landed on their feet. But they could no longer ascend to the sacred presence of Fetupad. They were not humbled by their fall, however. Oh, no. They told each other, 'We will make our own sky homes, and we will still catch the flying things, and we will still sing on the roofs of houses when the Tide Mother shines without the sun.' And so they have continued until this very day. And that is why cats climb."

Faia nodded. "A very pretty story."

"I wanted the cats to have wings, Mama. I thought ol' Fetupad was mean to them."

"I see. So my daughter declares herself a god and gives our cat wings. This doesn't surprise me. What does surprise me is that you helped her."

Witte blushed. "She was so excited about the idea, and I must admit I thought it would be charming."

"You thought it would be charming to give Hrogner wings? Hrogner the Thief? Hrogner the Firebug? Hrogner the idiot cat with hands?" Faia shook her head in disbelief.

"I like your cat. I find him a delightful animal, and a creature after my own heart."

Faia arched an eyebrow. "I don't want to think what that says about you." She shook her head. "Which gets us as far as the cat's wings. What about the swallow?"

"The cat, as soon as it had wings, flew into the air and caught a bird in front of the child."

Kirtha's eyes grew bright with tears, and one rolled slowly down her cheek. "Hrogner caught the bird an' *ate* it, Mama. Bad ol' cat!"

"So you made the next bird you saw breathe fire."

Kirtha pointed an accusing finger at Witte. "He *said* if birds could blow fire on cats, cats wouldn't bother them. He *said!*"

"Did he?" Faia turned to Witte.

He shrugged. "I was trying to make the child laugh. She was so upset when the cat killed the little bird. I had no idea—"

"On the contrary," Faia interrupted. "You did have ideas—and you shared them with a five-year-old." She sighed. "That was the problem."

She began to think having Witte as a continuing houseguest might not be the unadulterated bliss she'd hoped. Perhaps she ought to push herself in order to take him to the First Folk ruins soon. It was a pity there was no way she could just do it in the morning, but if she went all the way to the First Folk ruins, but wasn't prepared to stay, she would never hear the end of it from any of her friends. She definitely needed to get under way soon, though. Meanwhile, she needed to have a talk with Witte—before he had any more amusing ideas.

He was a charming man. But he was, she began to suspect, well-meaning trouble; the sort of person who stirred things up by not thinking—then stood back with his eyes wide and his hands clean, bemusedly watching the subsequent disaster.

Even well-meaning trouble was more trouble than she wanted.

Chapter 4

Faia slept poorly, and what little sleep she got was full of dreams of cats with wings and a little man dressed all in red who danced from place to place in front of her, while calamity followed.

She woke to darkness. She tossed for a while, trying to find a comfortable position, but discovered she was wide awake—and soon she wearied of waiting for sleep to return. She rose and walked through the house. Neither Kirtha nor Witte were up, but outside, morning noises had begun. Cattle clop-clopped through the cobblestone streets, heading back from the pastures where they had grazed. Antis-bells rang in the center of town, and the criers from the local temples began their ululations. The fish cart rattled by, the fishman singing, "Feeeeesh, fresh feeeeesh!" All of Omwimmee Trade acted as if morning had already begun.

She stepped into the street and looked east, toward the far hills. The first rays of dawn should have pinked the horizon, but the sky remained black and the stars glittered coldly.

Instead of the sun, Faia saw the giant sphere of the Tide Mother dressed out in black with a gold corona around her.

It was then, when she saw the vast bulk of the Tide

Mother dark and fire-edged, that Faia realized the sun would not rise again for fourteen days. The Month of Ghosts was upon her, and Faia, too busy with her sick visitor to notice the preparations the townsfolk made for the holy days, had done nothing to ready herself for its coming.

She ran back inside, to her workroom. It had once been a sitting room, but she'd changed it after Medwind and Nokar were gone. It was now full of candles and herbs and oils, bundles of flowers drying upside down, unspun wool, skeins of yarn dyed and undyed, a spindle, a lap-loom, and an ancient and terribly heavy worktable. She gathered up the white candles and set them against the north wall beneath the shuttered window; north was the direction of the realms of the dead.

Then she went and woke her daughter. "Kirthchie, it is time to help the ghosts of our loved ones find their way to the Wheel."

Kirtha woke slowly, rubbing sleepy eyes. "Yes, Mama." She trotted down the hall and knelt at her mother's side in front of the makeshift altar.

"Light candles for the Lady and her Lord," Faia instructed. That was the part of every ceremony Kirtha got to do. Faia hoped it would give the little girl respect for the magefires she commanded. Kirtha closed her eyes, and flames appeared on the wicks of the two deep-green candles.

To the hill-folk, the simple darkness of night was the Lord's time, when he walked through the hills, calling the spirits of the dead to commune with him. And the special darkness of the Month of Ghosts was the time when, after he had learned what the dead had done with their lives and what they still needed to learn, he took them back to the Wheel so they could begin again.

From the time Kirtha could first walk, Faia had taught her the hallowed songs, including the songs of the dead,

and explained to her the importance of remembering
those who had gone on. But Kirtha was still so young.
Faia wondered how much of this Month of Ghosts the
child would remember—this one, where all of Faia's
family and most of her world were moving between the
planes.

"Do you remember the words of the Ghost Song?" she
asked her daughter.

Kirtha nodded. Solemnly, mother and daughter knelt
on the floor in front of the two glowing green candles
and the forest of plain white tapers, and sang.

"Father Dark, watch over me
As the long night comes.
Nothing now will frighten me
As the long night comes.

We remember those now gone,
Souls that through the darkness roam.
Light our candles, one by one,
To guide our loved ones home.

Father Dark, love all of them.
Do not let them fear.
Guide them and watch over them,
Do not let them fear.

We remember those now gone,
Souls that through the darkness roam.
Light our candles, one by one,
To guide our loved ones home."

Faia was grateful for the darkness of the room, because
Kirtha would not see her weep as she lit the spirit candles.
One for her mother, one for her mother's father, one for
her sister and each of her brothers, one for each of her
sister's children, one for Rorin, one for Bayward, one big
candle for the rest of the village of Bright, and another

for those who had died during the second Mage/Saje War in Ariss. One for Nokar. And though she suspected it was sacrilege, one for each of her two dogs, Chirp and Huss, and one for her goat Diana.

The room grew brighter, and glowed yellow and warm with the spirits' guidelights. Faia stared into the flickering flames, and wept silently. She realized she beheld more spirit flames than she knew living people.

This was the first Month of Ghosts since the plague in Bright that had killed everyone she had ever known. Faia had been fifteen years old during the Sacred Month before that. She and her mother and her brothers and sister had burned candles for her father and her mother's mother—both of them dead of old age. Two candles had seemed to be so many, when in Bright many families burned no candles at all. She and her mother, her brothers, and sister had cried over those two flames, and sang the songs to lead the spirits to the Wheel so they could circle back to a new life, and tried not to be bitter because they had lost so much. But in the Month of Ghosts her sister had conceived a child, and one of her brothers had sired one—so her father and grandmother had been offered new homes among their loved ones, if they chose to accept.

Faia stared into the mass of flames and whispered, "I have no lover, and I bear no child. I can offer no new life for any of my family."

She was old enough; if she had been in Bright—if there still *were* a Bright—she would have taken part in the Celebration of New Souls. But Faia and Kirtha were alone in the world except for each other. Faia's mother, her brothers and sister, her nieces and nephews, her lovers and friends—all of them would have to find a place among strangers. She prayed that they would find families who loved them and cared for them.

"Were they nice?" Kirtha asked softly.

"They were wonderful," Faia said. "I wish you had known them. I wish they had lived to meet you."

"Me, too, Mama."

Faia closed her eyes and remembered her mother the last time she had seen her—the two of them standing in the yard and saying good-bye before Faia and the dogs took the sheep into the highlands for the summer.

Would I have gone, if I had known they would all be dead when I got back? she wondered. Or would I have stayed and died with them, so that I did not have to be so alone?

Then she looked over at her daughter, who sat staring at the many flames trying to understand. Loose curls blew around the little girl's face, and her hair gleamed red and gold in the candlelight. She seemed tiny to Faia, but already her fingers were long and tapered like her mother's, and she was nearly a head taller than the village children her age. She was beautiful, Faia thought. Beautiful, and perfect.

Faia leaned over and kissed the top of her daughter's head. I would have gone, she thought. I would have gone to the mountains and lived, so long as I also knew that I would someday have you, little one. My mother would have loved you so much.

A chill descended on the room. The doors were closed, and the room was not drafty, but the candle flames winked and danced in a sudden faint breeze.

She is very lovely, Faia, a voice whispered. *She looks like you when you were her age.*

Faia had not heard that voice in years, but she could never forget it.

Mama, she thought. You sound so near.

Kirtha had turned around. "Who are you?" she asked someone.

I am Faia's mama. Your grandmama.

Faia turned and stared at the misty shape standing near the door. "Mama?" she whispered.

You've done well, Faiachin, her mother said. *You listened, even when I thought you had not. You remember to be kind—and you are a good mother.* Risse laughed. *There was a time when I thought you would only be a good mother to your flocks. I am very proud of you. But you need to find someone. You have been too much alone.*

Faia was stunned to see her mother again, looking just as young and beautiful as she had remembered. At first, she could not believe her eyes. Her father had not come when the family burned candles for him. In truth, Faia did not know of any spirits who appeared among their families during the Month of Ghosts. But there her mother stood, and if Faia's mind was uncertain, her heart was not.

Faia rose, trembling. "I know, Mama," she said. She wished she could hug her mother, wished there was some way to touch her. She had missed her so much.

Risse moved over to Kirtha's side and crouched next to her. *Hello, Kirthchie,* she said softly. *I have enjoyed watching you grow up.*

"Hello, Gramma," Kirtha said. "Mama said you were always with us." She reached out a hand to touch Risse, and her fingers went right through her. "Oh!" she said, startled, and drew her hand back quickly.

Risse looked overwhelmingly sad. *This is the best I can do, dearest,* she said softly. She reached out as if to stroke Kirtha's hair, then stopped herself. She looked up at Faia.

I cannot stay long, Faia—and there is something you must know. You cannot keep hiding in this village. You have the Lady's power in you—and the time is coming when you must use it.

"Everyone has the Lady-gift of magic now, Mama. No one needs me."

Daughter of mine, Arhel will not survive without you. Everything you have lived until now has been practice for what will come. You will have a test—a test of your courage and your will—and, too, of your love for your friends, and for all the people of Arhel. You alone have both the magic and the spirit to do what must be done. Her mother stood and sighed. *Oh, Faia, how I have missed you.*

"Oh, Mama . . ." She stopped, the lump in her throat choking off further words. She had so many things she wanted to tell her mother—so many things that had happened, and she could not even think of where to begin.

Faia thought she saw tears in her mother's eyes.

Risse whispered, *The long night of the spirits is finally here, and my time as Risse is over. Where once I was dead, but not gone, now I shall be gone but no longer dead.*

"But I will remember you, Mama," Faia whispered. "I love you."

And I love you—but once I pass to the Wheel, I will forget. I must, Faiachin. If I remembered, I could not bear to go on.

"I know, Mama. I know." Faia wept. "I am so glad we get this time. I have so much to tell you—I never thought I would even have the chance to say good-bye."

Her mother stiffened, her eyes suddenly focused on some far-distant place. *The Dark One calls, and I must go,* she said. *Good-bye, Faiachin. Good-bye, sweet Kirthchie.*

"No!" Faia begged. "You cannot go yet. Not so soon, Mama. Please, tell Father Dark you cannot leave yet. You just came—"

Her mother began to fade in front of her eyes, began to stretch and swirl into the chill breeze, growing paler and fainter. She tattered, slipped—

Not again. Faia would not lose this chance to say good-bye again.

And, choking, sobbing, she still managed to whisper, "Good-bye, Mama. Find new life and happiness."

Her mother's voice echoed in her ears long after Risse vanished. *Find happiness, daughter. Find meaning, and find love.*

Chapter 5

The candles guttered, and Faia's legs were numb from long kneeling. She had no tears left; she'd pled with Father Dark to let her mother come back just once more—but Father Dark remained as unbending as stone. In the perpetual dark, time had ceased to mean anything. Faia only knew she'd prayed long, and without answer.

Sudden pounding rattled the workroom door, and a desperate voice shook her out of her near-trance. "Faia!" Witte shouted. "Faia, come quick! Help!"

She staggered to her feet and tried to run; stabbing pain shot through her legs and feet, and she nearly fell. She opened the door and clung to it while her legs came back to life. "What?"

"FAIA! You've got to come out of there! You have a terrible problem! You have . . ." Witte looked up at her and paused. She heard distress in his voice, and saw fear in his eyes. "You have *gods* in your garden."

"Gods? In my garden?"

"Gods." He nodded vigorously. His face looked pale in the candlelight, and his eyes were round.

Faia had been frightened by the urgency and panic she heard in his voice, but her fear became disbelief and annoyance when he insisted on the impossible—on the ludicrous. She leaned against the door frame, crossed her arms over her chest, and gave him the same look she gave Kirtha when Kirtha said oogins ate the last handpie. "Truly."

"Upon my word. You have only to look and you will see." He seemed sincere. Perhaps he was having some sort of relapse and was feverish. She left the candles burning, picked up Kirtha, who'd fallen asleep in a pile of undyed yarn, and came out, pulling the door shut behind her.

"Hurry up, hurry up," Witte said. He danced from one foot to the other, impatient. "They might be gone before you get out there."

"If they are, then I will no longer have a problem, will I?"

"I wouldn't stake wagers on that."

Faia shook her head. It was time she came out anyway. Father Dark had already given her more than she had a right to ask of him. She needed to thank him for the few moments she'd had with her mother. Those moments would have to be enough.

She limped down the breezeway with both feet tingling and coming awake; she lugged Kirtha into her room and tucked her into bed while Witte paced. Then she turned to the little man. "Well. *Now* I am ready to go see your gods."

Faia followed him down the breezeway and into the garden—and suffered a shock. This was not fire-breathing birds or flying cats, nor any other prank Witte had concocted. She had a garden full of gods.

She recognized the patron deity of Omwimmee Trade, Galtennor; the townspeople had erected a statue to him in the center of town next to the government building, and he looked just like it. He was shouting and waving his top two sets of arms around. His third set he'd crossed over his massive chest, while he'd set the fourth akimbo. Thessi Ravi stood arguing with him—Faia recognized her because her hair was on fire and her breasts looked like spear points. There were pictures of her about town, as well. Faia knew she was the patron deity of warfare in one of the local religions, but could not recall which one. The only other two Faia recognized, Hada and Bnokt, were amatory gods with some fertility duties. They were carrying out their official functions in the middle of her vigonia patch. Others she did not recognize at all.

"What are they *doing* here?" she whispered.

Witte gnawed on his lower lip. "Quite a lot."

Faia shivered, though not from cold. Her skin prickled, and she felt the little hairs on the back of her neck and her arms stand up. "That is not what I meant to ask." She tried not to stare at Hada and Bnokt. What they were doing should not have been possible with only two arms and two legs apiece. She caught herself trying to see if they had extras, and, embarrassed, turned away. "Where did they come from? And why did they choose my garden to . . . to do whatever they are doing?"

Witte shrugged. "Why don't you ask them?"

Thessi Ravi and some statuesque blonde had joined forces and were backing Galtennor through the garden toward Faia.

"I tell you the Dreaming God holds all of reality in his dream, and we too exist because he dreams us!" Galtennor roared.

Thessi Ravi's face twisted with anger, and sparks of lightning flew from her fingertips and sizzled in the greenery. "What sort of sniveling godlet are you? The Dreaming God is myth!" she screamed. "*Myth*, I say! I owe allegiance to *no* other god! None!" She waved an arm around to drive home her point, and caught the thatching on fire.

"Heresy!" shrieked the buxom blonde.

"Oh, no!" Faia yelped. She gathered up a cloud—as she had when the bird set the roof on fire before—and

doused the roof with rain. Her emotions surged, though,
with the stress of discovering her uninvited guests, and
what she had intended to create as a single cloud was
born instead as a torrential downpour, complete with
thunder, lightning, and screaming, twisting winds. The
rain soaked the gods, and the lightning struck them, and
the thunder drowned out their arguments.

She dissolved the storm as quickly as she'd created it,
but the damage was already done. The gods stopped what
they were doing, and one by one turned and stared at Faia.

"Oh, my!" Faia whispered.

"Indeed," Witte agreed.

Slowly, as if they progressed in a dream, the gods began
to glide toward her.

Faia covered her hand with her mouth. Her heart raced,
and she backed up. "Oh, no!" she whispered, horrified at
what she had done.

"Precisely which upstart god are you?" Thessi Ravi
glowered at her, and Faia saw the sparkles of lightning
crackling between the god's fingers.

Faia became aware that Witte was tugging urgently on
the leg of her breeches. She looked down at him, and
saw renewed terror in his eyes. He beckoned her to his
level with a hand. She crouched, and he whispered in
her ear, "Lie to them."

"Lie?" Startled by the suggestion, she glanced back at
Thessi Ravi, who moved closer, with the other gods, all
angry, following behind her.

He nodded vehemently. "Lie! Tell them you're a god.
If you don't, they will do terrible things to you. Mortals
don't go around dousing gods and smacking them with
lightning bolts without expecting retribution."

Faia thought about that for an instant. It made sense—
though she wished she had some idea what the gods
intended to do to her if they decided she *was* one of
their number.

She had no time to worry. The gods expected an answer. She stood, and glared at all of them—and for an instant, she felt as she had all those years ago when she walked into the Greathall at the University in Mage-Ariss, and faced a room full of hostile strangers. She took a deep breath, lifted her chin, and said, in the coldest voice she could manage, "I am *Faia*, of course. And just who are you, and what are you doing here uninvited?" She put hands on hips and looked down her nose at them, as if they were vermin she had just discovered in her pantry.

Her answer might have been a bit vague, she decided, but she had the tone exactly right. The gods stopped moving toward her, and one after the other, they muttered, "Oh. *Faia*. I recognize that name," while their faces registered nothing but confusion.

One of them said, "Faia—isn't she the goddess portended to bring death to all the gods?"

"Or perhaps one of the goddesses of hearth and wisdom," another whispered nervously.

"If you don't know who I am, you aren't important enough to know," Faia told them coldly. "Go back to whatever holes you crawled out of, little gods, and infest my house no more."

Then one of the gods glared at her, anger dark on his face. "But we were invited. All of us were invited."

Faia hid her discomfiture as well as she could, and kept her response icy and superior. "*I* did not invite you."

But the angry eyes were not fixed on her this time. Instead, they were focused on her guest—Witte A'Winde.

He was responsible for this? Don't be ridiculous, she told herself. Of course he's responsible for this. Gods don't appear in gardens any more often than wings appear on cats. He'd called himself Witte the Mocker—but that did not seem to define the little man appropriately right at that instant. Witte the Troublesome would be closer, she thought darkly. Or Witte the Prankster. Or even Witte the

Soon-to-be-Sleeping-in-the-Street. She glowered at him.
He gave her a shrug and a weak smile.

"Did you do this? Invite this rabble into my home?"

Witte threw himself prostrate at her feet and wept. "Oh,
please, please don't smite me!" he howled. "Please have
mercy, O Benevolent Faia. Don't blast me! Don't rend
me limb from limb! I meant no harm—truly."

Faia pulled her ankles loose from his armlock and did
not kick him in the head, though she was sorely tempted.
She looked back to the gods, intending to ask them to
leave—only to discover the last of them was at that instant
creeping out through her front gate, his forked tail quite
literally tucked between his legs. As she watched, the
tiptoeing god reached back and quietly pulled the inner
gate shut behind him.

She jammed her hands into the pockets of her breeches
and studied the gate thoughtfully, then looked at the still
prostrate and weeping Witte.

"You can get up now," she said, her voice dry. "They've
gone." She looked back at the gate again, and tipped her
head to one side. "Though I haven't the slightest idea why."

Witte jumped to his feet, all pretense of remorse gone
as though it had never existed. He chuckled while he
brushed the dirt off his silks. "They fell for that one?"
He shook his head ruefully. "What a bunch of rubes. City
gods would *never* have gone for that bit—" He looked
up at her, a thoughtful expression on his face. "Though
you did a nice turn as the great god Faia. Where did you
come up with the haughty act?"

She was still pondering the mysterious and panic-tinged
flight of the gods. She only half-heard his question at first.
"Hmmmm?" she murmured. Then she thought back to
what he asked her, and shrugged. "Well . . . I've dealt
with snobs before."

"Nice. Very nice. You could have fooled me if I hadn't
already known what you were." He laughed.

Something about the way he said that grated on Faia, and she glared at him. "You know *what* I am? What?!" She snarled, "Let me tell you what I am, Witte A'Winde. I *am* the woman who owns this house. I *am* the woman who took care of you, who nursed you back to health, who invited you to stay in my home, who offered to take you to the First Folk ruins out of respect for the memory of my friend Nokar. Finally, I *am* not happy about this."

Witte frowned, then turned and stalked away from her.

She strode after him and grabbed his shoulder. "*Why* did you invite the gods here? How did you find them, how did you call them? I want answers, and I want them now."

Witte turned slowly and removed Faia's hand from his shoulder. "I wanted to find out what they knew about the Dreaming God," he said stiffly.

Faia frowned. "Some of them were arguing about the Dreaming God when I went out there."

"Yes. Most of them agree the Dreaming God is real, but minor."

"Some of them did not agree, I noticed."

"Well, some. But Thessi Ravi is a hothead. She thinks with a bit more push, she can become one of Arhel's majors—though I don't think that's too likely. None of the better gods took her attitude."

Faia leaned against the wall and studied the little man. "Why does it matter, anyway?" she asked.

His eyes narrowed, and went cold and hard. "Because the oldest religions claim the Dreaming God is the god from whom all magic springs—and I've found evidence that he isn't a god at all."

"Not a god?" Faia arched an eyebrow. "It sounds like the sort of riddle my brothers and I used to ask each other; 'When is a god not a god?' And what is the answer to this riddle, Witte the Mocker?"

Witte smiled slowly. "When he's Edrouss Delmuirie," the little man said.

The silence seemed to crackle in the dark breezeway. *Edrouss Delmuirie*. Again. Edrouss Delmuirie, creator of the blasted barrier that trapped Arhelans on their little continent and denied them the endless seas beyond. Edrouss Delmuirie, false god. Edrouss Delmuirie, author of an infamous series of diaries, seducer of hundreds of willing women.

Edrouss Delmuirie. She could see the man in her mind as clearly as if she still stood in the First Folk catacombs; he knelt on one knee inside a pillar of golden light, sword out, chalice lifted, with his plain face tilted upward and illuminated by a beatific expression. Every time she thought of him, her stomach tightened and twisted, and her heart raced. Thirk Huddsonne had worshiped Delmuirie— had almost sacrificed Kirtha to him. None of that was Delmuirie's fault, but Faia, remembering both men, could not separate her justifiable anger with one from her linked anger with the other.

Witte did not seem to notice her silence. He paced in front of her, talking. "I have a great deal of proof, you see, that Delmuirie *is* the Dreaming God . . . or rather, that he became known as the Dreaming God after he disappeared. I have proof, too, that it is because of his dreaming that the magic of Arhel has begun to run rampant. My theory is that Arhel will return to normal when someone wakes him. But waking him will take an act of will and magic unlike anything that Arhel has ever seen."

Faia's ears caught that phrase, and she frowned thoughtfully. *An act of will and magic*. And her mother's words came back to her.

You will have a test—a test of your courage and your will—and, too, of your love for your friends, and for all the people of Arhel. You alone have both the magic and the spirit to do what must be done.

"Of course," she whispered. This act of will and magic—waking Delmuirie, setting right the wrong, wild magic overrunning Arhel—certainly this was the destiny about which her mother had spoken.

She smiled slowly. Her destiny was not just to lead Witte A'Winde to the First Folk ruins. She could feel the truth of the real need in her very blood. She closed her eyes; at last she would have a chance to be Arhel's hero, to remove the stain on her name that the burning of Bright and the near-leveling of Ariss had left. She would wake Delmuirie, and return Arhel to its rightful state.

"Good," she whispered. "When this is done, there will be none in Arhel who curse my name."

Witte looked up at her and his bushy brows knit together. "You look awfully pleased by all of this," he said. "I'd like to know why."

"I'm looking forward to seeing my friends again," Faia lied. "But I've decided we need to get ready and go to the ruins now."

Kirtha wandered out into the hall. "It's still dark, but I'm not sleepy anymore, Mama. Can I get up now?" The little girl rubbed her eyes with the backs of her hands. "Did Gramma come back?"

"You can get up." Faia scooped her daughter up and hugged her; she was grateful for the interruption. "It is going to be dark for a long time. Gramma did not come back. I don't think she will." She swallowed the sudden lump in her throat and said, "I think she told me what I needed to know."

Witte's eyes narrowed. "Your mother stopped by?"

"Yes." Faia did not wish to have her wonderful miracle questioned, so she said nothing else.

"Gramma is a ghost," Kirtha said helpfully. "She's very pretty."

Leave it to Kirtha to blurt out Faia's secret. "My mother appeared to me as I was lighting candles for the spirits of the dead. She told me something that confirmed much of what you say."

"Your mother's *ghost* confirmed . . . ?" Witte frowned, and shook his head slowly. "I don't like the sound of that—not at all."

Faia shrugged. Odd that the little man would remark on what her mother said, but not the fact that her mother had been there in the first place. Then she considered . . . he'd summoned gods to her garden. The ghost of a lone mother must seem pretty unspectacular to him.

Witte gnawed on the tip of his braid and glowered into the darkness. "It doesn't matter," he said suddenly. "Are you ready to leave now?"

She had hoped to get a birthing present for Roba, who had surely delivered her baby by this time. She'd hoped to take gifts to Medwind and Kirgen, too. But this sign that her destiny awaited her was more important than finding gifts. She felt the thrill of anticipation, of waiting adventure, of the promise of a fulfillment she would never find in Omwimmee Trade. "I have to dress Kirtha and myself in warm clothes, and pack a few supplies. And talk to Matron Bendreed about feeding Hrogner."

Witte smiled slowly. "Bring your cat, why don't you? It will be a short trip—and I have to believe a cat named Hrogner would be lucky for me."

Faia snorted. "Not for me. Hrogner is a four-legged disaster."

"The best kind. I'll watch him—I *like* that cat."

"He will stay here," Faia said firmly. "He's too much trouble—and Kirtha and I will be gone a week or so. He would be hard to keep up with in the mountains for that long."

When Faia met Witte back in the garden, she and Kirtha were already sweltering in the winter garb of the hill-folk—heavy boots, leather breeches, thick wool tunics, laced jerkins and sturdy hill-folk *erdas*, which were ugly square overwraps of waxed felt. Mother and daughter wore wide-brimmed leather hats, and Faia wore her waist kit-pack, and lugged her heavy supply pack over one shoulder. She carried a brass-tipped staff, while Kirtha had a simple wood walking stick. Faia almost felt silly wearing winter gear in the summer—but even in the lowlands the temperature had dropped with the absence of the sun, and in the mountains, bitter false winter would have already arrived, not to be banished until the sun crept out from behind the Tide Mother.

"I look like Mama, don't I, Witte?" Kirtha asked.

"Yes," the little man agreed, looking from child to mother and back to child again. He looked up at Faia in disbelief. "By my blessed bones, woman, what are you doing with all of that? We're going to make a quick jaunt into the First Folk city. I'm sure your friends will be happy to entertain you for the few days you'll be there."

"Anyone who travels to the mountains and doesn't anticipate trouble will be sure to find it," Faia told him. "I know the mountains. I grew up in them."

"Woll, I can certainly see taking a few precautions . . . but you have a *sling* in your belt."

"And spiked wolfshot in my waist pack."

"You could melt any bedamned wolves we met with a flick of your fingers."

Faia sniffed. "That is not the Lady's way. With wolves, I prefer wolfshot. Magic has its uses—but so do the skills of hand and eye."

Witte laughed and wrapped a fur-lined silk cloak around him. "How silly." He held out a hand. "If you have magic, you don't need anything else. Hold tight, and picture the place in your thoughts," he said.

Faia swung Kirtha onto her hip, grabbed her pack, then took his hand with her free one. She pictured the ruins, the domed whitestone worn by untold years of wind and rain and snow. Her stomach twisted, she smelled the sudden tang of bitter smoke, and that was all. One instant, she was standing beneath the stars in her garden, with the black Tide Mother over her head; the next, wind screamed around her and whipped snow into her eyes and down the loose neck of her erda. The white walls of the First Folk city towered over her head, and the curiously built, carved stone domes of the First Folk nestled below her. The three of them had appeared in the center of the circle of arches and pillars, on the high promontory above the main part of the city. It was very near the place where Faia and Medwind and Nokar had landed when they flew into the city only a year ago.

But everything about the place was different.

Chapter 6

Faia felt her heart begin to race as she stood on the narrow, rocky plateau and looked down into the lower ruins. Her skin and her nerves tingled with the charge of powerful, surging energy from somewhere nearby, and her heart raced. She could barely make out the forked shape of the library and the clusters of a few of the larger side-buildings through the darkness and the gusting snow. She was surprised she could even see those, so hideous was the weather; but below, the terrain gleamed with its own faintly golden glow.

The light was not from a campfire. It did not flicker at all. Nor was it mage-light, which was always palest white, with a cold sheen. It was a warm light, like the glow cast by a hearthfire, comforting to look at and oddly cheerful.

She studied that light and in the back of her mind, recent memories fell into place and she realized what she saw. She gasped, staring at the brilliant light. Horrified, she reached out tentatively with a thread of magic, and touched the light—then pulled back, her worst suspicions confirmed.

The golden light was the pillar of magic that had encased Delmuirie, now grown enormous in both size and strength. Faia stared over the bluff, trying to measure its spread; she realized it covered half the city that she could see, including all the areas where her friends lived and worked. The light was the source of the surging, prickling energy she'd sensed.

She remembered the way that pillar of light had rippled when she and Nokar, Medwind, and Roba had attacked Thirk with magic, and remembered as well that it had billowed out like a curtain blown by an invisible breeze when it swallowed Thirk at the end. The light had spread a short time after it swallowed Thirk, but then it had stopped, its boundaries larger but seemingly stable.

Evidently those boundaries hadn't been stable at all. Now the light spread to encompass much of the lower city, including the places where Medwind and Kirgen and Roba lived and worked. Her grip tightened on her staff.

Now perhaps I know why I haven't heard anything from anyone here in the past few months. Faia clutched Kirtha tight and stared down into that beautiful, frightening light.

I'm stronger, she thought—but so is that. Damn Delmuirie! How in all the heavens am I going to get through that?

She turned to Witte. "That light shouldn't be there!" she shouted over the wind. "That's what surrounded Delmuirie—"

"The cage of light?!" Witte interrupted. He stared down over the cliff at the unmoving sheet of light. "But I thought you told me it was a little pillar of light beneath the library! That's enormous."

Faia nodded. Strands of her hair, blown loose from her braid, whipped into her face and clung, damp with snow. She brushed them back—a futile gesture, for the wind never slackened—and shouted, "We can't go down there. If you move into that, it swallows you and freezes you. We'd never get out. We're going to have to find shelter though! We can't stay out here."

She started toward one of the few intact First Folk domes

that remained on their level of the city, up above the encroaching wall of Delmuirie's magic. Witte, though, tugged at the leg of her breeches and pointed toward the side of the mountain that backed them. "In there!" he yelled. "Cave will be warmer than one of those stone domes!"

She nodded and followed him. It was then that she realized she didn't have her big pack. She'd slung it over one shoulder when she left Omwimmee Trade . . . but it wasn't on her shoulder anymore. She looked around the plateau, and still didn't see it.

"Witte! My pack isn't here! What happened to it?"

Witte looked around, his face both puzzled and worried. "I don't know. I thought my magic was strong enough to transport all of us and our belongings here, but maybe it wasn't. The transport spell will drop inanimate things before animate ones—that's a safety feature. It might have gone over my mass limit!" He turned and headed for the tunnels, leaning into the wind.

An especially vicious gust, screaming down through the mountain pass, hit Faia broadside as she turned, and she staggered. She scooped Kirtha into her arms and hurried after Witte.

Into the tunnels, she thought. She knew they weren't caves—they were the labyrinthine lairs of the long-extinct First Folk. They wandered down through the mountains, their long, uncharted passageways honeycombing the whole of the ancient ruins. Into the tunnels—and perhaps she could find a way *through* those tunnels, using magic and intelligence. Or perhaps not. Perhaps there was no way through. None of the scholars had gone more than a few rooms into the maze in any direction or from any opening. No one knew how the rooms linked or where the tunnels led.

The wind cut instantly as she ran into the opening after Witte. The dark of outdoors did not begin to compare to that of the lightless tunnel. Faia stopped. She could make out none of the details of her surroundings—her eyes refused to adjust. She stood still and held them closed a moment, then opened them. Still she was blind.

"Faljon says,'*Only fools walk in darkness/ When light is at hand,*'" she muttered. She conjured a faeriefire. The bright spot of light cast long, dancing shadows, and showed her a rounded little cave with tunnels leading in three directions.

Witte seemed to have vanished. She worried that he might be lost, or that she might not be able to locate him if he wandered too far. "Witte!" she shouted. "Where are you?"

"Stay where you are!" Because of the echoes in the tunnel, Faia couldn't tell where Witte's voice had come from, but he was nearby. She waited, and before long, he popped out from a side passage, his own faeriefire following him. "I'm right here. I was beginning to wonder if you'd fallen off the side of the mountain." He grinned at her. "I was exploring a bit," he said. "Trying to figure out how this place is put together."

Faia nodded. "I have an idea about that. I can cast a seek-and-find spell—I used to do something similar when my sheep scattered. I can call hundreds of faeriefires that will seek through all the passageways, looking for a tunnel that goes where we need to go. When one finds the way, the others will follow it back. The spell is difficult, but I've done it before, and I think it will work here as well as in searching for sheep."

"That seems reasonable, but what will you send your spell in search of?"

Faia thought. "One of my friends, I suppose. Medwind, perhaps. I know her best, and can give the faeriefires the best description of her."

Witte smiled. "That should work just fine."

Faia closed her eyes and summoned the magic—easy, when the whole of the ruins thrummed and crackled with it. But while the summoning was easy, the control was hard; harder now than it had ever been when Arhel's magic was weaker. Still, she focused. She'd learned control in the past years—never again would she accidentally melt a stone village into glass.

Thousands of faeriefires appeared and swarmed for a moment around Faia, Kirtha, and Witte. The faeriefires coalesced suddenly and hung in the air. Then they burst apart, as if they were a flower budded and bloomed and gone to seed in an instant. The individual fires raced away in all directions.

"Just wait," Faia said. "This will take a while."

For a few moments, only Witte's and Faia's faeriefire lights lit the cavern. Then Faia noticed flickers along some of the cavern walls, and in a rush, the faeriefire swarm reformed. It hung in front of the three of them again, and after an instant, took off down one passage. Witte, faster than she would ever have imagined, turned and raced after it.

Faia shifted Kirtha around to ride on her back, and hooked her arms beneath her daughter's legs. Kirtha wrapped her arms around Faia's neck and shouted, "Go, horsy!"

"Not so *tight*," Faia grumbled. She took off through the labyrinth of connected stone caverns, all carved out of the living rock by the First Folk. Each domed room had three or four arched paths leading to other rooms. All of them looked exactly like every other one.

How could even the First Folk have found their way through this place? she wondered. Perhaps they had done it the same way she had—with magic. No simpler solution occurred to her.

Witte abruptly shot around a corner and dropped out of sight, chasing the faeriefire swarm that plunged ahead of him, into a low, wide tunnel that twisted downward, spiraling into blackness. Faia dashed after him and nearly toppled; the tunnel was uncomfortably steep. Just more proof that the creators hadn't been anything like humans—people would have built stairs. She found the sensation of chasing shadows in circles, with darkness riding hard on her heels, dizzying. Occasionally she'd catch a glimpse of Witte's braid bouncing as he ran down the steep grade ahead of her, but she never had more than that tiny reassurance that he was still ahead of her before he raced out of her line of sight again.

She passed one exit—she assumed it led into another layer of connecting chambers, but had no time to peek out of the tunnel to see. Witte and the faeriefires raced downward.

Finally, the tunnel leveled out into a sand-floored chamber. The rooms and tunnels there did not curve in the winding stone web of the upper layers. Instead, corridors ran off in four directions, perfectly straight, with the dark arches of carved doorways lining the corridors at regular intervals that ran on to the vanishing point.

Faia no longer needed her faeriefire light. The corridor that led straight in front of her and the one that ran off to her left both gleamed with the same warm golden light she had seen from the promontory.

The cluster of faeriefires hung in the air at the periphery of this golden wall, swarming and flickering. Those individual fires that at any instant were closest to the barrier darted into it and back out again; it was obvious to Faia that the faeriefire swarm was waiting for Witte and her to move forward. Faia looked around for Witte; she found him sitting against the arching far wall, wearing an expression of intense concentration on his face. His breathing was steady, though Faia gasped for air after her run. She considered that fact for an instant and found she didn't care for it. Witte had returned to remarkably good shape for someone who had been begging passage to Father Dark's domain only weeks before.

The little man twisted absently at the tip of his braid. "We have a problem," he said. "We can't get through here. Our way out is blocked."

"I noticed that, actually." She couldn't keep the edge from her voice. She tried to figure out why her spell had failed—and wondered why the faeriefires could go in and out of the barrier of light that she dared not touch. Even standing near Delmuirie's light, Faia found the energy of the magic wall almost unbearable. It thrummed through her bones from her head to the soles of her feet, and pulsed in time with her blood. Her skin prickled and her breath came fast. She felt as if she were going to explode.

She slipped Kirtha off her back and crouched on the sand floor beside her. "Sit right here and don't move. Mama has to find a way through this."

Kirtha nodded solemnly, eyes round and lips pursed.

Faia formed the image of Medwind Song in her mind. The young, sharp-featured face, skin sun-darkened; hair white as light itself from a Timeride of heroic distance; eyes pale and cold as ice—warrior eyes. Faia held that image and recalled the feel of Medwind's magic. While she struggled to clarify the image and the feel, the faeriefires flashed in front of her, dancing in and out of Delmuirie's wall of magic and trying to lead her forward; when she didn't follow, they came back for her like well-trained sheepdogs trying to lead a recalcitrant shepherd to a missing lamb. She ignored them and focused, until her picture of Medwind Song was as clear as she could make it. Then she focused outward, using her magic to locate a match for her memories inside of Delmuirie's wall.

She failed. That endlessly surging current swallowed every tendril of magic she sent forward, until she started to feel feedback as the barrier magic followed her magical paths back to her, hungry for a new source of food. Faia broke off contact and stood, shivering and gasping, wondering what she could do next.

Witte said, "What's wrong?"

"I can't find Medwind in that mess, and I'm afraid to try again. The magic of that barrier acts like a living thing— and a hungry one. It tried to absorb me just now. I broke off contact before it could, but I don't dare touch it again, or it will swallow me." She wrapped her arms tightly around herself; tears welled in her eyes, and she swallowed hard, fighting the lump in her throat. "My friends are in there, and I don't know how I can get them out."

He nodded. "Let me try. I don't have the magic you do, but maybe that will just mean I won't look as tasty." Witte frowned and stared down at his hands. After a long, tense moment, he stood and gestured, muttering something Faia couldn't quite hear. A shimmer of silver appeared in front of Faia, like a window into the golden light. At first she saw nothing in the window at all— then Medwind Song appeared, somehow even more beautiful than Faia had remembered her. The Hoos woman stared upward, her lips curved in a smile of unimaginable bliss. She sat at a table with First Folk tablets in front of her, frozen—Faia couldn't even see a sign that she breathed. Golden light surrounded her.

"That's Medwind," Faia told Witte.

"Oh, dear," he murmured. "She looks like she's in a bit of trouble, wouldn't you say?" He waved a hand at the magical mirror he'd created.

The scene in the mirror shifted. Medwind vanished, to be replaced by Roba Morgasdotte, who knelt in the burial chambers. A wax tablet and stylus lay in her lap, evidently dropped at the moment the golden light had overcome her. She was hugely pregnant, and frozen in place; her expression was identical to Medwind's.

"Oh, Lady! That's Roba Morgasdotte," Faia said. "She was supposed to have had her baby months ago."

Witte frowned. "Tsk, tsk. This doesn't look good. Not good at all."

The view shifted again, this time to Thirk, toppled on the ground where Faia had last seen him. He'd fallen when Roba pushed him while saving Kirtha's life—he'd been trapped in that wall of light ever since. His equally blissful expression grated on Faia's nerves, but she was pleased that he, at least, remained frozen in place next to his idol, Edrouss Delmuirie. And Delmuirie—

Thirk's image faded, replaced by Delmuirie's. His was a face that would have looked at home in any back-country village—his heavy cheekbones and sharp nose should have made him homely. His eyes, staring upward with that same cowlike expression of contentment, didn't improve his looks either. He had, however, the most perfect smile Faia had ever seen. She wished she could punch it off his face. She stared at him, glowering. The entire mess was his fault.

"Idiot," she snarled.

Witte looked up at her, his expression hurt. "Me? An idiot?" he asked.

She pointed to the form in the mirror. "No. Delmuirie."

"Oh." He nodded. "That almost goes without saying." He waved a hand again and the view once more changed. Now the mirror showed Kirgen, who sat with a stack of drypress beside him and a scritoire in his hand, stopped in the middle of the translating work he had come to love so much. Faia bit her lip hard enough to taste blood—if she didn't love Kirgen, he still remained one of her dearest friends, and the father of her daughter. Somehow, she had to save—

"My da!" Kirtha shrieked, and leapt to her feet before Faia could stop her, The child bolted across the floor of the chamber and leapt through Witte's window—straight into the enveloping golden light.

"NO!" Faia screamed and lunged forward after her

daughter. She, however, didn't reach the light. Suddenly her feet seemed to grow to the floor. She couldn't move— couldn't take a single step.

Kirtha ran as if moving through deep water, one step, two steps, and then a third—and then she froze, just inside the wall of light, one foot still lifted as if she were going to complete her next step at any instant. As she came to a stop, the light of Delmuirie's wall grew even brighter and more intense, and billowed out again, coming to rest after a moment only a few fingersbreadths from the place where Faia stood, trapped.

Behind her, Witte sighed. "Yes," he said. "Yes, precisely so. Things proceed apace."

Faia tried magic to free herself—but every time she attempted to ground and shield herself so that she could break away from the invisible bonds that held her, her use of magic served only to make the bonds stronger. Finally, despairing, staring at her trapped and frozen daughter, she begged Witte to do something. "Help me!" she pleaded. "Witte, help me. I can't move! I have to go after her!"

"Well, of course you do," he said. "But not just yet." He walked over to Faia's side, to where she could see him clearly, and he looked up at her—and when he did, he smiled, and his eyes glittered. "Right now you're exactly where I need you, thanks to your lovely little daughter. Children are so useful sometimes."

Faia felt her stomach lurch—she felt as if the floor were falling away beneath her. "What!?"

"Useful." He winked at her. "I assumed that when Kirtha saw her daddy, she would charge right into the barrier. And so she has—and now you are committed to helping me. Even though I thought probably you would do what needed to be done when you saw your friends trapped in the emeshest—the god-aura—I couldn't be sure. I *knew*, though, that you wouldn't leave your daughter a captive without making your best attempt to go in and free her. With her trapped in the Dreaming God's aura, you have no choice but to do what I want."

Faia's blood felt like it had frozen in her veins. Her heartbeat thudded in her ears. "You—you planned this?"

"From the moment I appeared on your doorstep, dear lady." He hooked his thumbs into his belt. "Even a bit before that."

The room pressed in on Faia from all sides, so that she felt she was running out of air. Bile burned in the back of her throat. She tried to keep calm, though she wanted to scream. "You conniving, dung-eating, sheep-futtering slime's son!" she growled. She had to force the words out through her suddenly constricted throat; her rage made breathing an effort. "You're no friend of Nokar's, are you?"

His eyes widened in feigned surprise. "Such language. Naughty, naughty. Nokar . . . no, he never met me— though I, of course, knew him. And . . . no, I wouldn't say we were friends—exactly. Let me introduce myself," he said, "by the best known of my many names. Folks do call me Witte A'Windo, of course, and sometimes Witte the Mocker. I'm the Mocking God, too, and Ranchek the Trickster. I'm best known, however, as Hrogner, chief saje God of Mischief." He bowed so deeply his braid flipped upside down and dragged along the floor. "I am one of the great gods, *not* one of the minor deities."

A god, she thought, while her heart raced wildly. He was a god—the god Hrogner. She'd brought him into her house, and made him welcome. All the folktales said gods could not enter a home uninvited—but she'd *brought* him in. Welcomed him, cared for him . . . His mocking words echoed in her mind.

". . . you need equal measures of kindness and paranoia, dear girl. Otherwise, there's no telling what you might invite into your house someday."

She'd invited him in. And he'd tricked her.

"I want my daughter back," she said. She could hear her voice shaking—fear for her daughter mixing with murderous rage.

"We all want a lot of things," Witte said agreeably, while his smile stretched wider.

Faia nodded slowly. He'd betrayed her. From the very first—from the moment she'd rescued him from the street, he'd *planned* to betray her. Worse, he'd planned to use Kirtha, who had adored him. That betrayal burned in her mind more than any other.

Fury devoured Faia; the very universe seemed to narrow into a tunnel that connected her to Witte. She stared at him, and felt the rage that sang through her body—felt the power of earth and sky draw into her staff, until her body seemed full to the bursting point with magic. "Yes, we do," she said in a quiet voice. "We all want a *lot* of things." Her magic fought her when she tried to use it to help herself—but perhaps it would still work if she turned it on him. She pointed her staff at Witte's chest and willed the power of earth and sun to destroy him. "And I want you to die," she whispered.

Rich green faeriefire flames boiled from the staff's brass tip and blasted into Witte—and through him. Energy crackled around him; the wall of rock behind the little man melted, leaving a ragged opening into another chamber and a pool of glowing lava on the chamber floor. Faia poured magic steadily into her staff, drawing from the power of the earth and the sun, and from the emeshest— with an equivalent outburst, Faia had once turned a stone village to melted slag. But Witte simply stood there, watching her and grinning.

The wall on the far side of the chamber she'd just opened collapsed, and Faia heard the rumble of shifting stone over her head, and felt the earth shudder. Her fury withered in that instant. She could bring the mountain down on top of herself and her daughter, she realized. She could die, leaving Witte untouched. He was beyond her magic.

She should have known.

He chuckled. "That was a waste of effort, silly girl. You haven't the power to roast me. Not even you can kill a god." He stepped into the wall of light—the emeshest—and danced and spun merrily through it. It didn't affect the little god at all. He pranced around frozen Kirtha . . . and then right *through* her, and leapt back out again. "You can't touch me," he told her.

He sighed and flopped onto the stone floor again. "Of course," he added, "because I am a god, I can't touch that." He pointed to the emeshest. "No god can reach inside another's aura. So I needed a mortal to wake Delmuirie."

She stared at him, and wondered how a mortal could kill a god. In her mind, she swore to the Lady that if it were possible, no matter what it took, she would destroy Hrogner.

He laughed out loud and clapped his hands. "You can't kill me, silly girl." He'd read her mind. He bounded onto a boulder, and turned to face her. "You can't." He grinned at her, his eyes for once level with hers. "That's what being immortal means. You can't destroy me. You can't do *anything* to me."

But she would, she thought. For what he'd done to her daughter, she'd find a way to make him pay. First, though, she had to save Kirtha—and her friends.

Her mother had told her, *You will have a test—a test of your courage and your will—and, too, of your love for your friends, and for all the people of Arhel.*

This was worse than a test, though. This was torture.

She had one question for the Mocking God. "Why do you want me to wake Delmuirie?" she asked. "Since I'm sure you don't care what happens to my friends or my daughter, and since I can't imagine you caring about what happens to Arhel, either—what is in this for you?"

Witte chuckled and sat down on the rock. "I want to cause trouble. It's what I do." He crossed one leg over the other and swung his foot like a small, wicked child. "Delmuirie is no god. He's a man—and I want to see him grow old like a man, and die like one. His presence among the eternals displeases me."

"That's evil," Faia said.

"It's funny." Hrogner arched an eyebrow and his smile curled at one corner. He pressed the palms of his hands together and leaned forward. "Do you know what is even funnier? I don't know what will happen when you wake him. Isn't that delicious?" He laughed again—a high, mad, giggling laugh.

The laugh grated on Faia's nerves, but she forced herself not to respond to it. She breathed in and out slowly, until she felt calm and centered. She had to think—had to find a way to free her daughter and her friends. "Fine, little fiend. You'll get your wish. I'll wake the idiot Delmuirie. Simply tell me what I must do."

Witte shrugged and chuckled. His foot swung back and forth. "I haven't the slightest idea."

"What?" Faia's voice dropped to a dangerous whisper.

The little god shrugged and tipped his hands palm up. "I can't affect the emeshest, dear girl, any more than I can affect the Delmuirie barrier. If I knew what to do, I wouldn't need you. Now, would I?" He smiled brightly. "I'd tell you if I could, of course."

"My daughter is in there." Faia imagined ripping the diminutive god into tiny, bloody shreds; she liked the image.

Witte remained unconcerned, though. "Think of her as incentive."

Her anger grew cold—and made her strong. She would find a way to free Kirtha, and when she had succeeded, she would find a way to obliterate a god. She didn't care that no one had ever done it before. She would do it— she would make the vile Hrogner pay. She stared at the barrier of light, and at Kirtha, frozen in midstep on the other side—still looking as if she would spurt forward at any instant and race on to find her father.

She's alive in there, Faia thought. And if there's a way into the emeshest, there must be a way out. I can find it—if anyone in Arhel can find it, I can.

She clenched her jaws tight and squinted into the light. I have to.

She reached out, and tentatively touched the wall of light. It shimmered and pulsed beneath her fingertip, and she felt a jolt of pure, wild energy sing through her veins. She pulled her hand back and pondered the wall again. It seemed alive, that glistening barrier—alive and waiting. Deep in her belly, she felt terror at what she faced; she kept that terror in check, though, and let the energy of her fear spur her thoughts. The only thing she needed to fear was failure; and because her daughter was in there, she could not fail. She could not. She lowered herself to the ground and crossed her legs, then pressed both her palms against her belly and concentrated on feeling her breath moving in and out.

Use the fear, she told herself. Let it fuel the magic.

Faia studied the pulsing wall of light with senses both physical and magical. She felt out its perimeters. It soared as far above the surface of the earth as it burrowed beneath it; it sat like a fat sphere buried to its middle in the mountainside. Not all of it was visible energy, she realized—from the promontory, the light had flowed like a blanket over the surface of the ancient ruins, though the actual reach of Delmuirie's magic covered much more territory.

She could find neither a ley line power source, nor a link with earth or sun. The energy seemed truly to come from the heart of the emeshest—from the center, where Delmuirie sat like a fat, stupid spider in its web.

She could not break the emeshest's ties with its source

of power, then. She dared not physically enter it, or she would certainly end up in the same situation as her daughter and her friends—from the inside, she wouldn't be able to help.

Yet what could she hope to do from the outside?

She struggled to ground the energy she controlled—the impossible amounts of power the emeshest generated had disturbed her when she and Witte had arrived in the city. Physical proximity to the wall of light made the effects much worse. She tightened the focus of her concentration, until the world around her ceased to intrude on her thoughts, and only the magic and the emeshest existed for her.

Inside and outside. That was her answer; she needed to be both inside and outside Delmuirie's wall.

Hard discipline had taught her to pare away all of herself that was physical, and to break her spirit free—long practice gave her the strength to do what she needed to do in spite of her fear for her daughter, in spite of the distraction of the pulsing emeshest, in spite of her fury at the meddlesome, evil god that sat on the rock above her, swinging his leg. Slowly and cautiously, she separated her conscious self from her body. She floated above her flesh, so that for a moment she could see herself sitting on the floor, legs crossed, eyes closed. She turned away from her flesh-self, and as she did, she caught a quick glimpse of Witte sitting on his boulder, suddenly very still, watching her intently.

Forget him, she told herself. Think of Kirtha.

Then she moved her spirit-self into the wall of light. This time, there was no palpable thrill of pulsing energy—with her flesh left behind, the magic couldn't touch her that way. For the first time, she embraced the mind of the magic.

Chapter 7

As her spirit-self melted into the glowing barrier, an immense outpouring of energy filled her; the wealth of magic was so vast every touch of power she had experienced to that moment seemed as nothing. Her spirit sang with joy; she heard the joy as music, incredible music, and knew that song as the sound of creation—the singing of the very atoms of the universe. *I am*, they sang. *Everything is*. And over that exultant, complex melody, a thread of awareness touched her and embraced her.

You have come, it said. *I have been waiting since before the beginning of time for you. Welcome, heart of my heart and soul of my soul.*

She did not hear the words as a voice. Instead, she felt emotion—an outpouring of love, immense and overwhelming.

For an instant she welcomed it, as a woman would welcome a lover's embrace. There was about it a joy and a sense of fulfillment that was almost undeniable. But the more she opened herself to the touch of this other, the more the other surrounded her and engulfed her, until she felt smothered. Startled and bewildered, she tried to block off the source of that desperate, needy emotion. She couldn't push it away entirely, but she did manage to damp it to the point where she no longer felt it would submerge her individuality in its all-encompassing embrace.

Why did you do that? the source of magic asked. Again, Faia understood the hurt bafflement without actually hearing words.

Who are you? she asked. She didn't answer its question. *Are you Delmuirie?*

She felt a quick flurry of emotions then. The first was delight and recognition at the name. The second, which attempted to hide that delight, followed almost immediately; that emotion was flat denial, mingled with disgust. *There is no Delmuirie.*

Really? Faia implied disbelief.

I am all—I am the whole of the universe. I have awaited the touch of your soul since the beginning of time. The cloistering, too-sweet syrup of other-love flowed around her again. *You thought of me as the Dreaming God when you first arrived here, though that is not my name. You have always known me, Faia. And I have known you since before your birth. I created you to be with me.*

Don't be ridiculous.

Ridiculous? In the other, she felt a twinge of anger, quickly suppressed. *I brought the first of your people across all of space and much of time, to the here and now that I inhabit—in all the universe, I had found no others before your kind with whom I could truly speak. Once your people settled this world, I discovered to my dismay that they could speak to me, but they could not hear me. They were not truly of my kind—none exists of my kind. In the universe, I am alone. Still, the potential was there—and over centuries, I have touched your people with my power and guided their loves and desires, while with every generation, the children became more like me. You are the culmination of my art and my dreams. You can speak with me; you can become one with me . . . you can love me.*

Faia was unimpressed by the "Dreaming God's" grandiose explanation. She expressed sharp annoyance, and pushed at the confining bonds of his adoration. *You aren't asleep.*

Of course not. I have never slept. I have listened to the symphony of the universe forever, but I have listened alone. Now I have you with me, and I will never be alone again. How wonderful it is to talk with someone at last. You and I will share the eternal symphony of being; we will create worlds together, and share eternal bliss.

Faia recalled her daughter, and her trapped friends, and found within her spirit the anger she needed to confront the "Dreaming God." *I have no wish to be a god, and even if I did, I would have no wish to be a god with you. Your name is Edrouss Delmuirie, whether you want to admit it or not, and you're an idiot. You tried some stupid spell and got yourself frozen here, and here you've been for Lady only knows how long.*

I created you. I made you for me—to be with me. . . .

Faia was unrelenting. *No, you didn't, Delmuirie. You didn't make anything—except a stupid mistake. And even if you had, I wouldn't stay here with you. I don't love you. I don't want you. I have a daughter, and I have a place in the world. That place has no room for you.*

She felt his anger begin to boil around her. Heat mixed with lust mixed with fury mixed with bewilderment in an ugly fusion that threatened to suffocate her.

You—will—love—me. I have been alone forever, but forever has become a moment, a nothing, now that you are here. I searched the universe in the hopes of finding another like myself, but none like me existed. I was alone—I have always been alone. I moved stars in their orbits, and changed even the flow of time so that someday I might have you by my side, and now at last I have you. You will be my consort.

No, Faia said. Hard as crystal, cold as ice, she shielded

herself from the heat of his desire. *If you made me stay here, I would withdraw from you and be silent, and you would still be alone. You will not have me, and I will never love you.*

Then, to emphasize her point, she backed away. She followed her spirit lines back to her body, out of the seething cauldron of rage the universe within the emeshest had become.

Even when her spirit was all but free of the god-aura, she could still feel the "Dreaming God's" wrath clawing after her. *You cannot leave me! You cannot reject me!*

I can. She pushed him away. *I did.*

Then she pulled the last thread of her awareness free from the wall of light and slipped back into her body. Immediately the sensations of simply *being* overwhelmed her, as they always did when she returned to her physical self after long absence. The dull ache in her lower back, the tingling of her nearly numb legs, the roar of her breathing, and the pounding of her pulse in her ears; all of these brought her back sharply to the reality of human existence. Still, the heightened emotions from her time in the emeshest clung to her. Tears streamed down her cheeks; the loneliness of the "Dreaming God" still hurt—and she hurt for him.

Except he isn't a god, she reminded herself. He's a man. A fool of a man who has my daughter and my friends and my daughter's father trapped within the barriers of his stupidity.

The emeshest was no longer golden, and it was no longer still. It undulated along its border, whipping out tentacles toward Faia, pulsing dull red and mottled purple and dirty yellow—the colors of a bad bruise. It looks like pain, she thought. If I were going to draw pain, I'd draw it like that.

Faia scrambled out of the reach of the tentacles, back against the wall where Witte sat, gripping a rock. He was pale and shaking. Sweat beaded on his forehead though the tunnel was cool.

"This was a bad idea," the little god said. "I was wrong to do this. You have to calm him. You have to put Delmuirie back to sleep."

"My daughter is in there," Faia said softly. "Remember?"

Witte stared at her. He wore death in his eyes, and fear. "Please," Witte croaked. "Stop him." The wall of light flickered and he flickered with it, so that for an instant Faia could see the rock he sat upon through his body. "He wants you back. Delmuirie wants you back. I can feel it. He's—angry."

Faia's hands knotted themselves into fists, and the muscles in her shoulders tensed. "I want my *daughter* back, and I'm angry, too. What do I care if he's angry?"

"I'm going to die."

Faia stared at him. "Gods don't die," she said, her voice cold. "Remember? That's what you told me."

"I can feel it. I'm going to die. It's all going to end. Everything is going to end." The emeshest whipped and rolled and flashed, growing more ragged and erratic with every pulse. And with every pulse of the wall of light, Witte grew more transparent, and his voice became thinner and harder to hear. "Save me, Faia!" he howled. "I want to live!"

Faia clenched her teeth together until her jaws ached. The time she'd spent caring for Witte and liking him meant nothing to her, she told herself. He had killed every bit of compassion she might have managed. "I want my daughter back."

"Too late!" Witte's scream faded, too, until it vanished into nothingness. The caverns around Faia shuddered, and from somewhere in the distance she heard thunder boom, and a sound very like that of lightning striking a tree—a terrible ripping, cracking sound.

Then the light vanished.

Faia stood in total darkness and complete silence, blind and lost. After the flash of light and the awful boom, her hearing returned first. Even then, she could hear nothing but the sounds of her pulse and her own rapid breathing. Then she heard a little cry. "Mama! Where are you!"

She sagged against the rock wall, and fresh, hot tears streamed down her cheeks. Her daughter was all right, and free from Delmuirie's magic. "I'm right here, Kirtha!" She called a faeriefire to give them light, but none came. She reached into the earth for power, but felt nothing. Swallowed by darkness, blinded to the touch of magic, she felt more helpless than she ever had.

"Mama! Where are you! I can't find you!" Kirtha wailed.

"Stay were you are and keep talking," Faia told her daughter. "I'll find you."

Kirtha talked while Faia fumbled her way forward through the dark, over the sand floor of the cavern. At last she reached her daughter. She wrapped the little girl in her arms and held her tightly. Kirtha hugged her, and her round cheek, soft as silk, damp with tears, pressed against Faia's.

Faia held her and whispered, "Everything is going to be all right now, Kirthchie. It's going to be all right now. We're going to go home."

Chapter 8

It was not so simple as that, Faia realized.

The light was gone and the faeriefires would not come. She tried other magic—tried difficult things and simple things, all without success, until she was forced to admit that her gift was gone.

She had failed the Lady, she realized. She had been given her great gift of magic so that she could wake Delmuirie—but not so that she could anger him.

I should have bargained with him. I should have asked him to free my daughter and my friends in exchange for my own freedom. He would have given me that; I suspect he would have given me anything I'd asked, if only I had stayed.

She hadn't been willing to make that sacrifice, and she was being punished for it. The Lady had taken away the one thing that had made Faia special—her magic.

At least the Lady hadn't taken Kirtha from her, too.

Faia drew a deep, shaky breath. She had to get the two of them out of the maze of tunnels, into the main part of the ruins. Once there, she would be able to get help. She rummaged through her waist pack and found her emergency candle and quicklights. She used the flickering of the flame both for light and to determine the direction air moved through the tunnels.

Wide straightaways led off in four directions, each straightaway lined with carved doorways and intersected at intervals by other wide corridors. She followed the one that gave her the most breeze, until she ran into an area where there were no straight passages left. Then she and Kirtha went through a series of domed rooms connected by twisting tunnels, testing every tunnel and following the leaning candle flame.

She hoped the outside world wasn't far.

She and Kirtha stopped once to rest, and Faia blew out the candle. The dark swallowed them again.

Kirtha began to cry. "I want light, Mama," she said. "I don't like it this dark."

Faia sighed. "We have to save the candle, Kirthchie. We only have one with us, and I don't know how far we will have to walk to get out of these tunnels."

"I'm hungry and I wanna drink."

Faia thought of her pack, and of the jerky and hard cheese and black bread inside of it. Damn Witte! It had been no mistake that he'd brought her without it—she would have bet everything she had on that. He'd left her pack behind out of spite, out of innate wickedness. She had no food because of him, no water, no healing herbs—almost nothing. She could hear the sound of running water somewhere in the distance, but it wasn't in the direction she and Kirtha were traveling, and she was afraid to wander into the maze of passageways.

Kirtha suddenly asked, "Mama, where's Witte?"

Faia could not avoid seeing again in her mind's eye her last sight of the evil god Hrogner—the screaming, twisting form dissolving into air, begging for her help. She winced, grateful the darkness hid her expression from Kirtha. "He—he went away."

"Why?" Kirtha asked.

"I don't know." At least the truth would serve for that answer, Faia thought.

"Will he come back?"

Faia shivered. "I—I don't think so."

After mother and daughter were rested, Faia relit the candle, checked her direction again, and led them forward again. The air grew colder—a good sign. The temperature inside the tunnels would be steady; in Faia's experience, the temperatures in caves varied little with the seasons. But near the tunnel mouths, Faia thought the air would begin to reflect the outside temperatures.

"Hallo!" a man's voice shouted. "Help! I see a light! I'm not dead, then! Help! Please!"

Faia looked around. The voice was male, and accented slightly. It echoed weirdly through the place, so that she was unable to locate the man by sound. The single candle didn't throw enough light for her to find him by sight. She turned in circles. "Where are you?"

"To the left!"

She turned left, holding tight to Kirtha's hand.

"Nay! The light grows dimmer. I meant *my* left!"

Faia stopped, and carefully backtracked. She went to each of the tunnels in the room—this particular one had five, and held the candle into them one by one. Finally the man shouted, "Yes, I see your light better now!" Faia and Kirtha walked along a round-ceilinged passage and into another domed room. This one differed from the others only in that it held camping supplies, a man, and some sort of heavy scaffolding that appeared to have toppled onto him. The scaffolding boards had fallen across him and wedged into the tumbled boulders and up against the ceiling, pinning him to the ground.

He stared at her with a dazed expression, then held his hands up and studied them as if he'd never seen hands before. "Light," he whispered at last. "It was so dark for so long. . . ."

He rubbed his hands over his face and his chest. "I'm . . . cold," he said. He looked up at her, then over

at Kirtha, then back to her again. "Who are you?" he
asked, and then, before Faia had a chance to answer,
added, "Can you help me?"

He was handsome, Faia noticed. Handsome and
powerfully built, with sad, faraway eyes and a wistful
expression that caught her imagination and made her heart
beat faster.

"Yes. I think I can."

"I thought . . ." he whispered. Then his voice broke,
and fear and desperation redrew the planes of his face.
Tears rolled down his cheeks—but silently. He cried as
men cried when they were ashamed of their tears. After
a moment, he took a long, shuddering breath and wiped
his eyes on a sleeve. "I thought I was dead," he told
her. Anguish overlaid his words. "I opened my eyes, and
I could not see anything. Could not see my hand in front
of my face, nor anything around me . . ." He stared off
into the darkness of the tunnels and paused—and Faia
saw him shiver. "I shouted for help. My voice was the
only sound I could hear. That and the moaning. I began
to believe that was the sound of other damned souls;
damned souls trapped here with me. I thought sure I
was one of them."

Faia frowned. "You heard moaning?"

"Aye. It's still there. Be still and you'll hear it only too
well."

Faia held still and listened. She did hear it; a far-off,
mournful throbbing sound that rose for an instant to a
keening wail, then grew soft and plaintive again. She
realized she was listening to wind moving through the
tunnels. She hadn't been able to hear that before; she knew
she had to be nearing the outside world.

For the stranger, though, trapped and helpless, that eerie,
wonderful sound that promised nearing freedom would
have been less than no comfort.

She changed the subject. "What were you doing in here?"

He lay there staring at her, then glanced around the room, up at the mosaics on the ceiling and down at the sand-covered stone floor, at the toppled boulders that had fallen from the far wall.

"How very strange," he said finally. "The last thing I recall, I was . . . hunting, high in the mountains and far from my camp . . . and a storm broke. I sought shelter in a . . ." He frowned. ". . . a cave, I suppose. After that, I remember nothing, until I woke to find myself in darkness, unable to move."

Faia pulled at the boards that pinned him in place. Those boards lay across his chest and trapped one leg in a hollow between two tumbled boulders. "You'll remember the rest," she said. "You probably took a bump on the head. Such a bump can knock the memories loose for a bit. But memories come back."

The boards resisted her—but she was no delicate city girl. She grew up plowing fields and chasing sheep and carrying water to horses and cows and goats; even after years of softer living, she was strong. She pried the scaffolding loose, and freed his chest and then his leg.

"Ah," he sighed, and lay flat on the floor. "That hurt a bit."

She nodded. "I'm sure. Hold still and let me look at your leg." She rolled down the top of his boot—it was made of good leather, she noted, if oddly cut—and unbound the leather wraps of his leggings so she could slide the soft cloth up his thigh. The wrapped leggings weren't of a style she knew well, either. Foreign, she decided—the accent should have told her as much.

The leg itself was bruised and scraped raw over the shinbone. She pressed hard on the edges of the wound, then lifted her fingers quickly. The flesh blanched, then pinkened: a good sign. The blood still traveled through the leg to the foot—the scaffolding hadn't pressed hard enough or long enough to do permanent damage.

"It could be worse," she told him, and frowned. The leg would heal on its own, she thought, but it would hurt him, and perhaps develop infection—and both pain and infection were so unnecessary. If only she still had her magic. She closed her eyes and turned away.

"Are you ill, then?" he asked.

"No," she told him. "Unsettled, perhaps. It doesn't matter. I'm just upset that I cannot do anything more to help you." She looked at him again, and her heart pounded in her breast. She felt her cheeks grow hot, and was grateful the candle threw so little light. Otherwise, he would surely have seen her blush.

"Don't worry about me," he said gently. "My leg hurts, but I feel well enough to stand and follow, I think—if you know the way out of here."

She told him the trick she used to find the exit to the tunnels.

"Clever lass," he said. "I don't know if I would have ever thought of that—even if I'd had the right kind of supplies." He looked around him. "Let me go through my pack and see what I do have."

Kirtha had been looking over his things on her own. "You have lots of clothes," she said. She squatted back on her haunches and watched him as he stood. "What's your name?" she asked him.

He gave Kirtha a brief flash of a smile which became a grimace as he hobbled forward. He stopped and took his weight off his injured leg, and managed another broad smile. "Gyelstom ArForst. But you may call me Gyels, young miss." He sketched a slight bow in the little girl's direction and she giggled.

Gyels went through his belongings—he found a cat-eye lamp full of oil, and lit that. He had spare candles, too—Faia took one to use for finding the way out, because hers was burnt nearly to nothing and the flame of the cat-eye, shielded from breezes, would not bend away from the tunnels.

Gyels threw his possessions into his bag. He was clearly as eager to escape the tomblike caverns as Faia. When he was finished, he shouldered his pack and the three of them followed both the sound of the wind and the bending of the flame through the tunnels. He hobbled, and Faia moved near him so he could put an arm on her shoulder to steady himself. He smiled down at her.

"My thanks, lovely lady. My thanks for your assistance, and for my rescue. I owe you my life—and if I could, I would show my gratitude. . . ." He raised one eyebrow. ". . . in a way your . . . husband? . . . could not take amiss."

Faia knew the meaning of that carefully posed question, and pondered her answer. She'd been ostracized in Omwimmee Trade because she'd admitted she'd had Kirtha without taking a husband in public bond first. If Gyels was hill-folk, the question would be unladen with that unspoken question of Kirtha's legitimacy. If he were of Flatterland stock, she needed to word her answer carefully.

And she didn't recognize his accent at all.

"I am now without a husband," she said. She told the truth, but implied a lie. She didn't like herself for that— but she didn't want the man to look at her the way Flatterland men often did, with their sly, speculative smiles.

"My sympathies for your sorrow." He glanced over, and in the dim and flickering light, his eyes seemed full of sadness.

She nodded. Then, so she would not have to add to her lie, she said, "Look. The candle flame bends further."

They stopped walking, and all three stood quietly, watching the flame dance and bend—the breeze had become strong enough that Faia could feel it brushing against her cheek.

"We're close," she whispered.

Kirtha said, "Listen to the ghosts, Mama."

The moaning of the wind was louder—Faia could almost catch words in the voices of the wind. Those eerie voices sounded sad—and yet they spoke to Faia of freedom.

"That way," she said. She pointed, and Gyels nodded.

A few more steps—a turn and then another turn—and suddenly snow whipped against her cheeks, and a gust of wind blew out the candle. The flame in the lantern lasted a moment longer, while the three of them trod into the middle of a snowstorm. Then it blew out, too.

After the light, her eyes had to adjust to darkness again. The golden glow of the emeshest no longer overlaid the city. Faia looked for landmarks. Their tunnel opened to the lowest aboveground level of the ruins. She could see little because of the storm, but the towering bulk of the ancient First Folk library was unmistakable.

The library held many of the answers to the mysteries of the First Folk; until slightly more than a year earlier, the scholars of Arhel had assumed that the first civilization on Arhel had been a human one. It was a reasonable assumption—the only people in Arhel were human and no one had found anything that would have suggested that things had ever been different. At least, no one had ever found any evidence of that sort until the expedition that uncovered these ruins—the most complete anywhere in Arhel. And the astonishingly well preserved mummified corpses of First Folk, hidden in a secret burial ground below the library and accessible only through a hidden passage in one of the back rooms.

Scholars were still reeling from the ramifications of that single find. If the first civilization in Arhel wasn't human, then when did human civilization begin . . . and how? What had happened to the first settlers, now extinct? Had the human and First Folk civilizations grown up together, or had one risen and died before the birth of the second? Faia had wondered about all of those things herself, and

"You've come! You've come!" she sobbed into the thick wool of Faia's erda. "Oh, please, please! You have to help Mama! Please!"

Faia picked up Kirtha and glanced over at Gyels, whose forehead creased in a worried frown. Faia shrugged. "What's the matter with her, Choufa?"

"I do not *know!*" the girl wailed. She turned away and buried her face in her hands, and Faia could see her shoulders heave as she sobbed.

Faia felt sick dread knot her belly and dry her mouth. She tried to be reassuring. "Whatever it is, I'll do my best to help." She was bereft of her magic, though—whatever help she might give would be strictly mundane.

Choufa got herself under control, though; either reassured by Faia's words or out of tears, she beckoned both Faia and Gyels toward the smaller rounded doorway that led into the second room of the ancient First Folk dwelling, and to the side of a crone who sat huddled next to the fire burning in the brazier on the floor. Faia looked for Medwind; she saw no one else in the room.

"Faia!"

That single word from the old woman's lips dragged the ice from outside to freeze the blood in Faia's veins. The wavering old voice was sib to one Faia knew nearly as well as her own. She looked into the ancient's eyes—eyes that were pale as the moon, intense as magefire, even though they rested in folds of wrinkles and the shadows of deep hollows.

The crone smiled and struggled to her feet, and said, "Thank every god in Ariss you're here. And Kirthchie—by Thiena's tits, she's grown. And him . . . ?" Her sharp gaze raked over Gyels, and the old woman shook her head. "I don't know him."

Faia tried not to show her dismay. "Medwind? Is it really you?" She rested her hands on the woman's frail shoulders, and looked down at her. She could see only the faintest traces of the young woman she had known—the Hoos warrior who had turned mage and scholar. But in the old face the young eyes remained unmistakably fierce and proud, and Medwind still showed unmistakable traces of her former barbaric beauty. "Oh, godsall," Faia whispered, "it is you!"

"It's me. Hell of a mess. Do you remember when Nokar was dying, after we escaped from the Keyu?"

Faia nodded. She would never be able to forget any of that nightmare time.

"I couldn't stand to let him die," Medwind said. "I loved him so much, and I hadn't had him for very long. So I studied the remains of the spells he'd used to prolong his life, and saw how I could repair them—if I used part of my own life energy as a sort of . . . glue."

The old woman shook her head ruefully. "I gave him part of my life, but I had no way of knowing how much. It would seem from the evidence," she held up her bent, age-spotted hands and frowned, "that I gave up most of whatever time I had." She looked away, and her voice grew quiet and sad. "And he died anyway."

"When did you grow old?"

"Only just. When damned Delmuirie's pillar released me—"

"That was the emeshest," Faia interrupted.

"Really?" Medwind's eyebrows rose, but after a moment, she nodded. "That makes sense. More probable the light is the aura of a god than anything else." She sighed. "Anyway, we first noted some additional spread in the boundaries of the . . . the emeshest . . . some weeks after it caught Thirk. Kirgen went down to study it, trying to fathom the reasons for its encroachment. He noted and documented an increase in available magic—not a large increase, but still, measurable. But Delmuirie's pillar showed no further changes, and after a while, we tired of watching it do nothing at all. All of us, including Kirgen, went back to our regular studies. Then two idiot Bontonards came to these ruins to study; they nosed into everything, disrupted our work, and I don't doubt did whatever it was that set the pillar off again. One minute I was working, the next, trapped in light and music and a sensation of infinity. Very peaceful, that, but too much like what I suspect death will be. But then, though no time seemed to have passed at all, we were released again."

"That was because of me," Faia said.

"Good." Medwind nodded again. "I should have guessed that you would realize something was wrong and come after us. I imagine we would have been trapped in there forever had you not come. And I'm glad you did. The emeshest was such a joyous place it almost hurt to be set free—" Medwind turned away, and walked back to the fire. "—But it wasn't living."

Faia saw her friend's shoulders slump, and heard her say, "This isn't much like living either, though. Because I rode the Timeriver, my body never showed signs of age. With magic I could have prolonged my existence for perhaps several hundred years; but now my magic is gone, and the touch of the Timeriver is gone—and I'm old. I've only lived thirty-six years, Faia—but look at me. My body could be ninety." Medwind looked down at her dried, frail body with disgust. "I'd be lucky to live out the year like this."

Faia clenched her hands into fists and willed herself to silence. Medwind's spirit seemed to have grown as old and weak as her body. If the eyes remained young, they were all old age had saved of the Medwind Faia knew— it did not seem possible that the same woman who rode the Timeriver and charged headlong into the search for the First Folk could be the same timid, despairing creature who huddled by the fire bemoaning her fate. Could mere age so completely destroy a great spirit?

Faia felt tears start at the corners of her eyes. She wanted her old friend back—and she was helpless to restore her. "My magic is gone, too," she admitted.

"All of it?"

"As far as I can tell. I can't even conjure a faeriefire anymore. I refused the Dreaming God—well, Edrouss Delmuirie, though he thought he was the Dreaming God. I refused to stand up and face my destiny—and the Lady cursed me for my cowardice."

"Destiny, eh?" Medwind turned back to face Faia, and her eyes sparkled. "That's rarely something we recognize when it spits in our faces. So what was this destiny of yours, girl?"

Faia quickly told her about her suspicion that she had been fated to stay with Delmuirie in order to free her daughter and her friends.

Medwind snorted. "Pah! That would be a silly destiny! The gods don't waste the talent of their best followers on grandiose gestures of self-immolation. That's the sort of nonsense you'd hear in those peasant songs of yours."

"The Lady leads, and I follow," Faia huffed. "Most of the time, anyway."

"The *Lady*. She's a cowardly excuse for a god, anyway."

"Just because she doesn't lead me to collect heads or futter goats like those monstrosities you worship—"

"Futter goats! Etyt and Thiena futter each other, thank you, and leave the goats to your *ecuvek* hill-folk shepherds!" The old woman glared at Faia through narrowed eyes.

Faia glared back, crossing her arms over her chest. Perhaps Medwind had become senile as well as old. She certainly seemed ruder than Faia remembered.

Gyels cleared his throat and both women turned to see what he wanted. He coughed and said, "I think I'll be waiting out in the, ah, cold." He ducked out of the room.

Faia felt heat rush to her cheeks when he departed. "Oh, that was childish."

Medwind sighed. "It was. I apologize."

"Me too."

The two friends looked at each other across the fire, and Medwind began to chuckle. "Childish . . . that has some possibilities. What about Kirtha? She had quite a bit of ability. Does she still?"

Faia said, "I didn't even think about what Kirtha could do! I suppose I wasn't thinking at all." She knelt beside her daughter and asked, "Can you light a fire for me, Kirthchie? Just a little one—" She fumbled through her waist pack and came up with the candle.

Kirtha nodded. "Yes, Mama." The little girl smiled, pleased to be able to show off one of her tricks in front of adults. She stared at the candlewick, and her face grew serious. A moment passed, and then another—and then she frowned. "I can't find the light lines, Mama," she said. "Where are they?"

Medwind and Faia exchanged looks. "Her too, then," Medwind said quietly.

"Mama!" Kirtha said. "Fix it! Bring back the light lines!" The child's face clouded—Faia could see a temper tantrum coming.

"I can't, littlest," she said, hoping to prevent the explosion. "I can't fix anything anymore."

"I *want* the light back, *Mama*!" the child yelled, and closed her eyes—as if to summon the thunder. But the thunder came no more readily than the fire, and the child, in a rage, threw herself on the floor and screamed and cried.

"I know how she feels," Medwind said, watching the display. "I'd do the same thing if I didn't think I'd shatter my bones trying it."

"Bedtime," Faia announced, and picked up her daughter.

She glanced at Medwind, who said, "She can sleep on my mat. I don't think I'll dare sleep again. Too afraid I'll never wake up." The ancient Hoos woman sighed deeply, and seemed to shake off her despair. "Call the man back in. Let me talk to him."

Faia stepped out, to find that Gyels hadn't gone to stand in the snow and the dark after all. He sat by the fire in the main room, talking to Choufa. Faia called him back, and he returned to Medwind's private chamber.

The old woman waited until he seated himself, then asked, "So—what of you? You have any magic to speak of?"

"Me? Magic? No. I never did have any magic. I'm a hunter. I track game—capture it live for breeders or kill it for food and hides."

Medwind frowned again. "No help there. No help from the rest of the people here, either. We met when we were released from the emeshest. There is no magic left among us."

Faia frowned. "That doesn't make sense. Why would the Lady curse all of us?"

The old woman clucked her tongue. "You and your Lady . . . she didn't curse *any* of us, Faia. I don't think your Lady had anything to do with what happened here at all. I would guess this spot has become *taada kaneddu*—a god-desert . . . a taboo place. One or the other of the gods has declared the ruins *taada* and the rest have pulled all magic away from this place—and everyone in it."

Faia brightened at that idea. "Then all we need to do is leave here, and walk until we're outside of the—"

"*Kaneddu.*" Medwind supplied the word Faia wanted. "It means a zone empty of magic."

"Exactly." Faia smiled. "We walk out of the ruins, and out of the *kaneddu*, and you'll be back to normal. We both will."

Medwind pursed her lips and nodded slowly. "If the circle of the *taada kaneddu* is small, that will work. Kirgen or one of those damned Bontonard scholars can check as soon as the storm stops. You'll meet them soon enough, I'm sure. Bytoris something and Geos something else. They eat like a herd of starved goats, and skulk around poking into everything. I can't stand 'em." She sighed, and the spark of anger that had given her face some animation died. "If the circle of the *kaneddu* is large, though, I'll never survive the trip." She leaned forward and rested her hands on her knees.

"I want to ask a favor of you, Faia. If the circle is too large, go outside of it for me—and when your magic comes back, figure out a way to bring me to you." She closed her eyes, and an expression of pain ran across her face. "Help me get my life back. I'm too young to be this old, Faia." She whispered, "And I'm not ready to die."

Choufa had come back into the room with Gyels. She sat beside Medwind and put an arm around her. She looked at Faia with desperation in her eyes. "Please. Save my mother." She bit her lip and looked like she was going to start crying again.

Faia crouched in front of her friend and rested a hand on her shoulder. "You saved my life once," she told the old woman. "I don't know that I will be able to turn back time. But whatever I can do, Medwind, I will do." She took a deep breath. "I swear by my Lady, whatever is in my power, I will do to give you back your life."

Behind her, Gyels said softly, "You are very brave, Faia. Very brave."

Chapter 9

Faia left Medwind sitting by the fire with Choufa tending her, and Kirtha sleeping on the mat. She went into the large, cold greatroom and sat by the hearth fire in the room's center—she'd intended to be alone, but Gyels followed her out and settled next to her on the rugs.

"I meant what I said," he told her.

She didn't answer him. She hoped he would leave her alone, but that did not look likely.

"You're very beautiful, and very brave. And your daughter is a courageous little girl. You must be a good mother, too."

Faia looked at him sidelong. "Indeed," she said dryly. "I'm to be given a place in the minor pantheon of deities next Watterdae."

Gyels laughed, not at all offended by her flippant remark. "I'd worship at your shrine."

Faia chuckled in spite of herself. "I won't be taking supplications from my worshipers for at least a month—I have to get used to the work."

"You look very like a goddess of love to me. I could help you learn your duties." He leaned closer to her, so that she felt the warmth of his skin like a lover's touch.

He was, she thought, beautiful. His dark eyes were bottomless pools that drowned the light, and his lips were full and firm, curved in the slightest and most enchanting of smiles. She leaned forward—then caught herself and pulled back. She'd been too long without a man to hold—the hunger of her body could easily outpace the caution of her mind. He was a gorgeous creature, but she didn't know this one well at all.

So she flashed a dangerous smile at him and said, "Remember what happens to all the handsome young hunters who woo love goddesses."

He tipped his head to one side and grinned at her. "I don't *know* what happens to them. Why don't I kiss you, and you can show me."

"The goddesses turn the hunters into eels or fishes, and feed them to their cats," Faia told him. Her voice held the slightest hint of laughter.

His eyes widened and he backed up slightly. "Ah," he said. "And do you have a cat, lovely Faia?"

"I do." She smiled. "I have a cat named Hrogner—he's clever and wicked, and he has hands. He would never drop a fish I threw to him."

"Hrogner," Gyels murmured. "I never much *liked* Hrogner."

"Neither did I," Faia agreed, with perhaps, she thought, too much emphasis. So she added, "But he makes a good cat." She thought about the cat, and hoped he would be all right. Somehow, she didn't think she was going to be home by the next week.

"Being a cat would play to Hrogner's strengths, I admit," the hunter said. Then he sighed. "Perhaps your husband's . . . death . . . has been recent? You are not ready for someone to come courting yet?"

"No." Faia played with the tip of her braid, looking at the way the hairs looked very red when she held them in front of the firelight. "It isn't that."

"Then you simply do not wish to be love goddess to my mighty hunter, eh?"

That wasn't true either. Her body was more than willing—her mind, however, found that sudden physical desire more frightening than attractive. "Not tonight," Faia said politely.

"Ah." Gyels smiled. "There is hope in that statement, in any case. May I ask some other night?"

Faia stood and looked down at him. "I make no promises."

Exhausted, she retired to Medwind's room to sleep next to Kirtha. Gyels stayed in the greatroom; Faia looked back long enough to see that he was making a bed for himself out of the rugs spread near the fire.

He wasn't far enough away, she thought. His presence made her feel raw and naked and vulnerable. And even in another room, she could sense his presence.

Chapter 10

Faia woke to the sounds of heated discussion in the greatroom. She stretched and rolled over. Through the narrow smoke-slits in the domed ceiling, she could see stars—that meant nothing but that the storm had ended. From the raised voices one room away, she guessed that any storm that had been outside had long since moved indoors.

"You *won't* leave her! Not now!"

"I have to." That's Kirgen, Faia thought, recognizing the voice in spite of the unusual volume and stress of it. He sounded both angry and frightened.

"Faia knows the mountains." Medwind was keeping her voice calm and reasonable, but Faia could hear the forced edge to it. "You've learned something of them from living in these ruins, but you can't begin to think that a trek through the worst of the mountains in the Tide Mother winter will be anything like huddling around a fire in one of these cozy domes."

Time to go out and see what is happening, she thought. She wandered to the doorway between the rooms.

"I'll have to learn quickly, then, won't I?" Kirgen shouted. "The other alterna—" He looked up from his seat by the hearth fire and saw her, and whatever he'd planned to say died on his lips.

"Good morning, Faia." Medwind's smile was thin.

Faia nodded to Medwind, but her eyes were on Kirgen. Kirtha curled in her father's lap, playing with the gold-banded braids that hung to his shoulders. He looked very much the scholarly, stuffy saje—very little like the cheerful young man she'd so enjoyed that one night years ago. He seemed unaware of his daughter's presence, or of the worried look in the child's eyes—his anger with Medwind, and with whatever the two of them had been arguing about, was the only emotion Faia could see in his face.

"Hello, Kirgen," Faia said, keeping her voice even.

He nodded stiffly. "Faia." He looked into her eyes, and the room narrowed down to exclude Medwind, Choufa, the hunter Gyels, even Kirtha.

"Why the fight?" Faia asked him.

"Roba is near her time. I suggested to Medwind that you stay with her and help deliver her baby while I went in search of the end of the magicless zone." His face flushed, and his eyebrows lowered.

"I suggested he stay here with his wife, and let people who knew the mountains go tromping around in them," Medwind said.

"Perfectly sensible. Why *would* he leave her?"

"He thought you might be too fragile to make the trip."

Faia's voice went cold. "I told Medwind I would go— I did not offer to do anything I was not capable of doing. And in fact, I *swore* that I would seek help. Would you ask me to forswear myself?"

"Your daughter needs you here with her," Kirgen said.

Faia looked away from Kirgen long enough to glance at Gyels and Medwind. Then she glared back at him. "My daughter has her father here—she can stay with you, and you can stay with your wife. I would not take you from the birth of your child." She saw him flinch as he recognized the fury in her eyes. "Or do you also question that I will do what I promised to do?"

Kirgen flushed. He was a city boy—but he also came from the paternalistic side of Ariss. A woman's oath had, until recently, counted for little there, and no matter how much Kirgen had come to accept women as equals, Faia knew he was still a product of his upbringing. His mind might accept, but his heart still doubted.

The hunter had been looking from Faia to Kirgen, a thoughtful expression in his eyes. "I'll go with you," he said to Faia. "I admire your . . . courage. And I know the mountains."

"No," Faia said.

"Don't be stupid!" Kirgen glared at her. "If you insist on going, take help with you."

"There's no need. The trip may be very short," Faia said. "The magic-barrenness may end just outside the city walls."

"It doesn't," Medwind said. "The hunter went out for us many hours ago carrying a lightstaff. He ran the distance someone unused to the mountains could walk in a day, watching to see if ground-magic would light the staff."

Gyels said, "It never did. So I ran farther. I'm strong," he said, "and I can do things most men cannot do. I ran the distance of a second day's journey, along the high road—and still the staff did not light. So I ran back. If you go, you will have more than two days of walking to reach this place your Hoos woman thinks exists—if it exists at all—and in that time, many things could happen to you." His expression grew tender as he looked at her, and he said, "I would be honored to travel with you and offer my blade to protect you."

Faia felt again that overwhelming desire to be with him, to let herself slip into his arms, to feel the love of a man once more. Overwhelming physical desire; a twinge of nervous caution. She did not flatly turn him down, though; she'd learned enough guile to avoid that mistake. It only led to arguments, and arguments could be lost as easily as they could be won. Instead she said quietly, "I will consider your offer, Gyels. Thank you."

However, Medwind's expression grew puzzled. She narrowed her eyes and looked from Faia, to Gyels, and back to Faia again. Then she pointed a gnarled finger at Faia and said, "You and I must talk. Alone."

Chapter 11

Kirgen took Kirtha back to his and Roba's dwelling; Choufa went along to help Roba; Gyels politely made his excuses and got out from underfoot. When they were well gone, Medwind turned on Faia and said, "What are you doing? You're turning him down without even giving him a chance—"

Faia turned her back on Medwind and said, "We aren't going to discuss this."

"By the gods we *are*." Her friend's voice rose. "You've been living like a cloistered celibate since Kirtha was born, and I haven't said anything to you. But you haven't been happy, Faia—and now I can see why. You refuse opportunities without even considering them."

"You were right not to say anything." Faia turned and studied her friend. It was almost impossible to see, in the old woman facing her, the young woman Medwind Song should have been—yet Medwind Song was looking at Gyels with those young-woman eyes.

"I did consider his offer, Medwind. It takes everything I have in me to keep myself from throwing my arms around his neck and dragging him off to some dark, cozy corner and bedding him. Obviously you've felt the pull of his attraction, too."

"More than I would have believed."

"I noticed." Faia looked down at the backs of her hands, and rubbed her right thumb along the backs of her left knuckles. "But for all that he's a pure gem of a man, I don't entirely trust him." She sighed. "I'd like to trust him—and I have nothing but the convenience of our first meeting that makes me doubt him."

"Convenience? You met him in a cave, in total darkness, when he was trapped under a scaffolding cave-in."

Faia smiled slowly. "Exactly. How lucky for him that I happened by."

"Remind me that I don't want you doing any favors for me. You might decide, once you've found a way to make me young again, that it is entirely too convenient that you were able to help me—and that I must have plotted the whole thing to use you."

Faia arched an eyebrow. "I have reasons for my suspicion. I traveled to the ruins with Witte—who turned out to be none other than the god Hrogner. He was a vile little god— he used me, and made a great deal out of the fact that I would never be able to get even with him. He said that no mortal could ever hope to kill a god."

"Of course not."

"Then he proceeded to die."

Medwind pursed her lips.

"And after I had nearly escaped the First Folk caverns with Kirtha, I run across a man so irresistible that when I am in his presence, I find myself able to think of almost nothing but touching him—a man I rescue from darkness and certain doom, who would have died had I not coincidentally happened along just the series of tunnels I did."

Faia took a deep breath. "I don't want to think this, but I suspect that Gyels is Hrogner, hoping to use me and make a fool of me yet again."

"Hmmmm." Medwind settled in front of the fire and stared into it. "Your hunter Gyels is as fine a bit of horseflesh as I've ever seen—and I've had ten husbands, Faia. Nine of them at one time." She raised an eyebrow and her grin quirked to one side. "*Briefly*, I had nine husbands at once. It became too much of a good thing. But, damnall, girl—so what if he is a god? If I were you, I'd take him—I wouldn't trust him, perhaps, but I'd have the pleasure of him. Hold your heart in reserve—but by Etyt and Thiena, girl, don't waste that body."

"I wish it were that easy." Faia rubbed her temples and closed her eyes. "I've been alone too long, though. I'm afraid he might come to matter to me in spite of all my caution."

Medwind clucked her tongue. "Hearts are made to break. Still, give yourself a chance. Take Gyels with you—you have no idea how far you have to go, or what you'll have to get through to get there. He'd be useful in the mountains. Don't bed him right away. If you would feel better with other people along, then take them—though I think you're throwing away a wonderful opportunity to be alone with him. Why don't you take the Bontonard scholars with you. We need to get them out of the ruins, anyway. Without magic here, and the Tide Mother's false winter sure to kill most of this year's crops, we'll need our stored food for ourselves." Medwind nodded. "In fact, if you and the hunter would lead them back to their city, that would solve a big problem for us here."

Faia nodded. "I can do that—but is their city in the right direction?"

"If my guess about the *taada kaneddu* is correct, then we're in the center of a circle. It shouldn't matter what direction you travel, so long as you go in a straight line." Medwind shrugged. "And if my guess is wrong, at least you'll get them home."

Faia considered traveling with Gyels. Her heart raced at the idea, and she wondered if she was insane to even consider it. Still, a hunter would be a useful companion.

Hrogner would be dreadful company . . . but as long as she suspected him, and didn't let herself rely on him, even if Gyels was Hrogner, he wouldn't be able to trick her. And with a few other people along, she'd be safe enough.

"I want to leave as soon as possible. Where can I find the Bontonards?"

"Check the library."

Chapter 12

The snow at the mouth of the dwelling's curved tunnel lay waist-deep—but it was dry and powdery, so that Faia had to wade through it, with no hope of going over the top. She stepped into a night of incredible beauty. The clouds were gone, and stars glittered in the clear sky from horizon to horizon. The burning halo of the Tide Mother, eclipsing the sun, hung directly overhead. She glimpsed it and looked quickly away. "It's midday," she whispered. It seemed impossible to believe.

She waded toward the library and her lantern swung in front of her, throwing a warm yellow glow that danced over the drifts and snow-covered rubble and made shadows that shimmied and stretched like things alive. Where the snow hadn't drifted, it rose to the middle of her thigh. The rolling white surface bore only deep tracks that ran from dwelling to dwelling; the rest of the city was covered by an unmarred blanket, with the hulking forms of the mountains rising high and dark out of it. The air was still; her breath hung in front of her like a fog. The drifts sprawled in fantastic shapes throughout the ruins, and the crisp, clean scent of the air brought back memories of winter in Bright.

Faia stood still for a moment, remembering playing with her dogs Chirp and Huss in a snow like this one, throwing them sticks and watching them plow through the white drifts trying to find what she'd thrown, exploding out of the powder and barking madly, then burrowing back in again. She smiled. It seemed so long ago. That had been—one?—no, *two* winters before the spring when she lost everyone. Her smile died, and she felt the familiar, painful lump in her throat. More than seven years ago in all.

She leaned on her staff and thought, How much longer? How long until I can remember them all without pain—with only happiness?

She doubted that day would ever come.

She waded to the raised, broken stone slabs that made up the First Folk road and climbed up. The wind had blown away some of the snow from the high, smooth surface—the road made comparatively pleasant walking. She trudged to the narrower road that led directly to the library, then stopped again.

The First Folk statues on either side of that road stared at her with their glittering black eyes. Their winged, taloned, arrow-tailed bodies were deformed into shapes even more monstrous than the original ones by layers of snow. They were at once hideous and comical and frightening. Faia held her light higher and stared, and the lantern flame reflected in the black stone eyes. Those eyes gleamed, bright and alert. The statues of the First Folk looked so frightening—and their glittering eyes watched her with an expression that seemed sly and fierce—and always hungry.

She shivered, only partly from the cold, and hurried down the long road between their ranks. They stared after her as she passed, and when she was beyond them, they still watched.

She went through the gaping stone maw of the library doorway, through the drifts of snow that covered the stone floor, and walked down the long central corridor. The noise of her booted footsteps and the tapping of the brass tip of her staff echoed weirdly, and her light made only a small, hardly comforting circle in the darkness around her—while her little sphere of light made the far shadows seem even blacker and more mysterious. The library was *wrong* to her human senses. The angles were awkward, the scale far too large—and her light kept picking up flashes from the live-looking eyes of the brightly painted stone gargoyles that leered at her from the tops of stone shelves and the recesses of unexpected nooks.

"Hallo-o-o!" she shouted into the cavernous spaces. Her voice bounced back to her, echoing from the vaulted wings on either side of the main part of the library and from the vast open spaces in front of her. Echo layered on echo, her chorus softening to whispers—her single voice became in an instant a choir.

She tipped her head and closed her eyes, listening— intrigued by the permutations in that one shouted word, until the last hushed "hallo-o-o" died to silence. She smiled slowly, and in a quiet voice, sang:

> *"Oh, fair was my love—as the summer, the summer*
> *As sweet as the rich ripened fruit on the vine."*

The echoes sang with her, adding depth and richness to the folk tune. Faia grinned, and sang a little louder.

> *"As cool and as strong as a river, a river,*
> *And heady as autumn-pressed wine."*

She liked the rich reverberation through the corridors as she sang the old love song—she loved to sing, though her voice was ordinary. The First Folk library, however, made her sound wonderful. She started walking toward the back of the library, looking for the two Bontonard scholars—but she walked as slowly as she could, and sang as she walked.

"I danced with my love in the summer, the summer,
I danced with my love by the side of the sea.
We danced in the dark 'til a sailor, a sailor . . .
He came and took my love from me.

"So I wait as the winter grows colder—grows colder,
I wait for my love as my hair turns to grey.
I wait where he left, by the sea—by the sea,
For the sea shall return him some day."

She could imagine herself, on the stage in the square in Omwimmee Trade, gorgeous in one of the low-cut, flower-decked dresses the Omwimmee Traders wore at festivals. Her audience would be rapt. She stopped walking and closed her eyes and imagined the stunned townsfolk watching her, whispering that never had they heard the song done with such feeling or skill. She belted out the next verse, putting a lot of passion in it.

"And now the sea blows the waves higher—and higher,
And now a ship founders beyond the cruel reef.
For now my love's come back to me—come to me,
But the sea brings me nothing but grief."

She heard a soft scurrying noise from the library's depths. So the scholars were in one of the little side rooms.

I can't imagine why they haven't heard me yet, she thought, and then she grinned. Scholars got lost in their studies so deeply, they would likely not hear the world end.

Now she knew how to find them. And if they weren't listening, she could go for a big finish without embarrassment. She tore into the song's last verse, soaring through the lilting melody, and the walls of the ancient library rang with her amplified voice.

"Don't LOOK for your love by the sea—by the SEA,
For the sea loves the sailor and WON'T let him
GO-O-O!
If ever he leaves her she'll KILL him—she'll—"

"Hel-l-l-l-l-ppppp!" someone screamed. "By all the gods and demons, help!"

The song died in midnote. Faia froze and looked around.

Help?

The screams came from just ahead. She heard a rumble—rhythmic pounding on something that boomed like thunder. Then the noise stopped and the screaming began again.

"Help, for the love of the gods!" Whoever it was sounded ragged and desperate.

Her mind raced ahead of her body as she tried to recall emergency rescue procedures, and as she tried to imagine what sort of trouble the two scholars could have gotten themselves into. What could have happened to them? She broke into a run, her lantern swinging in front of her.

"I'm coming! Where are you?" she yelled.

"They heard us!" a second voice shouted. "By the gods, they heard us!"

And the first shrieked, "Here! We're here!"

But the echoes in the library made it impossible for her to tell, just from sound, where the two men were. She lifted her lantern at each doorway, and checked each side room, hurrying as fast as she could.

"We're in the tunnel!" one of the men suddenly shouted.

The tunnel? She knew of the passageway that led to the ancient First Folk burial grounds. It was hidden behind a secret panel in one of the statuary rooms at the very back of the library—but surely the two scholars would not have gotten themselves trapped in *there*. The panel had a latch that led in, but nothing that permitted anyone inside to let himself back out. Everyone had been very careful of that tunnel, always making sure that someone waited outside to open it.

A single icy finger of fear traced its way from her neck down her back, and she stopped, shivering.

The scholars hadn't gotten themselves trapped in the tunnel.

Edrouss Delmuirie and Thirk Huddsonne had wakened.

They're awake—they're awake—awake—awake. . . . Little voices welled up from deep inside her, like ghosts from the Lord's long night, whispering. Awake, they said—and now you have to face them, Faia. You have to face the man who tried to kill your daughter, and the man who tried to take you away from her forever. They're awake—and now that they are, you can never pretend again that your world will go back to being normal.

"I could leave you in there," she whispered. "I could walk away—but then you'd just come after me, wouldn't you?"

She walked into the statue room, where the First Folk had hidden the passageway to their burial grounds. The towering statues of the First Folk, carved of stone in heroic poses and still covered with layers of bright paint, leered down at her, obsidian eyes glittering. Their wings formed arches over the passageway that led to the secret door; their tails curled like serpents down the sides of the pedestals on which they sat. Walking among them, she wondered what the world had been like when they'd been in it.

She heard the men on the other side of the concealed door, and she pushed thoughts of the First Folk out of her mind. Thirk and Delmuirie shouted and pounded on the stone, their muffled voices pleading to the gods and to anyone who might be listening for immediate release.

Faia stood beside the lever that would roll the door upward. She caressed the cool polished stone with her fingertips; if her fingertip had been a single snowflake falling into the room, she could not have rested it on the hidden lever more lightly. She waited and listened to the shouting men begging for rescue, begging with voices of increasing desperation as she did not respond and the hidden door did not open. They shouted instructions on where she would find the lever—on how she would operate it. She knew all of that; her dilemma was not in discovering how to free the men, but in convincing herself that she should.

It would be so simple to walk away. Thirk Huddsonne and Edrouss Delmuirie would never get out without her help. They would die in the warm, waterless, sand-floored stone burial chambers of the First Folk, and someday someone would find their bones resting among the mummified remains of Arhel's extinct first people.

But Faia had never cold-bloodedly killed anyone. Turning her back on the two of them would put her on a level with Thirk—and she was not like him. She swallowed hard, then pressed down on the smooth stone panel, and a section of the wall rumbled and began to slide upward— and the tone of the men's voices changed from desperation to rejoicing.

"Saved!" they screamed. "We're saved!"

Then Thirk's voice rose over Delmuirie's. "Don't follow me or I'll kill you!"

"Why would I want to follow you, you lunatic? I do not want the cup back." Delmuirie's accent sounded like Faia's maternal great-grandmother's—only thicker. It was what the city-bred folk of Ariss referred to, with great derision, as a "back-hill frog-eater" accent. Faia, when she'd first arrived in Ariss, had spoken with a similar accent.

Funny she hadn't been able to pick that up when they were communicating in the emeshest. She might have liked him a little better the first time they'd met had she been able to hear him speak.

"You don't think I'd believe *you*, surely." Thirk's snarl still turned her stomach. Faia heard him scrambling behind the slowly rising doorway. "Light. Ah, gods, I see light," Thirk shouted.

Faia saw hands under the stone panel that slid upward into the ceiling high above, and then heads, as two men scrabbled out on hands and knees. She didn't stay to watch; she turned and headed for the front of the library. She didn't want the thanks of either man—she would be happiest if she never saw them again.

"Heya!" Edrouss Delmuirie yelled after her. "Lass! Don't go!"

She turned, and the lantern threw long shadows around the room, shadows that for an instant seemed to bring the sculptures of the First Folk to life. Faia looked back between the rows of statues, arch-necked and bright-eyed. She looked from Thirk, who clutched a metal chalice in one hand and gripped the pommel of a sword with the other, to Edrouss Delmuirie, who looked confused and lost. Delmuirie smiled tentatively, while Thirk's face went hard and cold while his eyes narrowed.

"You!" he yelled.

At least the bastard remembered her. "Me," she said, feeling bitter, and turned to walk away.

Thirk swore something under his breath; she heard his heavy footsteps thudding toward her at a run. She bolted, but not fast enough; Delmuirie shouted and the next instant pain blossomed in her lower back and she went sprawling, slammed into the stone floor by an unyielding weight. The lantern flew out of her hand and smashed against one of the statues. Flames licked along the spilled oil, casting a wavering light that blazed brightly for an instant; then the flames guttered low and died, leaving Faia in darkness—and pain.

A fist struck her full on the side of the face as she raised her head, so that she took two ferocious blows—one from

Thirk and the rebound blow as her head hit the stone floor.

She lay stunned; Delmuirie shouted something and Thirk answered, but while she could make out the voices, she could not make herself understand the words. Then the weight lifted from her back with an awful suddenness that somehow made the pain worse.

Faia couldn't move. The agony of her right side burned so ferociously that every tiny breath was torture. She wondered if Thirk had run her through with his sword, and if she was dying. She hoped, if that were the case, that she would die quickly—she wanted nothing more than for the pain to go away. She lay curled in a ball on the icy stone floor; she felt the running footsteps of both men racing toward the outside world and freedom.

I should have left them trapped in there to die, she told herself.

Then a single set of footsteps grew louder again, returning at a walk.

"Lass? Did he hurt you?" A darker shape knelt beside her in the darkness, and a hand rested on her shoulder: Delmuirie's hand.

"Go away," she mumbled. She wanted nothing more than to die in peace.

He slid his arms around her and scooped her into a sitting position, and the terrible pain, impossibly, grew much worse. She clenched her teeth to keep from screaming. No matter how badly she was hurt, she wouldn't give Edrouss Delmuirie the satisfaction of helping her.

She forced herself to remain upright, and with one hand tentatively felt along her side and up her back. She found no bleeding, no holes in her side—but the lightest touch along her right ribs made them feel like she was trying to cut them out one at a time with a dull whittling blade.

"I'm fine," she told him, though even the breath she needed to speak those three words cost her more strength than she had suspected she had. Those ribs were broken—

she didn't doubt that for an instant. Her jaw throbbed, too, from where Thirk had punched her.

"Yon madman got away from me when I pulled him off of you—I tried my best, but I couldna' catch him."

"Too bad," Faia muttered. "If you had, you could have killed him." She moved her arms forward slowly; then closed her eyes while red agony washed over the insides of her eyelids.

"You know him, then." Delmuirie offered her his hand. She didn't take it, and after an instant, he pulled back. "I suppose I could have killed him when we were trapped in the Klog burial grounds, but I thought him merely frightening—not really dangerous." Delmuirie's voice grew thoughtful. "He tried to be worshiping me at first. It was the uncanniest thing—he knew my name, and all manner of tales about me, though only some of them were true. But he kept asking me to show him magic, as if he thought I were some *ourzurd* from a child's tale. He would not believe me when I told him I was only a man like him."

"I'm not surprised. You didn't believe it when I told you the same thing."

There was a long silence. "We have met before?"

"More's the pity."

A sigh. "We have met before *and* I managed to offend you." Another pause, another sigh. "You must be pretty, then. Every time I open my mouth to a pretty lass, I say something I should not . . . though I am never entirely certain what I say that is so wrong. No matter. Please accept my apologies for whatever fool words I threw on you."

Faia had no intention of accepting his apology for his attempt to trap her in the emeshest forever. "You were talking about Thirk."

Delmuirie sighed again. "Bad enough that I am not to be forgiven, was it? Ah, well. It usually is." He paused. "About the madman, then—" Faia could hear bewilderment in every syllable. "—though I cannot hope to tell you why he did what he did. He stole my cup and my sword, and would not give them back. Called me a fraud, and said he would use the 'holy relics' to create a 'new age of magic in Arhel.' In my whole life, I have never heard a stranger thing."

Faia shook her head. "Holy relics?"

"He meant the cup and the sword, but I know nothing of holy relics, girl. The sword I bought from an armorer in Bog-Ariss, the cup I found in the burial grounds. I'd hoped it would have water in it, but it was dry." His voice trailed off, and for an instant he said nothing. "Everything was dry." His voice grew stronger again. "The madman had wine—he gave me some of that when we . . . when we woke."

Faia shoved her right arm tight against her side and went to one knee, then leaned into the staff she held in her left hand, and tried to push herself to her feet. The pain, which had seemed unsurpassable, instantly became worse, and she screamed.

Delmuirie lunged to his feet and slid an arm around her waist to support her.

"NOT THE RIBS!" she howled, and he let go.

"I thought you said he didn't hurt you." The voice was accusing. Faia was glad it was too dark for him to see her; pain tears poured down her cheeks.

"I lied."

"Why?"

"Because I didn't want you to know."

She heard the exasperated sigh. "Why by Falchus not?"

The pain was making her queasy. She wanted to find a hole and fall into it. She wanted the pain to stop. She wanted Edrouss Delmuirie to go away. The last she thought she could probably have. "Because all of this is your fault," she snapped, "and I didn't want you to have the satisfaction of knowing I needed help, Edrouss Delmuirie."

She heard the sharp intake of his breath, and felt momentary satisfaction that she'd at least hurt his feelings. Then he said, "Huh. You sound nearly as mad as he did. I had hoped to have sense from someone." He sighed. "Perhaps the whole world has gone mad. For the Klogs to have left Skeeree dark during the Long Night, it could almost be so." He clucked his tongue and brusquely slid his shoulder under her left arm. "Come, then. You cannot walk on your own—I can see that. Tell me where you came from, and I will take you back there."

He walked slowly, and Faia hobbled beside him. From time to time as they worked their way back to the front entrance he clucked his tongue and made comments about the disrepair in the library. Once he said, "By Falchus! *Kekkis* scattered on the floor. Keeven will claim the skull of the flirt that did that!"

Faia hurt too much to ask him to explain.

As they neared the entry, though, Delmuirie's steps slowed. He began to look constantly from side to side, and Faia heard his breath quicken. "Where are the *gallens*?" he asked at last. Faia heard distress in his voice.

"The what?"

"The *gallens*. The *GALLENS*!"

"Shouting it doesn't tell me what they are."

"The Klogs' wood panels. To . . . keep . . . the . . . snow . . . out. The *gallens*."

"If they were wood," Faia said coldly, "I don't suppose they exist anymore."

Delmuirie fell silent, but his head continued to turn— left, right, left, right. They reached the doorway; the stars and the corona of the Tide Mother cast enough light to give the snow that covered the ruins a pale sheen. The sight would have been far lovelier, Faia thought, if her pain had not been so intense.

Beside her, Edrouss Delmuirie came to a dead stop. For one long moment, he was silent, while his breath made quick, feathery plumes in the darkness. Then he croaked, "Where is it?"

"Where is what?"

"The city! The *city*, y' damned silly girl!" In the open air, his face was a pale blob, with dark shadows for eyes and mouth. Faia couldn't make out his expression—but he *sounded* like he was near tears. "What happened to the stinking *city*?"

"This is it." Faia didn't appreciate being called a "damned silly girl." She clenched her jaws and looked from him to the ruins. "This is all there's been for hundreds . . . and . . . hundreds . . . of years—since long after you last walked here, I'm sure."

"No," he whispered. Then he fainted, pitching forward down the little hill, dragging Faia with him.

As she lay on the snow-covered stone walkway, with the pain twice as horrible as the worst it had been before, Faia had a chance to consider both her words and her actions. And she came to a conclusion.

Maybe I shouldn't have broken the news to him in *quite* that way, she decided at last.

Chapter 13

Medwind Song was less than sympathetic. "You did a damn stupid thing, turning your back on a known enemy. You're lucky Thirk didn't kill you—and you would have deserved what you got if he did. Tighter, Choufa. Pull them tighter," she instructed, as Choufa wrapped Faia's ribs with strips of cloth.

Choufa tugged and Faia wailed.

"Hush," Medwind told her. "Your daughter will hear you and think we're killing you." She poked a finger against Faia's injured side, and Faia gasped. The pain was bad—but not anywhere near as bad as it had been. The wrapping helped. Medwind faced her and said, "So Thirk got away."

"Delmuirie ran partway down the main hall to catch him, but then came back to check on me. The whole business was very odd. He told me Thirk stole his sword and a cup he'd found, that Thirk called them relics."

The Hoos woman nodded. "They might *be* relics—at least the chalice might. He said he found it in the burial grounds, didn't he? If Delmuirie really did buy the sword at a market, then I don't think it would have any magical value. But Edrouss Delmuirie knows nothing of magic. Less than nothing—he doesn't even believe in it." Medwind crossed her arms and settled herself cautiously against the edge of her worktable. "I'm puzzled. He talked

114

about the First Folk as if they were terrible—called them Klaue and Klogs and smiled every time he realized there aren't any of them anymore. And he was unshakable when he insisted there was no magic in Arhel in his time. I don't think I convinced him *we* had magic, but he was willing to act polite."

"Delmuirie isn't at all as I thought he'd be," Faia said.

Medwind agreed with a single sharp nod of her head. "There is a certain . . . well, I don't suppose I can say an aura about him . . . but he does make one believe he's trustworthy. That's all, though. He's a nice-looking, likable young man like any of a thousand you could pull out of your back-hills villages. He's ordinary. I think Thirk realized that, too—and I think he figured out what really happened. Delmuirie somehow triggered a spell attached to the chalice, and unwittingly brought the Delmuirie Barrier into being."

"Unwittingly—perhaps," Faia grumbled. "But you forget, I spoke with him in the emeshest. He believed himself to be a god."

Medwind nodded. "I know. But if he did before, he seems not to now. I can think of several explanations for his confusion—"

"So can I. He's lying."

Medwind shrugged. "Perhaps. It's one explanation, but I don't think it's the best one. He doesn't have the feel of the liar about him." She cocked her head and stared at Faia. "The best liars don't, of course—but damnall, I find that I want to believe him."

Medwind sighed. She turned and looked through the doorway and into the other room, where Edrouss Delmuirie slept on a mat near the fire. "I cannot understand why I like him so much. In person, he's unprepossessing."

"You flatter him." Faia didn't say that she, too, found herself liking Edrouss Delmuirie, in spite of the fact that she had every reason not to.

"Well, you have the hunter to occupy your thoughts. Edrouss Delmuirie could almost be invisible if he stood next to Gyels," Medwind said. She looked back to Faia and her face brightened. "Your hunter went out after Thirk for us, incidentally. He seemed quite certain he could track Thirk down in spite of the darkness and the powdery snow." She sighed. "Gyels reminds me of several of my husbands. They were hunters, too—and randy as rutting billy goats." The old woman stared at her feet and clenched her fists. "I want to be young again," she said. "I want the pleasure of young men again."

"I promised," Faia told her. "You will be young again if I can make it so." Faia refused to be distracted by Medwind's speculations, though. "I don't like the fact that Gyels went after Thirk by himself. If he is the god Hrogner, he won't have any trouble finding and catching Thirk—but what will happen to us when he gets his hands on the chalice? A thing like that could make him more powerful than he already was."

"I doubt that he's Hrogner, Faia. He hasn't caused any trouble since you brought him here."

"He didn't initially cause any trouble in Omwimmee Trade." Faia frowned. "He made up for that, though."

The wind seemed to be picking up again. Faia paused, certain she'd heard it howling down from the mountain pass again. Of course, what she thought she heard could have been something else. She put a finger to her lips and held still, not even breathing.

Medwind, watching her, froze too.

The sound came again, somewhat louder. "No-o-o-o-o!" A shout from far away echoed from mountain peak to mountain peak and down into the valley where the First Folk ruins lay. Both women exchanged glances, and Faia mouthed the word, "Thirk?"

Then a blast of power swirled around them like a river undammed—magic, radiant energy, the absent sun briefly returned. Medwind's skin smoothed, her back grew straighter—and then the wonderful power dried up. As quickly as Faia felt it, it was gone again.

Medwind stared down at her old-again hands, and tears ran into the creases of her cheeks. "The chalice must be the key," she whispered. "Then truly, there is hope."

Faia tugged at the tip of her braid. "Perhaps. It depends on who has the chalice now, and who screamed." Faia slid off of the second worktable and carefully put on her erda, trying at the same time to move her injured side as little as she could.

"Where are you going?"

"To find out if Gyels got the chalice."

Faia stepped again into the freezing darkness of Arhel's long night, darker now that the Tide Mother had set. The stars blazed brightly—not winking as they did in Omwimmee Trade, but burning with a steady, harsh light. The air was thin and viciously cold—her eyelashes frosted again from the steam of her breath, and she wrapped a woven cloth around her cheeks and nose to keep her skin from freezing. The powder-snow crunched beneath her boots. She hiked slowly toward higher ground, heading for the ramp of the one unbroken tower that remained in the ruins. She didn't get far enough to find out if the frost-rimed stone slope was climbable, for a deep voice shouted after her as she trudged across the open spaces; she stopped and looked around.

Gyels slid down an ice-covered stone road from a higher level of the city; his hands were empty, and he was alone.

"What happened?" she asked when he got closer.

Gyels looked away from her, back the way he had come. "The bastard got away. He's stolen supplies from the stores, and taken off over the High Road. I nearly caught up with him, but when I got close, he did some sort of magic with that cup he stole and nearly flung me off the mountain."

Faia sucked in her bottom lip. Perhaps the cup *was* the source of magic, and Gyels only the mortal hunter he claimed to be. If he had been able to return with the chalice in hand as the conquering hero, she felt certain he would have. If he were just a man, and not Hrogner masquerading as one, perhaps she could permit herself to get to know him.

She gave Gyels a tiny smile; then full realization hit her and she turned away and swore. "By the Lady's heart and blood—Thirk has the chalice!"

Thirk—the malicious, obsessed madman. Her mother had told her she was supposed to save all of Arhel. Had she meant Faia was to save it from Thirk?

Faia wished her mother had given her a specific prophecy telling her exactly what she was supposed to do and with whom she was supposed to do it. Instead Faia faced Gyels, a hunter who might be a god; Delmuirie, a man who'd only recently thought he *was* a god; and Thirk, a power-hungry saje who, with the chalice, might become almost a god. And how the three of them related to her and Arhel's future, she hadn't the first idea.

Gyels had been studying her. "You've some skill at magic, haven't you?"

"I did have," she told him, "though I can do nothing now."

"If you got the chalice, could you make it work?"

Faia pondered that. "Perhaps," she said at last. "I don't know how to use it—but if I had it in my hands, maybe I could figure that out. Or maybe Medwind or Kirgen could."

Gyels looked back the way he'd come, up toward the ancient First Folk road he'd called the High Road. "I can track him," he told her, "if you can handle the magic when we catch up to him. But we'll have to leave as soon as we can get supplies together. Along the High Road, any sign he leaves will deteriorate quickly."

Faia's ribs throbbed and the bitter cold ate into her bones. She faced a trek into the mountains in winter—the false winter of the Month of Ghosts, but no less deadly than the real season. She had to find the magic that would save Medwind; now she had to stop Thirk, too.

Did she trust Gyels enough to head into the mountains with him? Not alone, she decided. She was willing to take a chance on him . . . but definitely not alone. "I'll be ready as quickly as I can."

Chapter 14

"Here's a bag of bonnechard," Medwind told Faia, and tossed a gut-wrapped bag full of thick, furry, gummy-looking leaves on the floor beside her. "For the pain in your side," she added. "Don't chew the leaves unless you have to—they'll take the pain away, but they'll also make you so drowsy you'll be likely to fall off the side of the mountain."

Faia studied the contents of the little packet. "How many?"

"One at a time—they're strong. An old Hoos warrior remedy." Medwind chuckled. "Besides, you won't want to chew more than one. They taste like shit."

"You've compared?"

"I'll make you chew one now if you don't take that back."

Faia grinned. "I take it back. Thank you." She put the packet aside so she could store it on top for easy access. She wasn't sure she'd even need the drug—the tight wrapping around her chest kept enough pressure on her broken ribs that even when she was kneeling and packing, the pain was merely bad, not intolerable.

Medwind settled onto a hassock and rubbed her arms briskly. "The damned body gets cold so fast now." She shook her head, annoyed. "Not as cold as *you're* going to be, I expect. Of course, alone in the mountains with Gyels, huddled together in a single tent for warmth—"

Faia didn't look up from shoving supplies into the pack she'd borrowed. "I'm not going to be alone with him. I've been to see your Bontonard scholars. They're mildly curious about the chalice, but mostly they want to get back to Bonton, and they think they'll have a better chance of surviving the trip if they're with a skilled tracker. Edrouss Delmuirie insisted that he was going to go along, too. I think, after being trapped in the burial grounds with him, Delmuirie wants Thirk's painted skull to keep on a shelf."

Medwind blew out a disgusted breath. "Moron."

"Edrouss Delmuirie isn't all that bad, and Thirk is worse than a moron. He's insane."

"I wasn't talking about Delmuirie *or* Thirk. You had the perfect chance to be alone with a positively magnificent man—a gorgeous animal—in a situation where you'd almost have *had* to get to know each other well. Sajes seven hells, Faia, men like that don't come along often! And you're *wasting* him!" Medwind stopped and looked closely at what Faia was shoving into the pack. "You don't have enough dried meat, and you've taken too much grain."

Faia kept packing. "I've done this before," she said evenly.

"You need more meat if you're going to be traveling in high altitudes—the thin air and the cold require more than your horse food."

Faia threw a gut-wrapped pack of dried meat to the floor and glared up at Medwind. "I grew up in high altitudes—I spent most of my life in mountains higher and more dangerous than these. Do you want to do this?"

Medwind snapped back, "I wish to Etyt and Thiena I could! I wish this bedamned body could go over mountains! I wish it could seduce men! I wish it wasn't going to *die* on me at any minute!"

Faia hung her head. "I'm sorry. I'm so sorry." She looked

up at her friend. "But, Medwind, I cannot live for you. I cannot do the things you would do because you can no longer do them. I have to live *my* life. I have to decide about Gyels in my own way and my own time—and I didn't grow up wanting nine husbands at the same time. I need to be more sure of what I want before I act."

Medwind stood very still for a moment. Then she nodded once, brusquely, and gave Faia a tiny smile. "You're right. Go. Do what you have to do—bring the magic back for us. I won't say anything else about you and men."

Faia laughed. "You won't have time to." She shoved the last of the foodstuffs and quicklights into the pack, and buckled the straps down. She turned, then, serious, and faced her friend. "Have you thought about the chalice—and what it means to the magic?"

"I have." The old woman sighed. "I might have been wrong about the *taada kaneddu*. If Arhel's magic is tied to the chalice, and Delmuirie's spell is broken, then there may be no magic in all of Arhel, at least until someone resets the spell."

Faia swung the pack onto her shoulder. "Maybe not. After all, it's hard to imagine all of Arhel's magic tied to a single metal cup. Perhaps it was only the magic in this area." She strapped on the belt that held the bottom of the pack snugly to her waist and shifted to be sure the struts didn't poke into her hips and that none of the bindings or buckles rubbed wrong.

Medwind for an instant looked even older and smaller and frailer. "If the cup is the key to Arhel's magic, though—nothing had better happen to it."

Faia hugged her. "Maybe the others will be ready," she said. "I'll be back when I can."

"Safe journey to you. Courage, success, and happiness." The old woman added, *"Dli kea'bemfoska akota'tyaaka-ne puku kea'tabboka-beku."*

Faia stopped. "What?"

Medwind smiled slowly. "It's an old Hoos wish—it means, 'May the bones of your enemies become a bridge beneath your feet.'"

"I'd wish you the same, but I'd have to swallow a live cat to say it." Faia laughed and shook her head. "Do the Hoos have *any* sayings that aren't about people's bones?"

"The ones about sex."

"Ah, yes. Sex." Faia hugged her again. "Be well. When I come back, I'll try to bring you a man."

"If you bring me back my youth, I'll catch my own man."

Chapter 15

Outside the library, the Bontonards argued over the distribution of some of their load. Delmuirie watched them, plainly disgusted. Gyels balanced like a dancer on his snowshoes, quick and graceful, impatient to be off.

Faia picked up Kirtha and hugged her.

"I don't want you to go, Mama," Kirtha said.

"You'll be fine with your da." Faia looked over at Kirgen, who stamped his feet to keep them warm, and gave her an encouraging smile. He'd take good care of Kirtha, Faia knew. He and Roba would do fine—and if Faia didn't survive the trip through the mountains for help, then they would raise her well and love her. "Be a good girl, Kirthchie. I love you."

She didn't want to think about not coming back. It could happen so easily—the mountains were dangerous, and Thirk even more so. She kissed Kirtha and handed her to Kirgen. "Take her inside," she told him quietly. "It's too cold out here." She swallowed hard. "And Kirgen—if I don't make it back, please help Kirtha burn a candle for me next Month of Ghosts."

Kirgen nodded, his face suddenly solemn. "Safe journey," he said. "And safe return. We'll be here waiting when you get back."

Faia pressed her lips together tightly and looked away.

Tears froze on her cheeks. "Tell Roba I hope the birth goes well, and that I wish I could have seen her before I left." Faia could imagine Kirtha with a baby brother or sister; could imagine her daughter with Kirgen and Roba—growing up without her. She wished right then that she didn't have such a good imagination. She shivered and wiped the streaks of ice from her face.

She looked back to see Kirgen trudging through the snow, back to his home, with Kirtha hanging over his shoulder, waving good-bye. "Your mama will be fine," he was telling her. "Now let's go in and sit by the fire, and I will tell you a story."

Faia waved until the two of them disappeared from view. Then she took a few slow breaths to regain her composure, and walked over to join the men with whom she would be traveling.

Besides Edrouss and Gyels, there were the two scholars from Bonton. Both were as tall as she, though one was dark and lean and the other was broad and solid and fair, with curly coppery-brown hair. She'd learned that the dark one's name was Bytoris Caligro, while the fair one was Geos Rull. She knew nothing of either man—though in the few minutes she'd had to talk with them, she hadn't thought them as loathsome as Medwind seemed to find them. They seemed nice, if ordinary.

Edrouss Delmuirie watched the two Bontonards, who were arguing over a particularly awkward piece of equipment that both men wanted to take but neither man wanted to carry. Delmuirie turned to Faia and, in a bemused voice, said, "I can't believe all of you came here and not *one* of you brought a pack animal. Not *one*."

"We flew." Faia gave him a dark look.

"You *flew*." He shrugged his shoulders to reposition his pack and adjusted the wrap that wound around most of his face—he'd had to borrow winter gear from Kirgen, and Delmuirie was broader through the shoulders and a bit taller. He looked uncomfortable in the borrowed gear.

Gyels moved to Faia's side and rested a hand on her shoulder, the gesture uncomfortably proprietary. Faia saw Delmuirie's eyes flick from the hand to Gyels's face, and then to Faia's.

"Well, Faia—are we ready, then?" Gyels asked. "Or are we going to stand around while *they* repack their gear one more time? Every minute we waste is another minute the wind and the weather get to destroy our sign."

The Bontonards, it was obvious, had never packed for a hike in their lives. They probably weren't up to the trip, either, but Faia was unwilling to leave them behind. "Oh, they wouldn't repack again," she murmured, then realized that it appeared they intended to do exactly that. Faia wanted a crowd with her—or as close to a crowd as she could get. But catching Thirk had to be the first priority.

She looked from Delmuirie to Gyels and sighed. "Let's go."

The three of them started off. Her heart felt as heavy as her pack—but she was afraid the first would grow heavier even as the second grew lighter.

Gyels took the lead, heading uphill toward the break in the First Folk wall. He set a brutal pace. Faia's ribs began hurting almost immediately. She wondered how she could possibly keep up—but she could understand Gyels's haste. Thirk wouldn't wait, and neither would the prints he left in the blowing, powdery snow. She forced herself to keep her silence—she wouldn't let anyone know how much she hurt unless she could no longer go on. She did, however, think longingly of the bonnechard in her pack.

The three hikers in the lead had made it to the first steep rise that led to the break in the wall when Faia heard the Bontonards shout, "Wait! We've only got to balance our loads a bit more evenly."

"Keep going," Delmuirie said. "Or they'll be balancing their loads while the grass grows up to their knees."

Faia chuckled and she and Edrouss kept moving. She hadn't wanted to stop anyway. If she went too slowly, she knew she would fall so far behind Gyels that she would lose sight of him.

Ignoring the Bontonards seemed to be the best policy, and in fact, not long after she heard their first plaintive yell, the two foreign scholars ran up behind her, slipping and stumbling and cursing. Faia wondered if they might jump into the lead if she pretended not to notice they existed at all.

"Slow down a bit to let them catch up—but don't look at them." Faia kept her voice low enough that it wouldn't carry beyond Delmuirie. "Let them think we'll go on without them if they don't keep up."

She tried to watch the Bontonards out of the corner of her eye without making it obvious she was doing so. She figured if she pretended to ignore them, they couldn't do much to try to convince her to stop while they repacked.

Edrouss winked at her and nodded. He slackened his pace almost imperceptibly. She followed suit.

Edrouss Delmuirie seemed happy enough at the moment, Faia thought—his equanimity was quite a change from his reactions upon discovering he'd been held in the emeshest for uncounted hundreds of years. When he first regained consciousness, he'd raged. Then he'd withdrawn into himself and said almost nothing, finally curling up by the fire to sleep while Medwind had patched Faia's ribs.

But the moment the rest of the would-be travelers decided they were going after Thirk to try to retrieve the chalice, Edrouss Delmuirie volunteered to go, too. He'd said nothing else about the world he'd lost, and had quickly packed the winter gear he'd been able to borrow, and had immersed himself in the business that occupied all the rest of them. Faia couldn't help but think about the fact that he'd lost his entire world and everyone he'd ever known in an instant; his loss had been more complete than hers when she'd returned home to her village to find all in it save one dead of plague. Yet somehow he carried on; he was able to smile and talk and act.

Faia discovered that she admired him enormously for that.

They reached the place where the inner portion of the city wall had crumbled, the gods only knew how long ago; it was the only place along the inside wall that made a passable ground route out of the city.

We should have known from the first time we saw this place that the First Folk were fliers, she thought. *What other sort of people would build a city with walls but no gates?*

The travelers shed snowshoes and strapped them on their backs, then clambered up the loose rubble of stones—the fallen rocks were snow-covered and in places slick with ice. Dangerous. Faia lost her footing once and smashed her knee into a square-edged stone; she swore under her breath, then began to laugh as she realized four other people were at that moment stumbling and slipping and swearing. No—three. Gyels went up the rubble like a goat, then stood on the top of the wall glaring impatiently down at the rest of them.

Delmuirie, struggling beside her, whispered, "I could grow to hate him."

And Faia, ribs and knee and hands hurting, couldn't help but agree.

"How did you get in and out of the city before?" Faia asked Delmuirie. She assumed the wall had been in good repair when he had last seen the place.

"Klogs—what you have called First Folk—let us set up rope ladders to climb in and out; the young ones were forever jeering at us as we went up and down them, or flying overhead to dump dirt and grass and the like down on us. They despised us, and only permitted us the ladders because we did not have wings."

"Why did you come here, then?"

"Part of the agreement with the bastard Klogs. Humans— Annin, they called us . . . in their tongue it meant anything that couldna' fly—had to have 'ambassadors' in their cities whose presence guaranteed that Annin wouldna' hunt Klogs—or our lives were forfeit."

"You were *hostages*."

He looked over at her and arched an eyebrow. "You do not think you would find it sufficient honor being ambassador to the Klogs?" He grinned. "I did not, either. That is how I got myself in such a fix." He reached the top of the rubble before Faia, and held his hand out to assist her to the top.

She hesitated only half an instant, then accepted his proffered hand. He smiled down at her. She scrambled the rest of the way up, and the two of them stood atop the wide stone wall, watching the Bontonards climb.

He looked down the rubble and shook his head. "So you flew in here, did you?"

"Well, the Bontonards flew." Edrouss Delmuirie was having a hard time accepting the very concept of magic— Faia did not think he was ready to hear about the saje magic of transporting.

Questioning magic did not appear to have been his intention right then. "I would love to fly," Delmuirie said softly. His wistful expression made Faia think for an instant of Kirtha wishing for a flying castle. "I think if we had been fliers, the Klogs would have accepted us as equals."

"I've done it often enough. Sometimes it's pleasant, but sometimes things go wrong. The ground is usually safer—at least this time of year. In the summer you wouldn't want to walk down there." She pointed over the opposite edge of the parapet to the snow-covered ground far below. "You can't see it now, but there's a killing field just below this wall," Faia said. "The kellinks use the wall as a corral; the bones down there are waist-deep in places."

The Bontonards reached the top, panting from the climb.

Delmuirie looked where she'd pointed and said, "They always did. So there are still kellinks, are there? Too bad. With all the Klogs gone, I had begun to think this new life I fell into was heaven in disguise."

Faia smiled ruefully. "There are still kellinks. I wish I could say there weren't." The kellinks, poisonous six-legged pack hunters, were among the few big predators in Arhel that considered humans fair game. And they were plentiful in the jungles north of the Wen Tribes Treaty Line. "There are all sorts of dangerous things in Arhel."

Delmuirie chuckled and set off at a brisk pace, hiking along the wide wall, southeast and uphill. "There always were."

The party followed along a fairly level uphill track, until they reached the place where the wall intersected the First Folk road. The road, carved out of the living rock, rolled along just below the mountain ridgeline, a broad ledge sheltered from the prevailing wind, covered with blowing snow but safe and well out of the reach of predators like the kellinks, who did not venture into the mountains even when the weather was good. The monuments left behind by the road's builders—white standing stones worn down by wind and weather—stood like jagged, uneven teeth.

Gyels stayed ahead, and the Bontonards lagged behind, more interested in talking to each other than in getting to know their companions. Faia found herself walking with Delmuirie. After they'd been on the road for a while, Faia told him, "I want to know something."

Edrouss Delmuirie smiled. "I would like to answer. What would you wish to know?"

"You said you got in trouble with the First Folk because you didn't want to be an ambassador to them, right?"

"Indeed. 'Twas how I ended up stuck like a bug in sapstone in their burial ground for gods only know how long."

Far ahead, Gyels dropped to one knee. He looked like he was having trouble finding sign of Thirk's passage.

Faia noted that, then returned her attention to Delmuirie. "So . . . what did happen?"

"The Klogs held a grand meeting—called it the *eahnnk gurral*. The words mean 'burning memory'—I never found out what the meeting was to be about. To my knowledge, they had never had another like it in their history—but the damned Klogs would not tell any human what was on."

Delmuirie swung the tip of his walking stick and struck it on the ground as he walked. The swish and thud as it hit the stone beneath the powdery snow punctuated his speech. "On the first morning of the *eahnnk gurral*, every Klog in Arhel left the cities they had built, whole flocks of them taking off with the babies clutching the backs of the birds or flitting along in the care of the young hussies, and flirts and rangers soaring ahead, so that the sky was dark with them. The Klog scholars left last, after making sure everything in their blessed library was secure. 'We will return by first of spring,' they told us. 'Entertain yourselves as best you can while we are gone, and keep the beasts fed and cleaned.' Then they pulled up the ladders after themselves, and went away."

He sighed. "I was one of the ambassadors expected to work with the librarians and scribes on documents that affected Klaue and Annin. I knew the library, and I knew there was a secret passage into it. If the Klogs knew I had found that passage, they would have killed me, I know; every once in a while, an 'ambassador' would stray into the wrong part of Skeeree and have a little accident, and the Klogs would fly his body home, all teary-eyed and sympathetic."

Faia leaned into her walking stick as the road wound over a steep rise. "Doesn't sound like the sort of work people would be lining up to get." She panted and braced her free arm against her ribs to splint them. That helped.

Delmuirie's laugh was a short, harsh bark. He said, "It was not. We drew lots among those who were qualified to serve, actually. Losers had to go, so that the rest of Arhel's humans could live in relative peace. My number came up after a friend of mine was brought back dead from service."

"That's terrible." Faia thought about having to go work for someone who had killed a friend, and thought she'd probably try to find a way to revenge him.

He nodded. "It was terrible, and I lived in fear of meeting my friend's fate. Still, once the Klogs were gone on their secret trip, I went into the library and back to the hidden passageway. I let myself in, thinking I would find something in there that would give me an edge on the Klogs. I was just sure when they came back, I would know a way for the Annin to beat them— to send them off so that we humans would have a place of our own."

"But there's nothing at the end of that passage but a graveyard," Faia blurted. "And once you get in, there's no way out."

"Aye." He gave her a rueful smile. "We know that now, do we not? But I did not know it then. I went down there, and I was trapped. None of the other ambassadors knew where I was, the Klogs would not be back for nearly two months. I would be good and dead before they got back, and if I were not, they would be sure to kill me when they got back. Oh, I was in terrible trouble."

"What did you do?" Faia asked, drawn in and sympathetic to his plight in spite of herself.

"He prayed," Gyels muttered. Faia had not realized that they had almost caught up with him, or that he had been listening.

"How did you know that?" Delmuirie stopped dead and stared at the tracker.

Gyels was unflustered. "It's what every man does when he gets in trouble. No need to look so surprised. When people get themselves in a fix, the first words across their lips are 'Oh, god, help.' "

"That's true," Faia agreed. "That's usually the first thing I say—though I call to the Lady."

Edrouss Delmuirie nodded thoughtfully and started along the road again. "He's right. That's what I did. I lifted the empty cup I found, begging for water, and swore on my blade that I would do anything for my god if he would just get me out of the mess I was in." He fell silent, and walked along the road, swinging his staff into the snow with almost angry emphasis.

Faia gave him a moment to continue, but when he didn't, curiosity overrode patience. "So what happened?"

He looked at her, and shrugged. "I dinna' know. One instant, I am trapped in the Klog catacombs; the next, I have fallen into a place of light and music, happy as can be and not a thought in my head." He looked into Faia's eyes, and she shivered at the hollow, haunted expression she saw in them. "And an instant or an infinity later, the light and the music die and I find myself trapped in the catacombs in the dark with a lunatic who keeps praying to me to save him."

Faia felt lost. "But what did you do to create the Barrier—or had you already done that?"

"The Barrier . . . that madman Thirk kept insisting I had to lower the Barrier. . . ." He frowned. "What *is* it?"

"It's . . ." Faia struggled for the words. "It's magic—a

sort of wall of magic that goes all around Arhel, and nothing can go in or out of it."

"Good lord above. And people blamed that on *me*?"

"Yes."

"Whatever for?"

Faia sighed. "This is from my reading, mind you, and from classes I took at the University, and discussions I had with Medwind and Nokar. I am *not* a scholar, merely an interested layman, so I may not have this exactly right." She cleared her throat and considered how to explain what she had learned as logically as possible. It had never seemed like a particularly logical story to her. "There are records in some of the old tomes attributing the thing to you. They are copies of copies, of course, and the original sources are obscure, to say the least. But the name Delmuirie has been linked to the Barrier since the oldest records anyone has. The records are of two opinions—they say either that you were a hero protecting Arhel from some unnamed evil of unimaginable proportions who sacrificed your life to build a magical barrier; or else they say you were a complete idiot playing with forces you didn't understand, and that those forces overwhelmed you and trapped all of us here."

"No middle ground in there, is there? I am to be either hero or buffoon. And is there a theory that some other person was responsible for this Barrier?"

"Some blame it on natural causes, but most attribute the Barrier to you."

Edrouss Delmuirie laughed. "No doubt because I could not make a case for my innocence."

Faia grinned wickedly. "Men have been attributed with great things for lesser reasons."

But Delmuirie had stopped laughing. "Wait," he said. "Tell me again where the Barrier goes."

"All around Arhel," Faia told him.

"All around Arhel," he repeated thoughtfully. "So then, Vit and Kaz—what of them?"

"What are Vit and Kaz?" Faia asked.

Delmuirie nodded, and sucked on his lower lip. "Indeed, that tells me what has happened to them . . . and you have no Klogs, and an impassable barrier." He frowned. "Well." He fell silent, and began to walk faster, head down and shoulders hunched.

Faia scrambled to catch back up with him. "So what were Vit and Kaz?" She had little patience for mysterious behavior.

"Ah." Delmuirie sighed. "Places. Huge, wondrous, lovely places—not that it matters if we cannot get there. They were continents across the sea—where the real civilization was. No one bothered much with this outpost."

"Outpost?"

"Arhel. This was scrap land—marginal from everyone's point of view. Nobody wanted it—story is, when the Klaue granted this land to the Annin, the Annin named it 'Our Hell.' Truth is, it was not ours free and clear even then; the Klogs had their overseers back in Skeeree and in High Bekkust to make sure we Annin did not try to get above ourselves."

"You've mentioned Skeeree before."

"That's the Klog name for yon old city we just left. What you call the First Folk ruins." He started to laugh. "Skeeree was a sort of punishment post for the Klogs— none of the comforts of home, or damned few."

"Kaz and Vit." Bytoris shook his head, bemused. "It's hard to imagine a world bigger than just Arhel. And these places are out there? You've seen them?"

"I toured Vit once." He smiled sadly. "It was . . . seemingly endless. Fascinating. Ancient, even in my time—full of Kloggish history and Kloggish art. Wide-streeted cities with metal-banded towers soaring like needles toward the sky, thoroughfares lined with statues

of the Heroes, libraries that would swallow the tiny
one at Skeeree and a hundred like it. The great Klaue
debaters arguing philosophy in the streets, roaring at
each other from their pillars and spreading their wings
in threat-display, while their admirers flocked at the
bases of their favorites' pillars and cheered them on.
Vast, stinking meat farms; tone-deaf Klog orchestras
playing caterwauls and skirling pipes loud enough to
wake the dead and kill the living; Klog pirates swaggering
down the avenues with their rilles ringed in gold and
their claws tipped in obsidian, shouting at the young
flirts and hussies to come join their bands. The parts
of Vit I saw were unforgettable." He shook his head,
and turned so that Faia could not see his face. "And
everything I remember is gone. I thought I was going
to take all of this fine," he said. His voice was barely
louder than a whisper, and Faia heard it crack. She
could see his shoulders shake. "I thought that it would
not matter that my world was gone, because there was
another whole world here and now, and I would find
a place in it for me." He glanced back at her, and the
look in his eyes could have broken harder hearts than
hers. Faia knew what he was feeling. She'd felt that
same awful emptiness when everyone she'd ever loved
had died of the plague in Bright.

Delmuirie added, "It does matter, though. It matters more
than I ever could have believed."

He let his pace slack off, making it clear that he wanted
to walk alone. As he dropped back, Gyels also slowed,
until Faia was even with him.

"I was listening to the man," the hunter said. His voice
was flat, and edged with a burr of irritation. "He tells a
sad tale, doesn't he?"

Faia agreed, keeping her own tone neutral.

"His is the sort of woeful tale women love, isn't it?"
Gyels's face hardened into a frown. "You pity him, and

then you'll want to make him feel better, and the next thing anyone knows, you will have fallen in love with him." He growled, "I wish I knew such a tale to tell."

He hurried ahead, his shoulders stiff and angry. Faia watched him, disconcerted. He wanted her not to like Edrouss, she realized. Gyels was jealous.

Chapter 16

At last the travelers made camp. With no cycles of day and night to break their journey, they pushed themselves to the point of exhaustion—the Tide Mother with its brilliant corona had much earlier dropped behind the far forests and rolling hills. Faia had no idea how far they'd trekked along the High Road, but no matter how hard they pushed, they never caught sight of Thirk.

Perhaps he has found a way to use the magic of the chalice to fend off weariness, she thought. She would never have attempted such a thing with magic—the rebound was too horrible and too dangerous once the magic stopped. However, Thirk was obsessed; perhaps he didn't care about the price he would have to pay when he reached his destination.

Faia hurt. She thought with longing of the bonnechard leaves at the top of her pack.

I'll have some after we set up camp, she promised herself. When I am safely in my bedroll and have nothing to do but sleep.

All five travelers tied their tarps together, bound the struts to form two strong arches that crossed in the middle to hold them up, and left enough of a hole in the center for the smoke from their small campfire to escape. The bitter cold was going to make sharing heat essential until

138

the sun finally came back out from behind the Tide Mother—Faia thought sharing sleeping space with four men would be easier than sharing with one. She was glad she'd pushed for the companionship of Delmuirie and the Bontonards.

As it was, Gyels tried to spread his blankets next to hers—and only with difficulty did she manage to reposition herself between one of the Bontonards and the fire without making her retreat obvious. Once she'd done it, she wondered why she had. Every time she looked at Gyels, her pulse raced erratically and she felt the unmistakable stirrings of lust deep in her belly. She wondered if her real fear was that, starved for attention for so long, she'd find herself ravishing the man in the night—only to be caught by her other tent mates. The more she considered the idea, the less she could discount it.

So I want him, she realized. I suppose my problem with him is that I still don't quite trust him.

His jealousy bothered her, too. It seemed presumptuous of him to exhibit possessiveness toward her where other men were concerned when she had promised him nothing; when, in fact, he hardly knew her. It was probably a difference in culture, she reflected, but if it was, it wasn't one she liked.

All five of them passed around food—hard cheeses, traveler's bread, jerky, and honey-sweetened grain balls— and talked in a desultory fashion of their aches and their weary desire for sleep. Faia chewed her leaf, which tasted even worse than Medwind had promised. But the bonnechard worked quickly, and once the pain eased, Faia discovered she really didn't care how it tasted or how sore she was. She also discovered that instead of making her sleepy, the drug in the leaf seemed to wake her up.

Feeling suddenly sociable, she decided she hadn't properly met her Bontonard companions.

She lay back with her head nestled on her pack and grinned at Bytoris, the man sprawled beside her.

"Did you know I don't know a thing about you?" she said.

Bytoris's dark eyes were mysterious, and Faia liked the faint hint of dimples in his cheeks; he wasn't smiling right then, but he looked like he did often. He was handsome— though not, she thought, as handsome as Gyels. He grinned, and sure enough, his dimples deepened. "That's only fair. I don't know anything about you, either."

Faia laughed. The drug gave her the most wonderful floating feeling. "You first," she insisted.

He nodded. "My name is Bytoris Caligro."

"Well, I did know that," Faia said. "But I'm honored."

Bytoris Caligro inclined his head and said, "Of course you are." He smiled when he said it, and she laughed again. His voice was deep, and he rolled the syllables to those few words until they sounded like music. Faia caught indications of an odd accent, but nothing that she could put her finger on.

"And you," she said, pointing at the other Bontonard.

Geos Rull had been sprawled flat on his blanket, looking, Faia thought, either comatose or near death. But he lifted his head from the pillow he'd made of a spare shirt and said, "My full name is Geostravin Thermadichtus Rull." Geos had light hair that curled wildly, sticking out in all directions, and as many freckles across his nose and cheeks as Faia had. "I prefer to be called Geos."

"I can see why," she told him, then realized what she'd said wasn't very nice. She clapped her hand over her mouth and murmured, "Ooops!" She tried a solemn nod and told him, "My greetings," but her solemnity dissolved into a sputtering little giggle. She flopped back onto her makeshift pillow and sighed. "Why in the Lady's name were you tromping around in that stone wreck of a city?"

"We're premier scholars—some of the finest in Bonton,

which means the finest in the world." Bytoris said that without even a hint of a smile.

"We were studying the First Folk tablets—" Geos added with a nod.

Bytoris interrupted him. "Made more discoveries in our brief stay than the Arissers did in their entire first year. I, for example, discovered the Caligro Tablets—a series of documents in one of the back sections of the library containing not only First Folk script, but the same text in Old Arhelan, and also in Ancient Gekkish, the precursor of the current Hoos dialects. If it had been left to the *Arissods*, Arhel would have been another hundred years before finding the linguistic key to the whole site. Pittering around, they were, no more clever than pigs spinning on a spit."

Faia giggled. She could imagine what Kirgen would have had to say about that. The infamous feud between the natives of the city-state of Bonton and the grand old magical center, Ariss, was still definitely alive and well.

Edrouss Delmuirie sat up, though, interested by what the Bontonards had said. "The Caligro Tablets? And you found them in the library? I don't remember documents by that name."

"And why should you? I just discovered them—they're named after me. They were filed in the back of the library, where the *Arissludge* hadn't gotten yet."

"I know the library fairly well," Delmuirie said. "What were the file numbers?"

"File numbers?"

"Impressed into the stone on the side—Klog numbers."

Bytoris frowned. "Klog—what are Klog numbers? I wrote down the location markings—but those are in First Folk codings." He pulled a little tablet of drypress pages out of his pack and riffled through them. "Here. I found the tablets in double-three, three-two, four, one, double-two."

Delmuirie closed his eyes and began ticking things off on his fingers. Faia watched his lips move, and felt the urge to say something terribly silly, but she restrained herself. "Oh," he said at last. "You would have found those in a section with blue-green stone shelves, about midway down the wall shelf." He looked over at the Bontonards. "Yes?"

"Yes." Bytoris frowned, puzzled. "That's exactly where I found them. How did you know that . . . and who are you?"

Delmuirie smiled. "Let me introduce myself. My name is Edrouss Delmuirie. I used to work in that library."

The looks on the Bontonards' faces were so priceless, Faia pressed her face into her sleeve to hide her laughter and kicked her feet up and down on her bedroll.

Bytoris got his voice first. "*Edrouss Delmuirie? The* Edrouss Delmuirie? The Delmuirie of the Barrier? But you can't be. That Delmuirie lived two thousand three hundred eighty-seven years ago."

Faia found that statement too funny for words. "How do you know it wasn't two thousand three hundred eighty-six years ago? Or eighty-eight?" She rolled onto her stomach and chuckled. "Or *seventy*-eight? *Seventy*-eight, *seventy*-eight, *seventy*-eight." She loved the sound of those words—she thought she could say them all night.

All four men looked at her with enigmatic expressions on their faces.

At last Delmuirie said, "Well, it is a sensible question, if not sensibly put."

Bytoris stared at Faia. She grinned back at him, then schooled her face to seriousness, trying to make her expression as mysterious and full of secret knowledge as would be any scholar's were he in possession of a deep, important secret. Bytoris looked disconcerted—he kept his eyes on her while he answered Delmuirie. "Our calendar begins on the year of Edrouss Delmuirie's death. He was

a great Bontonard scholar and the author of many erudite
works on magic and scholarship—"

"Though his style was terribly dry and formal," Geos
interrupted.

"Only in his later period. His earliest works are models
of concision and wit."

"Personally, I always thought he read like six different
writers—I've suspected for years that every anonymous
work in the scholarly canon was attributed to him sooner
or later."

"Nonsense."

"I don't think so," Geos said. "It doesn't matter right
now, anyway. The point is, Edrouss Delmuirie is dead.
And has been for a fiendishly long time."

"Well, *I* am not dead." Delmuirie linked his fingers
together and stretched, cracking his knuckles loudly. "And
I resent being told that I am. And I *am* Edrouss
Delmuirie, but I was never a Bontonard—Bonton was
a cow pasture with a bunch of grubby cowherds living
in the middle of it when I knew it."

Bytoris's face went dusky. "Spoken like an *Arissod.*"

Delmuirie snorted. "*Bog*-Arisser, you mean? That
stinking swamp Ariss was home to stinking fish-eaters
and the ugliest women in the world."

"Well, we agree on that at least. Nothing good has ever
come from Ariss."

"I spent some time there," Faia said. "I thought it was
an interesting place."

Bytoris, however, was not interested in her travels. He
had returned to his previous subject. "The real Edrouss
Delmuirie . . ." The expression on his face became
unreadable. Faia thought Geos looked skeptical—but she
couldn't figure out what Bytoris Caligro was thinking at
all. He sat straight up and hunched his shoulders forward,
leaning toward Delmuirie. A weird fanaticism burned in
his eyes. "I don't suppose you could read the script of

the First Folk, could you? As proof that you are who you claim to be."

"First Folk script—I did not know they had a *script*. Or do you mean Klog-press?"

"The impressions they left behind in tablets."

"That's Klog-press. Of course I can read it. And write it. I speak and read Air Tongue, Stone Tongue, Blood Tongue *and* Water Tongue—that is what I was *doing* in Skeeree."

Bytoris's eyes narrowed. "He speaks it. He reads it." He stared down at his feet and rubbed the bridge of his nose with one long, graceful finger. When he looked up at Delmuirie again, his attitude was unmistakably condescending. "Would you at all mind giving me a demonstration?"

Delmuirie shrugged. "Does not matter to me. If there are no more Klogs, seems like a useless enough skill, but—"

Bytoris pressed his lips into a thin white line. "Useless. Of course. A moment, please." He rummaged through his pack, and came out with a sheaf of drypress sheets. He held one up, and beckoned Delmuirie over. "These are rubbings I did of the tablets so I'd have copies for my own study." He leafed through the sheaf and pulled out a single drypress sheet. He covered all but the top third with the other sheets, which he put facedown. "I know this part—I worked out the Gekkish. If you would start reading here." He pointed to a line on the page.

Edrouss Delmuirie nodded, and studied the sheaf. "This is the Graggha-Sondmon Treaty—the one before the amendments, you know. There is a more recent one back about four shelves." He glanced down, then back up again and opened his mouth. Instead of words, though, he began to cough and sputter and hiss and growl. Gyels lay back on his bedroll with his eyes closed, his expression one of boredom. Faia and the Bontonards looked at each other in disbelief, though.

Faia had thought Hoos sounded bad—but the sounds Delmuirie was making were like two mountain lions in a bag with their tails tied together. Two very *big* mountain lions.

"Stop!" Bytoris yelled after a brief demonstration. "What are you *doing*?"

"I'm reading it." Delmuirie shrugged. "In Klog."

Bytoris's face paled. "Translate," he growled.

"You did not say you wished to have me translate it. You said you wanted me to read it." Nevertheless, he ran his finger back to the top of the section Bytoris had marked off, and began again. "We agree," Delmuirie read, "we peoples of Klaue and Annin tribes, to make no more war on each other, to cease in all times and places from hunting each other for our skins or teeth or bones, to cease in all times and all places the stealing and eating of the peoples of each other's tribes. We, the Klaue, shall refrain from dropping stones on the heads and homes of our Annin neighbors. We, the Annin, shall refrain from coating landing towers with pitch and tar, or from lighting them when they become covered with trapped Klaue. We shall not make war on each other for sport, nor shall we demand slaves or heavy tributes. We shall make our peoples to live together in peace, to our mutual benefit, sharing our skills and talents and ruling jointly in a Council composed of the best representatives of all our people." Delmuirie sighed. "Then it goes into the actual articles of agreement. Do you wish me to read those as well—" He looked up and his speech faltered; he stared at Bytoris.

The Bontonard crouched on his blanket with his face pressed into his thighs and his arms wrapped over the back of his head.

"By all that is sacred," Delmuirie murmured, "what is wrong with him?"

Geos glared at Delmuirie. "An entire realm of scholarship, through which many, many scholars could have gained great wealth and fame, has just fizzled into a minor study of a dead, but known, language."

"How am I to repay my travel-study loan now, if not through my great discoveries?" Bytoris moaned. "I'll be in debt so deep my children's children will not be able to buy their way out of it. The assessor's office will have my house and . . ." He kept talking, but his voice dropped so low Faia could not make out the words—only the tone of his unhappiness.

Nervously, Geos changed the subject. "You've not told us *your* name, girl."

Faia quit staring at Bytoris and turned to the other Bontonard. "Faia," she said. "Faia Rissedote."

Bytoris stopped bemoaning his financial woes and raised his head to stare at her. Then both Bontonards glanced from Delmuirie to her, and Geos shook his head in slow disbelief.

"Then we are awash in celebrities. You *are* the girl who nearly destroyed Ariss?"

Faia winced and nodded.

Bytoris sat up straighter and gave her a half-smile. "Pity you didn't get it all while you were at it."

"I wasn't trying to destroy any of it. I simply did what I had to do to stop the evil."

Bytoris opened his eyes and studied her. "The Arissonese usually like their evil. I'm surprised you didn't do things to encourage it, like the rest of your countrymen."

"I'm not Arissonese," Faia said dryly. "I'm Kareen—hill-folk."

"Oh?" Bytoris smiled at her—the smile suddenly genuine. "I'm familiar with the Kareen—the hills above Bonton are full of them. Where are you from?" he asked her.

"North of Willowlake," she said quietly. She didn't feel like going into the details about the demise of her village, Bright.

"Why, I actually *knew* a man from up around Willowlake," Geos said, startled. "An old wool merchant who came into Bonton and sold his wool in my neighborhood when I was a boy. He always brought milk-sweets and hard candy with him when he came to town."

"My da told me all wool merchants carry candies in their pockets," Faia said. "The children run to them, and their mothers follow. It's easier to sell the wool that way."

Geos watched the smoke curl out through the vent in the top of their makeshift tent and sighed. He seemed not to hear her. "What *was* the old man's name? I knew it once." He lay back, evidently deep in thought, then said, "Well. I can't remember . . . but you probably knew him."

"Probably not. I was from *near* Willowlake."

"There isn't much at all near Willowlake—and this was a memorable old fellow. You're not so young that you wouldn't have known him," Geos insisted. "Tall as a tree, and always knew a good joke. Rumor had it he'd fathered half the children in the Virkitch-Sodin district—my neighborhood."

Bytoris said coldly, "Rumor-mongering is one of the Great Sins."

Geos laughed and slapped his knee. "Bytoris is from my neighborhood, too—and come to think of it, I never met your father. Went off during the wars; that was the story. Maybe—" he began to sputter and cackle, "maybe *your* mother knew the old trader, eh?"

Delmuirie and Gyels laughed, too. Bytoris, though, went pale. He turned his back on them, every stiff line of his body eloquent with wordless anger.

Geos stared after him, no longer even smiling. "I only jested, Bytoris. I meant no insult to your mother—she has ever been kind to me."

Bytoris kept staring off into the distance.

Geos bit his lip. Faia could see the regret in his eyes and his posture. He took a deep breath, then in a soft voice recited:

"By Witte, your wit shall draw our doom.
For e'er the jester wears his jest
And mockery brings the Mocker nigh,
Whose truth none love.

"That's Terrfaire, the great Bontonard poet, from *Three Lies and The Maiden*," he told Faia in a quiet aside. "Terrfaire also wrote, 'Make thy peace or find thy grave with honor unsullied.' " He frowned and looked over at Bytoris's back. "Dare I apologize?" Geos asked his fellow Bontonard.

Bytoris, though, didn't answer. Instead, he lay on his bedroll and feigned sleep.

To Faia, who'd discovered the bonnechard did make her sleepy after all, sleep seemed suddenly a wonderful idea.

Chapter 17

"I'll never take another leaf of that stuff again," Faia muttered under her breath. During her second day of trekking through the dark, she'd had plenty of opportunity to think about the giddy behavior she had exhibited while under the influence of the bonnechard—and she'd had plenty of time to regret that, as well as the pounding headache it had left her with.

She yearned for a cabin and a roaring fire and a soft bed. Her ribs throbbed but the bonnechard stayed in its pack, untouched, in spite of the fact that in this second camp, which seemed even colder and more exposed, the ground underneath her bedroll was rockier and more uncomfortable than it had been the night before.

The tiny fire in the center of their tarp-tent crackled merrily, though, and Gyels insisted they'd gotten closer to their quarry, so they were all in good moods.

The five of them ate, then drifted, as they had the night before, into talking—but this night their stories were about other places they'd seen and other journeys they'd taken.

Faia listened as first Edrouss Delmuirie, then Bytoris, then Geos, told tales that were at times full of adventure, at times funny or sad, and she grew wistful—not for their stories of the open road, but because those stories roused in her memories she had long forgotten.

At last she said, "My father always talked about the joys of the road, and the wonders of travel to faraway lands." She stared down at the fire, then looked back into the darkness again, feeling the weight of memories. Her father had loved to travel, and had passed his wanderlust on to her. When she thought of seeing new places, she thought of him, and she missed him. She recalled one of the Great Philosopher's sayings that her father had always liked, and repeated it to her comrades. "Faljon says, 'More friends / makes fewer miles.' "

"Faljon . . ." Delmuirie shook his head and said, "Are people still quoting Faljon?"

Bytoris said, "My father quoted Faljon. My mother said Faljon had been some back-country root-eater, and that he was nothing compared to Terrfaire—but I always liked his sayings."

Faia lay back on her bedroll and tried to find a comfortable position. "I learned Faljon from my father, too."

Bytoris smiled a tiny smile. "Faljon is the sort of philosopher fathers love, I suppose. Plenty of admonitions to work hard and avoid doing stupid things."

Geos chuckled. "You know who I remember quoting Faljon? That same old man I thought of yesterday. The wool trader. He quoted Faljon, and told stories, and gave us—"

"Milk candies," Bytoris interrupted. "I remember. Your entire life seems to have focused on those milk candies."

Geos snorted. "Not so. I liked the stories, too. He always started them the same way, with a little poem—and when he recited the poem, the children would gather round." He closed his eyes and frowned, quiet for a moment. "I remember some of it, but not the important bits. He always said, 'Little chickies and chirries, the world goes 'round like a ball, 'round and 'round'. . . ."

He paused, drumming his fingers on his thigh. "And

when one side's up the other side's down," he added after
a moment's thought. He sighed deeply again, frustration
written on his face.

"I can't remember any more of it."

Faia said quietly, "I can. It went:

> *'Like a ball the world*
> *Goes 'round and 'round.*
> *When one side's up*
> *The other side's down.*
>
> *When the good side's down,*
> *Then evil rules,*
> *And the world is a place*
> *Of villains and fools.*
>
> *But the good will triumph*
> *And evil will fail,*
> *And about it Kin Kinsonne*
> *Will tell you the tale.' "*

She clasped her hands together and swallowed hard.

"That was it," Goos said. He beamed and slapped his
thigh. "That was it exactly! So you knew him!"

Faia nodded. A few hot tears rolled down the corners
of her eye and she brushed them away with a quick
backhanded swipe, embarrassed that anyone should see
her cry. She caught Bytoris staring at her, and thought
she must look ridiculous, brought to tears over such a
silly poem. "He was my father," she said. "I didn't know
anyone anywhere remembered him." The tears slipped
down her cheeks, hot and fat. "It's almost like having
him back, to know that someone besides me still thinks
of him."

Bytoris coughed and looked down at his hands. "Your
father's name was Kin Kinsonne?"

Faia nodded.

"Do you have any brothers or sisters?"

"I did." It was Faia's turn to look away. "They all died with my mother, in the plague that destroyed Bright. I've been alone since, except for my daughter."

"Ah. I was my mother's only child." He rested the knuckles of one hand against his lips and stared into the fire. "The gods do love their tricks."

"The gods often get blamed for what can only be attributed to blind chance," Gyels interrupted.

Bytoris glanced at him. "I have heard some say that, but I don't believe it." He returned his attention to Faia. "Perhaps since you are without family now, you will not find what I have to tell you unwelcome. Perhaps."

Faia heard unexpected awkwardness in his voice. She raised an eyebrow. "What might that be?"

"Well, some of us knew Kin Kinsonne better than others." Bytoris glanced from Geos to her, and said, "My colleague's jibe the other day was nothing but truth, though he didn't know it. My mother always insisted I say my father died in the wars. But Kin Kinsonne was my father, too."

"But your name . . ."

"Bontonard children get their public names from their mother's patron deity. My mother's deity has always been Caligro Sehchon, god of engineers. She is a water engineer in District Virkitch-Sodin."

"You're certain he's your father?"

Bytoris looked like he wasn't sure whether to be amused or annoyed. "My mother seemed to be sure. And he always called me 'son' when he came into town."

Faia felt sure the world was going to drop out from under her. "You're my brother?" she whispered. The world seemed to sway beneath her.

"Perhaps I should have said nothing." Bytoris looked away, and even by the ruddy firelight, Faia could see his face grow duskier. "Maybe you didn't want to know this about your father."

Faia's heart pounded in her ears, in her fingertips, and as she took it in, she began to think she must surely burst. "I have a *brother*?" she asked again. "I'm not alone?"

"Then you aren't angry?"

Faia was crying. She shook her head vehemently "I left to take the sheep to the upland pastures for the summer. When I returned, I was alone—my family . . . my village . . . everyone I ever knew . . . died in that plague—"

Bytoris nodded; he seemed relieved by her reaction. "You'll find quite a large family waiting for you in Bonton. I have a wife and a multitude of children—and I confess myself pleased to discover that I have a sister."

She couldn't take it in. "I have a brother again," she whispered, over and over. "I'm not alone."

"You are very much not alone."

Even after the fire guttered down, after all the others in the tent were sleeping soundly, Faia lay watching the stars that crossed the little smoke hole at the top of the tent. Sleep eluded her—her thoughts circled wildly and would not quiet, no matter how she tried to calm herself.

One part of her was elated that she had a living brother, though Bytoris shared no past with her. She had grieved for her family, and in Bytoris she could see resemblance to her long-dead brothers and to her sister. With him alive, they seemed to her not so completely lost. Another part of her, however, was deeply unhappy. By the simple fact of his existence, Bytoris had taken away from Faia pieces of her past that she had clung to, and made lies of some of her memories. Her father was not the man she had thought he was. Bytoris appeared to be older than her, but younger than her oldest brother or sister. So there was no question that her father had kept his two families at the same time, in violation of even the liberal Kareen laws of public bonding.

Bytoris is my blood kin, she thought. Blood kin should

matter; Bytoris should be someone to rejoice over, not someone to regret.

But she lay there remembering her own brothers—her *real* brothers, she thought—and how it was growing up with them. Playing in the hayshocks; stealing handpies from the cooling racks; climbing onto the back of the neighbor's giant plowhorse as it ambled past the fence while it grazed, and sitting astride it pretending to be riding from town to town, selling wool.

She closed her eyes.

And all the towns we imagined were Bright. Over and over, endlessly—our world consisted of one tiny village repeated in our minds a thousand times, the back of a fat plowhorse, and the stories we told each other.

Mama and Da loved us; we had homespun to wear and good food to eat; we knew Bright would make room for us when we grew up. That was enough, and we were happy.

To give Kirtha the family and the childhood and the way of life I knew, I would have given up my magic, my accomplishments, everything I have ever had in the world until this moment.

And now I find that my world was not as perfect as I thought it; that if I had given Kirtha my childhood, I would have given her a lie.

Faia lay in her bedroll, watching the flickering lights of the fire and hearing the droning snores of the men. The world of memory held her while she searched through all she recalled of her own past, looking for signs that would explain the place where she found herself, and the truth she had discovered.

Chapter 18

"Up! Hurry! We must pack and leave, quickly, or the thief will get too far ahead!" Gyels untied the first of the tarps from the supports, so the icy mountain air blew across Faia and the rest of the sleepers.

Again.

She'd lost track of the number of camps they'd set up, and had no idea of how many actual days they'd been pursuing Thirk. Faia felt she'd been hiking forever; the journey got worse daily. First they'd run out of the First Folk road, and then, for no apparent reason, Thirk had turned east toward steeper, rougher terrain before heading south again. He seemed to have picked the most dangerous, horrible route he could come by. Faia wondered how he was even surviving—but then she'd think of the chalice. He had magic—of course he could survive. His pursuers, meanwhile, struggled endlessly, becoming too weary to think or to question or to do much more than just put one foot in front of the other, plodding in the wake of the hunter Gyels.

They camped on cliffs and slopes so steep each of them pitoned loops of rope into the stone and slept with the loops wrapped around them. They ate sparingly—their rations got slimmer the further Thirk led them from the lowlands, and they became daily more aware that they could run out of food long before they reached the gentler climes of the lowlands. Gyels killed a mountain goat once, and they all ate from that for several days.

Hardship piled on hardship. Faia's ribs got better, but her nerves got worse. Once an avalanche nearly buried all of them but Gyels, who was—characteristically—far ahead, tracking. They heard the rumble barely in time and ran forward, slipping and sliding. The torrent ripped past them, only handbreadths away, tearing rocks and scrawny trees from their beds and roaring down the mountainside with the debris.

Then at *nondes*, the night they ate the last of the goat, something above kicked rocks down at them; they got a bad fright, though only Delmuirie was hit, and he was lucky. The rock that struck him was small enough that it only bruised his leg instead of breaking it. Gyels went off looking for the cause and reported back that a goat had knocked the rocks loose—but Faia wondered. The rain of rocks had been so regular, and had felt so intentional.

What worried Faia more than starvation, more than danger, was the inescapable feeling that they were being watched.

She'd mentioned it to each of her fellow travelers. Gyels scoffed—he was, he said, as keen-eared as he was keen-eyed, and if anyone had been spying on them, he would have discovered it. Geos and Bytoris didn't believe it simply because neither of them could imagine anyone but themselves lost and wandering through the mountains in the endless, awful darkness. Edrouss Delmuirie listened to what she had to say. He didn't say what he thought, or give any indication whether he believed her or not—but he did listen, and he did start watching behind the group as it traveled.

"Onward, already," Gyels growled. He'd come up behind Faia and the rest of them while they finished eating a light *antis*; he was in a miserable mood, as he had been the past few days. He'd begun to make his advances toward her more obvious, and Faia had found his pushy certainty that she would come to her senses and fall into his bedroll sooner or later increasingly less attractive. At last she had flatly rebuffed him—and the entire expedition was now paying the price, by being forced to live with his foul moods and the increased pace at which he drove them forward.

Faia, sitting on a flat, cold stone, jumped; Delmuirie turned and snarled something about moving when he was good and ready; and Bytoris threw a tiny scrap of smoked fish on the ground in disgust and stalked off.

Only Geos remained outwardly unmoved. He ate the rest of his dried meat without saying anything, though the look he gave Gyels when the hunter turned away was murderous.

Gyels glanced back at Geos in time to catch the look, and his expression became thoughtful. He said nothing about it, though. Instead, he turned back to Faia. "You want to capture Thirk, don't you?"

"We're never going to find him," Faia said. She pressed her hands to her face and sagged forward. "This is hopeless and it's horrible. If he does something that is going to destroy the world, I suppose he is just going to have to do it."

"You want to turn back?" Gyels smiled—but his smile was cold and mocking. "Silly creature, we're almost to Bonton—surely you realize that's where he's been leading us."

"Leading us?" Bytoris snarled. "He's been wandering in circles in the mountains for gods only know how long. We've been following—but only a fool would say he's been leading."

Faia nodded agreement.

They loaded up in unhappy silence and started off.

Gyels's promise that they were near civilization meant nothing to Faia, for she couldn't bring herself to believe it. She was doomed to wander in darkness until she died. Doomed to the wilderness, and the cold, and unending night.

She felt that way for nearly an hour—and then the Tide Mother rose from behind the mountains, and the sky began to pale and grow pink. Faia saw the sliver of the sun peeking out from behind the Tide Mother's vast bulk. She and the Bontonards and Delmuirie stopped right where they were, on a shale-covered downslope, and hugged each other and wept. Daylight! It became possible to hope for a nearby city, for more food, for their success in catching Thirk and rescuing the chalice—for *anything*, with the Month of Ghosts truly past.

Only Gyels didn't celebrate. He glanced in the direction of the sun, and frowned, and moved on. When they stopped at a spring to fill their waterskins, Faia asked him why he hadn't been as happy as the rest of them about the return of daylight.

"Night is the time of the hunter," he told her shortly.

Delmuirie waited until Gyels was well in the lead again, then whispered to Faia, "I would think he'd be thrilled. It has to have been near-impossible to track in darkness, and at the speed he's been going. Daylight could only make it easier."

"Well, at least in daylight, I'll be able to see some of the signs he's been following," Geos said. "I've never been a great tracker, but I've read a lot about it."

"You wonder how he's been doing it?" Bytoris asked.

Geos said, "The question crossed my mind."

Faia had wondered at Gyels's abilities in tracking, too—but he had successfully hunted down game animals in the darkness, and had gotten them safely through passes she would never have found, in spite of having grown up in mountain country. He was more than competent—and she had come to trust his ability as much as she'd come to dislike him personally.

She had put concern about Gyels out of her thoughts, because she had been focused, instead, on the larger worry—Thirk and what he would choose to make of the world if he had the power of all magic in his hands. She had not mentioned to Bytoris, Geos, or Delmuirie her early suspicion that Gyels was Witte, disguised in a new form. In light of Gyels's exemplary behavior, she had been glad she'd kept such silly thoughts to herself. But with Geos's question fresh in her mind, she was forced to reconsider Gyels. He had not joined in the storytelling with his fellow travelers. He had told nothing about himself. He kept to himself and kept his own counsel, and if he pursued her affection with single-minded intensity, or the escaping Thirk with the same sort of resolve, he had never given anyone a sign of the motives that drove him.

It was something else to worry about.

Late that day, they reached a river that crashed through the valley in front of them, swollen with snowmelt. The reappearance of the sun was bringing the world quickly back to the summer it had abandoned for the Month of Ghosts. The air grew steadily warmer, especially as they worked their way down to the lower altitudes.

"Wait or traverse now?" Bytoris shouted over the roar of the water.

Gyels stood studying the raging whitewater. He yelled back, "Cross now. Tomorrow will only be hotter, and the day after that hotter still. The current will grow steadily worse if we wait."

The river was not very wide, but it was fast. Slippery boulders, worn round by ages of rushing water, jutted out like balls thrown by a giant. Gyels found a few boulders close enough together that someone strong and graceful could jump from one to the other—and he tied a rope tightly around his waist and did just that.

He made it look so easy—but Faia could see that the surfaces of the rocks were slippery—some were covered with moss, and all were wet.

She and Bytoris and Geos and Edrouss Delmuirie made quick counsel, and after looking at those mossy, slick rocks, decided to pass their belongings over the rope first, so that their burdens would not unbalance them as they crossed.

Delmuirie and Bytoris went down to stand on the riverbank and pass their packs across. Geos stood beside her, well back from the banks, holding his pack in one hand, waiting.

"You're quite beautiful in firelight," he leaned over and told her. "I have all this while admired the fineness of your face and the grace of your walk. Still, this is the first time I've really seen you in daylight, and now I see that you are even more beautiful in the light of the sun."

He rested a hand on her arm and said,

> *"The sweetest touch is woman's touch*
> *Nor can mind grasp her loveliness.*
> *There is no winter 'neath her gaze,*
> *Nor sorrow in her soft embrace."*

"Terrfaire?" she asked.

"No! Me. I just made it up."

Faia laughed, delighted at the scene—a charming man creating poetry for her in the fierce mountains near a raging river. "I like it," she told him.

He took a deep breath, and blushed bright red as he started to say something.

"Geos!" Gyels shouted from across the river. His voice, Faia noted, carried remarkably well. "I'm ready for your things now!"

Faia grinned at Geos and put a finger to her lips. She told him, "Tell me later."

Geos's pack went across without difficulty, as did Faia's.

With the packs across the river, the people had to cross. Faia was the lightest of all of them—she went first because the men decided Gyels would be able to pull her out of the river on his own should she slip from a rock and fall in.

She made a loop in the center of the rope, knotted it, stepped into the cinch she'd formed, and began picking her way across the wet boulders. Gyels held the rope on one end, while Delmuirie and Geos anchored her on the other. They gave her plenty of slack, so she ended up feeling very safe. The crossing wasn't as difficult as she'd expected, either—although the rocks were slick, she had a good sense of balance. The only really frightening part of the procedure was seeing that roaring water rushing past, slipping by under her feet as she jumped from rock to rock; that gave her a dizzy feeling, and she had to make an effort not to look at it at all.

"Careful, girl!" Delmuirie shouted. Geos shouted similar encouragements.

Then she was across; she landed on the solid ground of the far bank, laughing and exhilarated. "My mother always used to say I was half goat," she told Gyels.

He nodded politely as she untied the rope from around her waist, but did not smile. The men on the other side reeled the rope back. Faia looked from them to him; the look in Gyels's eyes as he studied the three men still waiting across the river was disquieting.

Faia shivered, realizing she was completely alone with him for the first time—and abruptly she wished she weren't.

Bytoris, though, didn't waste time. He came next, moving as easily as Faia had. Delmuirie stopped for a moment before he came across. He had a quick conversation with Geos, and Faia saw Delmuirie demonstrating the tying of the knot he was using to the other man. Then Edrouss Delmuirie crossed. He slipped once, and got his foot wet, but Geos on one side and Gyels and Bytoris on the other pulled the rope taut in an instant, and that supported him while he got his feet back under him and somewhat unsteadily completed the crossing. Geos didn't worry about pulling the rope back—he had no one to anchor him on that side of the river. But he waved and grinned, and wrapped the end of rope around his own waist. He tied the knot and jumped up onto the first rock.

He was as agile as she had been, Faia thought. She was surprised to see a man of his size move with such grace. He frowned, his concentration evident on his face, and jumped to the next rock—again, it was a lovely jump. He looked up, and directed his smile straight to Faia. She smiled back.

He jumped to the next boulder, still watching her—and he missed.

Time seemed to her to slow down. Faia tightened her grip on the rope, and felt the others do the same. Geos bobbed up once, screamed something, and went under. The current and the rope acted together to drag him below the surface of the water. He struggled up for air. Faia dug her heels against the rocky ground, fighting for purchase; the rope bit deeply into her palms, and the muscles of her thighs and along the backs of her arms began to burn.

"Harder!" Bytoris shouted.

The rest were shouting to Geos, screaming, "Swim! Swim!" and pulling for all they were worth. They made headway. He was more than halfway across the river, out of danger from most of the boulders that could pulverize him.

He burst to the surface again, arms flailing, spitting water, gasping for air—

And the rope around his waist unknotted, and the four would-be rescuers on the shore crashed backwards and landed on the ground in a tangled heap.

With a scream of anguish and dismay, Geos vanished beneath the torrents of icy water.

Faia scrambled to her feet and began running along the riverbank, trying to catch up to the vanishing pale form as the water swept him away. She heard other running feet behind her. The little level space where they were crossing soon gave way to another steep cliff— and the river to a steep, many-layered falls. She saw Geos go over the edge; saw his body crash against boulder after boulder, arms and legs splayed and flopping as he tumbled through the air; she saw him wash into the back eddy of a pool a hundred feet below—then his limp body washed out of the pool in the current and floated, facedown, into the deep channel of the river.

She stared after him until he vanished from her sight.

Then she turned away, and fought back tears.

If he hadn't been looking at me, he wouldn't have fallen in, she thought. He'd still be alive.

"Should we see if we can retrieve his body?" Delmuirie asked.

Bytoris looked grim.

At last he said, "There is no need. His body will go back to the All-Mother this way as much as if we found him and built a cairn over him."

He looked down over the cliff, watching the water crashing over its course. He began to recite, his voice lifted over the noise of the falls:

> *"The sun is gone from out the sky,*
> *And will not rise; the sun is dead.*
> *Laughter bury, bathe in tears.*
> *Beloved Brodatio breathes no more."*

Terrfaire again, Faia thought. With those two, it was always Terrfaire.

He was silent for a moment, then he added,

"..., *exists not*
His equal. Ne'er man was born,
Who, truer friend, did walk these streets,
Or set his hand to any task.
I owe my life; I greatly owe."

Faia looked down at the falls. She had no lovely words for her thoughts—nothing poetic came to mind as she considered Geos. She hadn't known him well, but she'd liked him. She said, "He made up a poem for me," and felt quick, hot tears burn at the corners of her eyes. There was nothing else she could think to say.

She walked away, avoiding looking at the three surviving men. She tried to remember the poem he'd created for her, but all she could think of was the rope around Geos's waist, and Edrouss Delmuirie showing him how to tie the knot.

Chapter 19

The sun set with a flourish that splashed colors across the sky and set to gleaming something golden on a far distant peak.

Bytoris, walking just ahead of Faia, stopped and stared. He pointed to the gleam.

Faia nodded. "I see it."

"That's the Temple of Horse-Dancers. It's just on the other side of the Wen Tribes Treaty Line, and about a day's hard walk from Bonton."

"We really are almost to the city, then?"

It should have been a moment of triumph. They stood, looking at the faraway point, and Faia felt no elation; she felt only weariness. One of their number was dead, Thirk was still ahead, her nerves insisted that something lurked behind, still watching, and now she discovered that she didn't trust any of the men with whom she traveled. Bytoris watched Delmuirie with eyes that grew increasingly more hate-filled—and if he was her blood kin, he was blood kin she didn't know; she had no idea if he would consider murdering Delmuirie, whom he blamed for Geos's death. Faia could not deny, either, that Delmuirie might have been responsible, though she could not think of a possible reason why he might have wanted Geos to die. She could not help but wonder that a knot tied in a wet rope would untie itself, when such knots tended, in her experience, to become so tight almost nothing could free them. Then there was Gyels, who made Faia's heart race every time she looked at him even though she didn't like him.

As true night fell for the first time in a month, the quartet set up camp beneath a few thin conifers on a grass-covered slope at the base of the next mountain they would have to pass. They hung their packs in the trees when they were done and pitched their tarps singly around an outdoor fire; they seemed to have come to silent agreement that they needed as much space away from each other as they could get. Faia studied the way they all watched each other warily as they ate. The tension around their little campfire became almost unbearable. And when the food was gone, they watched each other some more, but pretended not to, wrapped in their bedrolls and unwilling to sleep in spite of their exhaustion.

Bytoris sharpened his knife, spitting from time to time on the blade and working the edge carefully at an angle along the bit of rock he'd found. He held the knife up, studied its edge by firelight, snorted, and went back to his methodical scrape, scrape, scrape.

Gyels got up and walked away from the camp. Faia listened as he paced through the darkness, beyond the range where she could hear his footfalls, then, not too much later, picked up his heavy steps as he returned. He settled back onto the deadwood seat he'd vacated and sat glaring at the fire, until he decided instead to glower at Bytoris and Edrouss. His eyes narrowed and his lips thinned. When at last he stared at Faia, his eyes were full of longing and anger. She lifted her chin and looked at him defiantly. He frowned and got up—and walked out again.

Edrouss Delmuirie waited until Gyels's footsteps had faded into the distance the second time. Then he huffed out a quick breath and said, "I know you both think I had something to do with Geos's death—"

Bytoris cut him off. "No one accused you of anything."

"No one had to accuse me. I am not stupid. I saw the knot untie, just as you did, and saw the rope slip off from around his chest, and I was the one who showed him how to tie the damned rope." Delmuirie sighed heavily. "You have to believe me. I showed him the best, strongest, easiest knot I knew—he said he was a city boy, and did not know knotwork well."

"You could have tied it for him," Bytoris said. "Sent him over before you."

"I suggested that, but he wanted to go last."

Bytoris looked momentarily startled. "He did?" he blurted—and then his countenance became grim again, and he said, "Well, yes, you can *say* that, can't you?" He went back to sharpening his knife.

Faia thought Edrouss Delmuirie sounded sincere. She didn't particularly want to believe him—there was a part of her that still blamed him for the Barrier, and for his delusions of godhood while in the erneshest, and it would have fit her preferred picture of the man to think he'd also done something that had caused Geos's death. In spite of herself, however, and the grudge she bore against him, she felt he was telling the truth. "Geos tied the knot himself," Faia said at last. "If Edrouss had tied it, and it had come undone, it would have been easier to believe his death wasn't an accident."

"So?" Bytoris raised an eyebrow. "You think this man did nothing wrong?"

Faia took a deep breath. "Yes," she said slowly. "I think Geos's death was an accident."

Bytoris nodded stiffly and slipped his knife into the sheath at his waist. "You are entitled to your opinion." He rose and walked to his tarp, and before he ducked inside, made a show of wrapping one hand around the knife hilt. "I hope you and your opinions sleep well."

She and her opinions dreamed ugly dreams, of drowned men and waterfalls and something that watched, waiting. Once, she woke from a sound sleep to hear someone out in the packs, but when she looked out, she saw nothing.

In the morning, when Gyels woke them, everyone's belongings were scattered through the little copse, and their food was gone.

They stared at each other, and every face wore the same suspicious expression.

Gyels was the first to speak. He said, "I didn't make this mess. I left camp last night because I couldn't sleep, and I've spent the night trailing Thirk; I only just returned this morning. At least I bring good news with me. Thirk is very near."

"You don't look like a man who walked all night," Faia told him. "You don't look tired at all."

"I don't need as much sleep as you . . . you sluggards." He sniffed and his nostrils pinched tight.

Which was true, Faia thought. Gyels had stayed in the lead the entire time, breaking trail under dreadful conditions, and although she had seen him look bored plenty of times, she had never seen him look completely worn out.

"Perhaps Thirk doubled back to steal our food," Delmuirie said.

Bytoris looked at him as if he were insane. "He's almost to Bonton already. He has the magical chalice. Why in the names of all the mad gods would he troop *back* into the mountains to steal our sorry dried fish and hardbread?"

Delmuirie shrugged. "Why, if he has something magical, would he walk through the mountains instead of flying?"

That was a good point, Faia thought. Their mountain trek had been no pleasure stroll. If *she'd* had her magic, they would have flown at the very least. Thirk was a saje, and knew how to transport. Why had he not done so?

Gyels said, "No doubt an animal got into the packs while you people slept."

Faia had been looking over the ground beneath the trees where the packs had been. She found prints in the soft earth—but they weren't animal prints. They came from a human. She rested her foot lightly beside the clearest of the marks, and found that it was somewhat longer than her foot, but nearly as narrow. And the boot had a sharply pointed toe and a rounded heel.

She said nothing. Instead, she looked at the boots Bytoris, Gyels, and Delmuirie wore. Bytoris's boots were round-toed. So were Gyels's. And Edrouss Delmuirie wore odd square-toed boots with thick, black soles carved in geometric designs.

"Perhaps it is the person I've felt following us," she said.

Gyels looked at her and rolled his eyes. "I told you, no one is following us." He glanced at the ground beneath another of the trees where a pack had hung and said, "Night boles. Their prints are everywhere."

Faia started to dispute him and stopped. The hair stood on her arms and her gut tightened. Liar! she thought. But what did he have to gain with such a lie? His insistence on a point she could plainly see was untrue meant something. All she needed to do was figure out what. Why would it matter to him that everyone thought an animal raided their packs instead of a man? Why would he deny so vehemently even the suggestion that someone might be following them? Was that important? It was frightening, of course . . . but was it important? And if so . . . why? She held her peace, deciding she would watch Gyels, as she watched Bytoris and Delmuirie, until something began to make sense to her.

Chapter 20

The rolling hills and scattered groves of the countryside they reached two days later were lovely; as Faia waded through knee-deep grass full of day-blooming fox-roses and towering Maraid-flowers, she was overwhelmed with memories of the hills where she'd grown up. She felt that at last she'd come home. She breathed cool air redolent of crushed grass and sweet sage, and heard the bleating of sheep in a far pasture, and her heart ached.

The four travelers crested a hill, and from the ridge Faia saw gaudy flags flapping in the distance from the top of a grey stone wall. She guessed the great city—for she could see Bonton was that—at little more than an hour's walk. Her first thought was, There will be food in Bonton, thank the Lady—and someplace to bathe.

Her second was, I wish Kirtha were here. She'd love the flowering meadows, and the sweet, cool air. So different from humid Omwimmee Trade near the sea.

"Bonton," Bytoris said. He smiled, and when he did, Faia realized how long it had been since she'd seen a smile on his face.

Delmuirie studied the huge walled city and stopped. "It was nothing but cow pastures and mud huts . . . before," he whispered. "Truly, is that Bonton?"

"The greatest city in the world," Bytoris said.

"Well could I believe that, seeing it before me now."

Gyels said, "It is sad that we were unable to capture Thirk before he reached the city. Once inside, he will have little difficulty hiding from us . . . he may elude us for a very long time."

Faia waited. There was, she was certain, more to what Gyels intended to say.

He didn't disappoint her. "I am certain Bytoris Caligro will have to return to his work, now that he has come home. And Edrouss Delmuirie will need to find a place for himself, and some way to provide himself with food and shelter." He clucked his tongue. "Which will leave you and me to catch Thirk. There are people in the city who . . . owe me debts. We will be able to find lodging and food without difficulty, you and I."

Both Bytoris and Edrouss turned and studied Gyels.

"I had thought to continue the search for the man," Bytoris said. "I would not willingly give over such a vital quest."

Delmuirie nodded. "I did not come to Bonton to find a job," he said. "I came to find a thief and stop a madman. Once I have done what I came for, I will worry about other things."

"But where will you stay? How will you live?" Gyels asked. His smile was confident—and now Faia saw what his aim had been. She wondered if, all along, Gyels had been keeping them back so that Thirk would be able to maintain his lead. He intended to discard both men and be alone with her.

His tone infuriated Faia.

Evidently, however, she wasn't the only one put out by Gyels's assumptions. Bytoris said, "I have a large house in the city, with plenty of rooms. My newfound sister will have a place to stay and food to eat."

Faia looked at him, and tried to put her hopes and her prayers in her eyes. "What about Edrouss?" she asked.

Bytoris's lips thinned and his eyes narrowed for an instant. Then he said, "By all means, Delmuirie will stay with us, too." Then, with a cold little bow, he added, "Even you, Gyels, are welcomed beneath my roof, should you desire to help us continue our hunt for Thirk Huddsonne and the chalice—though of course we will no longer need your tracking skills."

The tone in his voice told Faia under no circumstances did he expect Gyels to accept his offer.

The next instant, Faia decided Bytoris should have ignored good form, for Gyels smiled and said, "Well, well—both invited and welcomed into your home. In truth, I am honored; I will carry your offer and promise close to my heart." But then he shook his head sadly, and she breathed a quick sigh of relief. "Nonetheless, there are in Bonton those who value my company, and who await my arrival with some eagerness. I suspect I should first seek them out, to see if they would help me."

"Help you to find Thirk?" Bytoris looked surprised.

"That is what we have been doing all this time, isn't it?"

Bytoris nodded his head stiffly and turned his back on Gyels, whose smile became at once both self-satisfied and sly. Bytoris pointed out across the meadows before them. "Beyond that next little hill, we'll cross the road. Be wary near it—the Wen's trees, in these past few months, have moved from the jungle to the roadside, and now hide within the normal trees that line both sides of it."

"The trees—moved?" Delmuirie asked. He looked from Bytoris to Faia, and his expression indicated he was certain they'd all gone mad. "Walked? Oh, come now. Surely not."

"Lurched along on their roots like giant fat spiders," Bytoris said. "I saw them do it—watched two of them moving toward the city while I stood on the top of the wall." He frowned at the horizon and said, "Ugliest gods-forsaken things I ever saw."

Delmuirie looked last at Faia, and leaned close, and said, "You don't believe this, do you? It can't be real."

Faia said, "The Keyu are magical trees. In the last few months, they've begun to walk—the survivors who traveled to Omwimmee Trade told stories of the trees hiding by the roadside and snatching up any who weren't quick enough. Those trees are both real and deadly."

"Trees," Delmuirie muttered. "*Walking* trees." He shoved his hands into the pockets of his breeches, and sighed. "I have never seen such a thing."

"You're about to," Bytoris said. "Be careful you don't die of the excitement."

The travelers stopped just short of the trees lining the road. A dreadful stench assaulted them—the stink of meat spoiling in the sun, of death. Faia saw the Keyu waiting among the nonmagical trees, squat and twisted and leprous-looking, hunkered down on their insect-leg roots with their fat, slimy white palps trailing along the ground. She shuddered, remembering her first encounter with those trees, deep in the Wen jungles that bore them. They'd been bad enough when they couldn't walk.

"How are we going to get around them?" she asked. "They're lurking much closer together than I would have supposed."

"Gods, those are ugly trees," Delmuirie whispered. "And they reach out and grab at you as you go past them?"

Faia nodded. "And then their trunks split, and they drag you into the hollow middle—" She stopped and closed her eyes; the memory of being caught in the maw of a Keyu, of being touched and bored into by silky, sticky threads, was suddenly fresh and real again. And now that none of them had magic, she didn't see how they could hope to pass.

When she opened her eyes, she saw Bytoris frowning at the Keyu.

"What is it?"

"You've seen them before, haven't you?"

She nodded. "Closely."

Bytoris pointed. "Look at them. They aren't twitching the way they usually do."

Faia studied the trees, and realized that, indeed, they were as still as normal trees. Puzzled, she looked back to Bytoris.

He picked up a rock and hefted it thoughtfully from one hand to another. Abruptly, he pitched it at one of the Keyu. It struck directly on the palp—and sunk in. The wound oozed gelatinous grey slime, and then, with a moist, sucking sound, the palp he hit fell off.

"Ugh!" Delmuirie muttered. "Disgusting."

"They've . . . they've rotted," Faia whispered.

None of the palps so much as jerked. Faia, bewildered, took wolfshot from the bag at her belt, tucked it into her sling, and hurled it at a different palp, on a different Keyu. The jagged shot bored in one side of the growth and out the other, and more of the grey slime spurted from both holes. That palp, too, ripped free and flopped to the ground with a sickening squelch.

"I think the Keyu are dead," Bytoris said.

"Couldn't happen to nicer trees," she told him, though she didn't dare to believe he was right.

She and her brother edged closer to the Keyu. Her heart pounded in her throat—she was just waiting to discover that it was a trick, and feel again the moist, sticky tendrils as they wrapped around her and dragged her toward a waiting, gaping maw. The smell of death grew stronger, and so did Faia's fear. Delmuirie walked along beside them, staring from them to the unmoving trees, until at last he gave an exasperated snort, and trotted up to the nearest one, borrowed sword drawn. He whacked off its palps, then strolled across the road to the other side, where he turned and bowed.

"I would guess they're dead," Faia said.

Bytoris gave a dry chuckle. "You might be right, mightn't you? Though I find myself wishing that one, at least, had been alive—to swallow him." He nodded toward Delmuirie. "Arrogant bastard."

Gyels strode forward. Faia put a hand on Bytoris's arm, and both of them hung back. When Gyels was out of earshot, Faia said, "I know you don't like Edrouss. But thank you for making room for him as well as me; the more I have seen of Gyels these past few days, the more I feel we are at common cause against him."

"You're welcome. There are few things about that hunter that I like."

They looked over to see Gyels walking past Delmuirie, hurrying toward the walled city—while Delmuirie stood transfixed, with his mouth gaping idiotically wide. Faia realized he hadn't moved since he turned and bowed. He stared at the tree—and suddenly an eerie, wordless keening noise tore from his throat; it brought the hairs on Faia's neck straight up.

"Uh-oh," she whispered. These Keyu were dead—dead. They had to be. She *wanted* them to be. But perhaps they were not as dead as they seemed. Perhaps Delmuirie was under the spell of some new form of their magic, some clever trap. She ran between the gauntlet of trees, keeping as far from any Keyu as she could manage, while her pulse roared in her ears and her breath came in short, sharp gasps. The trees didn't move, didn't grab her, didn't pull her in. They stayed dead, and she reached the far side of the road in safety, and turned to see what it was Delmuirie stared at.

When she saw, she turned away.

The tree he was looking at had fed well before it died; its maw gaped partway open, with the remains of a victim blocking the mouth and preventing it from closing. Inside, the bloated bodies of the Keyu's prey—men, women, and children—hung tangled in its silky webs. Hung and rotted; one it had captured recently had died still reaching for the freedom of light and air. The stench around the tree was unbearable, and Faia shoved her *erda* against her face and drew fresher air through the coarse felt.

"Get away from here," she said. "You can't do anything now."

Delmuirie was frozen—pale and shaking, he couldn't move. "You were telling the truth," he said.

"Of course I was telling the truth, you idiot." Faia grabbed his arm and dragged him after her, across what had once been a crop field—though now it was parched and overgrown with weeds. No doubt it had been neglected since the arrival of the Keyu. She heard Bytoris running in her wake.

She looked back just as he caught up with her; she saw fear in his eyes—but fresh fear, of a present danger. She stared at the Keyu behind her, but they stayed dead. "What—" she started to ask, but Bytoris merely shook his head and pointed upward.

"Run!" he croaked. "Find cover."

Delmuirie looked where Bytoris pointed and gasped—air hissed between his teeth. He lunged at Faia, grabbed her around the waist, and knocked her into a tangle of weeds and deep grass behind a small hillock. She pummeled him and shrieked, "You bas—" but he clamped one hand over her mouth and whispered, "Quiet, or we're dead."

He pointed, keeping his movements small, close, and careful. She followed the direction he indicated, and quit fighting.

"I thought you said they were gone," he whispered, and then he grew silent.

Faia got the chance to look up. High overhead, but dropping fast, monsters arrived on brilliantly colored wings. The air was suddenly full of leathery beating, of roars and rough deep bellows. Creatures from nightmare dropped out of the sky, screeching and thundering, bent on attacking the city. Faia saw Bytoris leap into tall grass nearby, and prayed that the monsters had not seen him.

The beasts were huge, lean, and muscular; their hides sparkled as if they'd been formed of gems—and indeed, the monsters came in every imaginable gemstone color, and a few besides: ruby red tipped in black, glittering emerald green, deep violet, striped orange and copper, richest sapphire blue, sun-bright yellow tipped out in emerald green, and more. But their eyes were stony, sparkling black, and their ivory teeth and adamantine claws were long and sharp.

The warriors on the wall fought back with a hailstorm of arrows, bolts, and fire, and a few of the monsters fell screaming into the moat or onto the embankment—Faia could feel the earth shake each time one hit—but the monsters had the advantage of flight and ferocity. They would not be turned. They snapped up and tore apart all the warriors they could catch, and seemed to revel in the screams and sobs of the dying. They chased after the wall defenders, bellowing as they flew mere handbreadths above the parapet; they swept bowmen from the wall with gutting slashes of their taloned forelegs, or picked them up and dropped them from great height to watch them spatter on the rock below. They dove and dipped and soared, beautiful and terrible beyond anything Faia had ever imagined. Though they had flattered themselves in their artwork, she knew what they were—she felt the certainty in her bones. They were the First Folk. Klaue. Klogs.

Faia pressed her face into the grass and cried silently; she was afraid—she could hear people moaning and sobbing from the battlements and from the ground around them. Terrible things had happened and were happening. The Klaue were going to find her. They were going to lift her into the air and rip her limb from limb. She would never see Kirtha again.

Beside her, Delmuirie moved an arm around her and

held her tightly—and she was grateful for the comfort he gave.

The earth beneath them shook, and nearby a Klog roared. That hellish roar was a sound that made a pack of hunting kellinks sound gentle by comparison. Faia prayed she would never hear it again.

Then the Klogs lifted as one, as if to a silent signal, and still screaming, flapped away with slow, steady wingbeats toward the east.

For long moments neither Faia nor Edrouss Delmuirie moved. Then Edrouss sat up and pulled her close. He held her for a moment, and she rested against his chest and shook. He was crying, too, she realized, and he trembled as well.

"I've never seen them like that," he whispered. "They were like animals."

"They *were* animals," Faia whispered with conviction.

"They weren't before," he said. "I knew them before. They were vicious bastards . . . but not like that."

They lay still a few moments longer, while the sobbing and shouting along the city walls went on and on. At last Faia felt her courage return, and she pulled free of Delmuirie's embrace. They rose. The hillock behind which they'd hidden was just high enough to make it good cover. Faia was grateful—without it, she and Delmuirie might have been dead. They walked to the top of it, hoping to see where Bytoris had hidden.

Right in front of them, red and black and half as long as Faia was tall, a monster's head slashed out at them from the place where it had been hidden by the other side of the embankment. The giant mouth spread open and teeth gleamed. The downed Klaue lay where it had fallen, mortally wounded but not yet dead enough.

Faia didn't think; she reacted. She hurled her staff as if it were a javelin, straight down the beast's throat. The Klog gagged and tossed its head from side to side; neither

Faia nor Edrouss Delmuirie stayed to see if it freed itself from the obstruction. They both ran full out until they reached the place where Faia's half-brother had hidden.

He crawled out from under the thorn shrubs where he had hidden as soon as he saw them, and wrapped his arms around Faia by way of greeting.

"Bytoris!" She was sincerely glad to find him unharmed.

"Faia!"

His dirt-caked cheeks were tear-streaked, but he managed a sincere smile for her. "We must hurry," he told her. "I have to check on the rest of my family."

Chapter 21

The cantilevered arch of the gate before Faia rose higher than the wall. Men of old had carved the forms of humans and beasts into its grey stone, and the eyes of those pocked and worn faces stared warily at Faia as she approached. This, too, was an ancient place, she thought—though not as old as the First Folk ruins. And it lacked about it the feeling of alienness those distant ruins had. Two burly men leaned beneath each side of the carved arch, their hands resting on the pommels of swords or the hafts of long spears. A fifth sat at a small table to one side. His helmet rested on the flat paving stones at his feet. He had weary eyes, Faia thought. Weary—and sad.

Gyels hurried ahead of the rest of them. He stepped up to the seated guard and whispered a word. The guard nodded, his face expressionless—and Gyels passed into the walled city and immediately strode through the midst of a group of bickering merchants, where he disappeared into the crowd.

Bytoris frowned, Faia noticed, but he didn't say anything. He walked up to the seated guard and addressed the man. Faia, standing in the background waiting, paid no attention to her brother—she stared up at the gate arch over her head, fascinated. More stone faces stared down at her—

the faces of imaginary demons and all-too-real monsters, their mouths open in silent, eternal screams. The hollows of their mouths extended further into the stone than normal carving could account for, and the teeth and insides of the mouths, bleached white in the otherwise grey stone, told her the rest of the story. She realized suddenly that those mouths were hollowed tubes. Weapons. The soldiers on the arch above could, at any time, pour boiling water or acid or liquid fire on the people below. She shuddered and looked away; those disguised weapons seemed to her a sly and evil use of art.

"What do you *mean*, I cannot take them in?" Bytoris suddenly shouted.

All the guards looked at him with eyes no longer bored or weary. "Rules since the change," the seated one snapped. "None but citizens or their families in."

Bytoris opened his mouth to protest, then shut it. "Come," he said to Faia and Delmuirie, and turned away from the gate.

They walked in silence alongside the wall. Bytoris was clearly angry; he clamped his jaw tightly, and Faia could see the muscles twitch. He stormed along, saying nothing. Delmuirie prudently kept quiet, and Faia decided to follow the same path of wisdom herself. She and Delmuirie nearly had to run to keep up. They came to a good-sized stream that fed into the moat. Bytoris led them along it, away from Bonton and toward a little bridge and a pleasant-looking copse of trees not too far away.

They crossed the bridge and achieved the cover of the trees. Bytoris threw his pack on the ground, opened it, and began rummaging for something. Faia watched him, puzzled. He had a cold smile on his face, and he kept muttering, "I'll show them. Won't let *my* people in, hey? Who do they think pays their salaries, tell me that?" At last he found the thing he sought. He gave a satisfied snort

and sat back on his haunches, and held up his find for
both of them to see.

"What is it?" Faia asked when her brother didn't explain.

Bytoris looked past her, to Edrouss Delmuirie. "Stick
this in your pack. It's your citizen's pass. When the soldiers
at the next gate ask, you're Geos Rull, collector and
language expert from the House of Antiquities and
Artifacts."

Faia felt her eyes widen. "I thought Geos was a scholar."

"He was." Bytoris looked suddenly grim. "He was also
employed—being a scholar pays nothing here in Bonton.
But there's money enough to be had in collecting curios."

Stealing them, more likely. Faia thought of the contents
of Geos's pack, which Bytoris had moved to his own
when no one was watching and had subsequently carried
without complaint. It must have been full of artifacts
from the First Folk ruins, she realized. And, likely, her
brother's pack had contained even more of the same.
Medwind and the other scholars would have been furious
had they known what the Bontonard "scholars" had
actually been doing in the ruins.

Edrouss Delmuirie nodded and shoved the little plate
into his pack.

Bytoris, meanwhile, pulled out a piece of drypress
and a scritore, and began scratching out a note of some
sort. He looked up at Faia once, assessing her, then began
to write again.

"What are you doing?" Faia asked him.

"Forging a bride-price paper. Says that Edro—ah, *Geos*,
here, picked you up from traders moving from Omwimmee
Trade to the Forst Province. That makes you Fisher—
they're the only folks who sell their women. So you can't
speak at all, right? Because I'm betting you don't speak
Spavvekith."

Faia nodded. "You bet right."

"And your name is Reeluu. Every woman I've ever met

from the Fisher Province had been named either Malleth or Reeluu." He sighed. "I'd take you myself, but I already have a wife and a whole crew of kids, and I can't afford the extra taxes another wife would cost me—even temporarily." Bytoris stood. "Anyway, that will be enough to get us through the gate. We'll have to make you and— er, *Geos*—" He frowned at Delmuirie. "You and Geos permanent. The laws of Bonton don't look kindly on men buying wives unless they then make them citizens—and we'll have to do that fast." He finished his forgery, told Delmuirie to sign it, then blew on the whole thing until the ink dried. When he was satisfied it wouldn't smudge, he handed the paper to Delmuirie, who put it in his pack with his own pass.

Faia frowned at Bytoris and protested, "But I'm your sister. The guard at the gate said family. I shouldn't need to have to pretend to be . . ." she spat the word, "*property*."

"You and I have nothing to prove that we are brother and sister," Delmuirie said. "And I'm betting more than one man has tried to claim 'sisters' or 'brothers' he didn't have in order to help friends outside the city get inside." He shook his head. "No. This is best. Just play along while we're here."

They rose, and Faia, patently unhappy, turned to go back the way they'd come.

Bytoris said, "We aren't going back to the Doweth Ecclesiastic Gate. The guards *might* be off their shift, but they might not be, too, and I don't want to take a chance of running into them again. Besides, I think we'd get better treatment from the guards of a gate that hadn't so recently been under attack by Klogs."

He led them through the woods along a well-worn path, down to a rutted cart-road that ran between fields of summer wheat and cherticorn. "Timnett Merchanter is a better gate, anyway," he added.

It was a very *different* gate, at least. Faia noted that the cantilevered arch was the same, but the carvings were of trade goods—bolts of cloth, pack and draft animals, herd beasts, fruits and grains, amphoras and jugs. The gate was prettier, the carved faces of the few people on it not so crazed-looking. Yet when she stood underneath it and stared upward—while Delmuirie and Bytoris talked to the guards—she could see that the bottom jugs were tipped and angled and hollow, aimed to pour destruction down on anyone beneath. She frowned. Ariss had not resorted to such mundane means of defense—the mages and sajes guarded the city magically.

"Reeluu!" Delmuirie said. Faia ignored him.

The mages and sajes *had* guarded Ariss magically, she thought. Then she wondered how Ariss, magically built on a magical hill in the middle of a nasty swamp, was faring. Probably the whole bedamned city had sunk beneath the water and everyone in it had drowned. She had hoped to do something that would make her welcome in Ariss again. Instead, it seemed more than likely she would never be able to set foot near that city—if any of it remained—for as long as she lived.

"*Reeluu!*"

She decided not to think about Ariss.

"REELUU!" Delmuirie ran over to her, grabbed her arm, and dragged her back to the guards. "I'm not sure she can even hear," he told them with an apologetic smile. "Perhaps that's why the Fishers sold her to me. But she's pretty, isn't she?"

The guards grinned. Faia kept her expression neutral and just a little puzzled.

"Tax officer will want more than ten percent for *her*," one of the side guards said. "She's the best-looking Fisher I've ever seen."

Bytoris frowned. "He got her for a good price—due to her defects."

The guard at the table chuckled. "If she can't hear and can't speak either, that would make her the perfect wife."

Bytoris and Delmuirie both laughed, and Bytoris said, "He didn't buy her to talk to, anyway."

The guard looked at the paper Delmuirie handed them, and nodded. "That was a good price. Pity they didn't come through here first—I'd have bought her myself." He handed back the paper and the metal pass, then pointed to the packs. "You people have anything to declare?"

Bytoris nodded and smiled. He pulled out a couple of carved stone rings from the top of his pack and held them up to the guards.

The seated guard frowned. "What are they?"

Bytoris shrugged. "I don't have any idea. I found them in the First Folk ruins."

"So they're artifacts."

Bytoris nodded. "Of some sort."

One of the other guards wandered over from his niche in the wall, and both he and the seated guard took one. They turned the rings over, ran their fingers along the edges, and squinted at them as if they thought squinting would make the artifacts make more sense. Finally, the guard in charge shrugged. "Small artifacts, unknown purpose, unknown value—let's say one rit each. Silver, though, not pressleaves. If they turn out to sell for more than that, the tax officer will surely drop by to pay you a visit."

Bytoris and the guard laughed, and Bytoris said, "Oh, surely. I imagine he will anyway—you know how they are about their taxes." He reached into his pack again and pulled out two small, octagonal silver coins. The guard checked both sides of the coins, nodded to the other guards, then waved them through.

"And that is all there is to that," Bytoris said with a chuckle as soon as they were out of earshot.

"What the man said about the Klaue worries me." Edrouss Delmuirie wasn't smiling. His dark eyes were thoughtful.

Faia hadn't heard any of the guards say anything about Klaue. "What was that?" she asked.

"He said they have been attacking that same quarter of the city every day since first sunrise. No one knows why. This is the first day any of the Klogs were killed, and there were fewer human casualties than any previous day." He shook his head. "That is not like the Klogs. They usually have a plan . . . and they usually win."

"Maybe they've changed," Faia suggested.

Edrouss shrugged, but did not look like he was considering the possibility. "Maybe."

Faia studied Bonton. It was nowhere near as impressive as Ariss. She recognized the peak of the Remling Tower, visible from time to time over the rooftops. Anyone who'd gotten paid in Dorrell Province would recognize that, though—its image decorated the obverse of every Dorrellian coin minted or pressleaf pressed. It wasn't as attractive in real life as it was stamped onto gold, either, she thought. And the rest of Bonton was even less prepossessing. The buildings, stone and baked brick and hewn timber, jumbled on top of each other closer and closer the further she and her companions penetrated into the city; deep in the backways, the inhabitants had built far into the streets so that in places the main road permitted only two people to proceed abreast. Traffic throughout was thick and rough; people fought past on foot or on horseback or in skinny little goat-carts. They all smelled of sweat and dirt. Their hair was greasy to a one, and their faces showed grime.

If the people were dirty, though, the city itself was worse. The cobblestones were slick with the droppings of horses and cows and other livestock, and the gutters ran with trash and dumpings from chamber pots. Faia noted rats and flies and thin, wary alley cats. The stink grew, and grew, and grew, the further they went into Bonton's heart.

Bytoris slowed. Faia watched the expressions that flashed across his face; bewilderment, disgust, confusion, and finally fear. "This is what this city has come to without magic," he said. He stopped completely, looking at the filthy streets and the grimed people who hurried through them. He shook his head. "This is vile. I need to get home."

He led them quickly down a twisting, close road, through a foul, stench-bathed alley, and at last into a little closed-off circle of tall, brightly painted houses. The paving-stone circle was awash with the same mire that befouled the rest of the city, though Faia could see how the little circle of houses might have been thought pretty, if the stink were not so overwhelming.

A boy from the top window of a tall, thin yellow house suddenly shrieked, "Mama! Mama! Papa's home!"

There was an instant of silence; then the house erupted with noise. "Papa! Papa!" a veritable chorus of young voices shouted, and a woman's voice cried out, "Bytoris?! Oh, gods, you're home at last." The floors echoed with the thunder of running feet; a slight blonde woman burst out of the front door first, leapt up, and wrapped her arms around his neck and her legs around his hips. "Godsall, I thought sure you were dead!" She hugged him close and smothered his face and neck with kisses; Faia couldn't help but grin.

"Renina!" Bytoris spun her around and hugged her. "I nearly was dead, love. Nearly was." He kissed her, then pulled away. "What's been going on here?" he asked, but he didn't have time to hear an answer. A horde of children—Faia counted six, but they were moving fast enough that she might have missed one or two—streamed out of the house and surrounded him. They, too, hugged him and shouted. The scene in the cobblestoned courtyard was mayhem; neighbor women ran out to see what the commotion was, and squealed when they recognized Bytoris. They and their children surrounded him, too, shouting and laughing and talking all at once.

It sounded like a huge flock of chickens in the henyard. Bytoris was popular; her brother seemed to be friends with everyone, and everyone stood around talking about how pleased they were to see him alive and how concerned they had been about him—and how worried about the winged kellinks getting him.

His wife Renina finally shooed the children back into the house—this time Faia was certain she counted eight— with an admonition to them to get back to work. Then she turned back to her husband with a laugh and flung her arms around his neck again.

Faia stood apart. She turned at the sound of a sniffle, and found Edrouss Delmuirie standing there, fists clenched and eyes suspiciously bright.

"What's wrong?" she asked.

"It just hit me—anyone who might once have run out of a door like that for me has been long years dead." His eyes unfocused, and he turned his head away.

"Your wife, you mean?" Faia asked. "Your children?"

For a moment he seemed not to hear her. Then he said, "No. I wasn't married. I had both my parents, and two brothers, and two sisters. Nieces and nephews, too."

"And a line of lovers that would reach from here to the sea," Faia said suddenly.

"What?"

"All those women who begged to share your bed, and attempted to seduce you."

"I never—"

Faia cut his protest short with a wave of her hand. "I read your diaries," she said.

Edrouss Delmuirie turned the red of a ripe roseberry and pressed his face into a hand. "My *diaries*?" he groaned.

"Scholars found and translated them. Hundreds of people—maybe even thousands—have read them," Faia told him.

He shook his head, and his face grew even redder, though Faia would have thought that impossible. He didn't seem lost in grief anymore, though, she decided. He seemed positively buried by mortification instead. She grinned. It was always pleasant to think she could help distract a man from his troubles.

In the pause, she heard Renina say, "—well, invite them in, dearlin'." Faia turned to see Bytoris's wife tuck a bit of the hem of her outside skirt into her kirtle and spin around. She danced up the steps, radiating happiness.

Behind her, Faia heard Delmuirie mutter, "Why would anybody read *my* diaries? I made up everything in them . . . almost."

Faia chuckled. She'd suspected as much when she read those diaries—*nobody* had people bowing and scraping the way Delmuirie had described; nobody was so invariably right at the expense of chagrined fools who'd disbelieved; but most of all, nobody got laid as often or as variously as Edrouss Delmuirie had claimed to get laid. The Delmuirie scholars had insisted the contents of the diaries were an unflinching look at the life of a great man; but then, they were trying to emulate that life.

Bytoris followed his wife into the house, and Delmuirie and Faia trailed after. Renina led them through a dark, narrow foyer, into the bright, window-lit interior of the house.

Glass windows, Faia thought, looking around. The individual panes were little and held together by narrow strips of lead—some of the panes were brightly colored so that the sun, blazing through them, left rainbow patterns on the floor. Faia had seen such windows before, but only in the great university buildings of Ariss—never in common houses.

My brother does make money, she thought.

The walls of the sunlit room were lined with shelves, and the shelves were covered with statues and plates and little stone carvings—all of them battered, most of them chipped or broken but expertly repaired, all of them obviously ancient.

Faia heard the low hum of children's voices from further back in the house. Then she heard the unmistakable sound of crockery smashing, followed by a moment of silence.

Then a girl's voice, shrill and angry, broke the quiet. "Oh, thanks," she yelled. "Why not just break the next into a thousand pieces, to see if I can puzzle them out? Why couldn't you just break the neck off?"

The boy's voice sounded both older and calmer. "I can't always just break the necks off. You don't think real artifacts always break that way, do you?"

"Look, Seluis, see how well I've rubbed the paint off?" yet another voice called.

"That's good, Jaychie. It looks very old."

Faia held her breath, listening. The voices had fallen to murmurs again. She looked to her brother, questioning.

He shrugged. "This is the use to which we put scholarship—those of us with families who insist we would rather eat than starve." He pointed to the rows of ancient artifacts. "My family makes these. I copy real artifacts, and carve molds of them, which my children then pour and shape and paint—and age. We sell them to collectors and traders—and Geos had a store where he sold them to people who wanted to think they'd gotten a bargain on artifacts created in the days of the old gods. We've done well enough."

Faia picked up one of the little statues and studied it. "That's dishonest."

Renina gave Faia a cold look. "It's work, and it's food.

When some people had great magic, and some of us none, things were bad enough." She looked at her husband, and pointed to the stocked shelves. "Things are worse now. Few are buying, and those few are more careful of the provenance of their goods."

Bytoris took his wife's hand and squeezed it. "I brought artifacts and rubbings from the First Folk ruins for us to copy. First Folk artifacts are rare enough we should get rits in plenty."

Renina's happiness seemed to have worn off. "If people keep spending rits for trinkets when food and water become scarcer by the day . . ."

Bytoris nodded to Faia. "She may be able to do something about that."

Renina looked doubtful. "Has she come to bring back magic, then?"

"Yes."

Renina glanced at her husband, looking to see if he mocked her; then, when she realized Bytoris meant what he said, she turned to Faia with hope in her eyes.

Faia felt the weight of the other woman's hope and everything that hope meant settle on her shoulders.

She cleared her throat. "There is a man——" she began, and faltered. "He stole something, and the magic of Arhel is tied to the thing he stole. I've come to—to find him, and get the thing back. I cannot promise——" She sighed. "In truth, kinswoman, I cannot promise anything. But I will not stop looking for this man until I have found him, or until I am dead."

"Kinswoman?" Renina looked to her husband.

"She is my sister," Bytoris said, "though we have not yet sorted out legal kin-claim. We might not need to."

His wife nodded. Both her attitude and her speech became formal. "Then, kinswoman," she bowed slightly, "may the touch of Kedwar the Finder guide your footsteps, and may the Dark Hunter sharpen your eyes, so that your journey will be crowned by success."

"My thanks," Faia said.

Renina turned and hugged Bytoris again. "I'm so *glad* you're home," she told him fiercely. "This is a frightening city without you."

Chapter 22

Faia and Edrouss, Bytoris and Renina sat around the good company table, eating by the flickering light of an oil lamp that threw the shadows of defunct magelights in their curving holders against the wall; the shadows looked like huge, jittery spiders lurking in the corners of the room. The dining hall must have been a cheerful place at night before the magic died, but it was far from cheerful at that moment. Faia could hear the children chattering while they ate in the other room; Renina did not feel the adult conversation would be any fit thing for children's ears.

The three travelers had taken turns telling the story of how they'd arrived in Bonton, while Renina sat wide-eyed. When they were finished, Bytoris asked, "What happened here?"

"I wish I knew," Renina said softly. She sat back in her seat and stared into the little flame of the lamp. "One instant, everything worked perfectly. The Festival of Darkness was on, and all the streets were full of dancers. Above us, fire-writers spelled out the prophecies of the wajeros for the new cycle of years in glowing letters against the dark sky, and the magicians in the beautiful flying castle moored to the west wall sent out fire-flowers by the thousands that burst over our heads and tossed their petals down into the streets. It was wonderful. The next instant, all the lights in the city went out, and the fliers fell from the sky, smashing into the roofs of houses and crashing down onto people in the streets . . . and the castle came crashing down." Renina nibbled at her lower lip. "It fell into Five Cathedral and shattered all the altars—which the Priests of the White shouted was a sign, while the Priests of the Five shouted that it was not. The earth shook as though it might split open at any minute."

She shivered and wrapped her arms around herself. "You never heard such screaming, Bytoris. I hope *I* never do again."

Faia closed her eyes. She was reliving that moment as she had experienced it far away, when the billowing emeshest went rage-red and came grabbing after her.

The magic ended when I refused the Dreaming God; when I broke down the barrier. But I only did what I had to do to save my daughter and my friends, she told herself. *I only did what I* had *to do.*

She could no longer doubt, however, that all of Arhel's magic had died at that instant. In her mind's eye, she could see Ariss on its magic-built hill sinking back into the swamp over which it had been built, and flying castles all over Arhel smashing into the ground. She could see the lights of an entire continent going out at once, while the darkness of an earlier, primitive time descended, perhaps never to be lifted again. She could hear the screams as clearly as if she'd stood there beside Renina.

Bytoris's wife was continuing her story. Her voice was oddly flat while she talked, her face strangely expressionless, as if she were recounting things that had happened far away to someone she didn't know. "—and we buried over three hundred people in a mass grave outside the city walls, and we only hope we've found all of them. Some of the things that came down took out whole houses—and everyone in them. It was . . ." She shivered, but still her eyes remained expressionless. "I never want to go through anything like that again. Ever."

Chapter 23

The merest flicker of power, the tiniest thrill of magic, coursed through Faia's nerves. She woke to find herself in a comfortable bed, in a warm but unfamiliar room, and for a moment did not recall how she came to be there. Then the murmur of a child who was sleeping on the floor brought the events of the previous day back to her. Bytoris's house. She nodded and got up carefully. She stepped silently over the piles of children who slept on padded mats on the floor and slipped downstairs, where she found the makeshift hearth—this was a house once run by the most modern of magical conveniences, now less convenient and practical than a poor farmer's sod hut. The embers of last night's cookfire still glowed, and a bucket of already-used water sat next to them, warming.

Faia took a rag and sponged off—the city was short on clean water, though engineers were desperately working on a system of aqueducts that would someday provide it. If they didn't get clean water into the city soon, the plagues would start. Faia, washing down from the tiny bucket of dirty water, shivered when she thought of that. If Renina never wanted to see a castle fall from the sky, Faia never again wanted to see the aftermath of a plague. She needed to get out soon—needed to get back to Kirtha while she could.

But first, she had to find Thirk. And the tiny promise of magic that had awakened her was her guidelight.

Faia heard people moving upstairs. She wanted to get out of the house before they found her and tried to talk her out of going alone. Alone, undistracted, she knew she could find the source of magic; if she had to deal with Delmuirie and her brother, she might not be able to concentrate.

Going alone would certainly be dangerous—but time was running out. Hundreds in Bonton had already died; thousands across Arhel were dead. And *tens* of thousands would die in the upcoming days and months, all because Arhel's magic was gone; they would die from hunger, as fields full of magically augmented crops withered and failed; they would die from panics and riots when the cities ran out of food; they would die from diseases; or they would die from wars as one have-nothing city-state attacked another in the hopes of garnering anything that might help it survive. All those future deaths had in common two things. They didn't have to happen. And Faia could, perhaps, prevent them.

If she could find the chalice, she thought she would be able to control it, and revive Arhel's magic; that might stop the disasters that were coming. She believed she was the link between Arhel's past and its future.

She dressed, strapped on her knife, tucked her sling into her waistband, and borrowed her brother's spear-tipped staff. Hers had been better, but it had gone down the throat of a Klog, and nothing would convince her that hadn't been worthwhile. She wasn't planning on leaving her brother's home for good—but she had no idea how much time she would need in order to do what had to be done.

It will take until I find Thirk, she told herself. Until I figure out some way to make him give me the chalice.

Faia slipped to the front door and lifted the latch, which squeaked as it rose. She bit her lip and looked back—no one had yet come downstairs. Carefully she eased the door open and slipped out, into the cool grey dawn. A light rain misted the cobblestones, washing them but doing little to alleviate the stink of the effluvia in the gutters. The rain made the paving stones slick, too—the leather soles of her boots slipped and she nearly fell into the mire.

She strained the muscles of her right hip when she caught herself. The hip burned, and she swore softly as she limped out of the circle and down the twisting, dark back street.

The strength of the rain picked up as she walked. She pulled the brim of her hat down so that it kept the back of her neck dry, and kept the water out of her eyes. She slogged along—she didn't want to think about what she was wading through.

She turned onto a main thoroughfare. Already the streets were crowded with farmers and traders and merchants—the early risers in every town and city. Faia didn't want crowds, though—they would distract her. She closed her eyes for an instant, feeling again the tiny, warm flash of magic—she used that flash as a guidelight and aimed herself toward it. When she opened her eyes, she stood facing the entrance to a smaller street; she headed into it. It meandered as every street in Bonton seemed to meander, turning back on itself in big, twisting loops so that sometimes it led her toward her goal, and sometimes directly away. She looked for signs, but the few she found were written in the ancient and defiantly unreadable Bontonard ideographs instead of the progressive Hortag-Ingesdotte script developed by Arissonese mages. Her street intersected with another little street that veered off at a sharp angle to her left, and to her right became the entries to a dozen little alleys.

Faia had seen something like these streets before, though she couldn't recall quite where. She took the turnoff that didn't go into all the little alleys—she didn't like the looks of those—and found herself switching back and forth up the side of a hill.

It clicked then. Cows. Cowpaths. She'd wandered along them when she'd been a small child, in the hills around Bright—and the streets of Bonton were nothing less than paved, glorified cowpaths. The city had been laid out by cows—and not nice, sensible ones that wanted to get home in time to be milked, either. These had been cows that had gotten into the corn mash and were weaving around after making a night of it, with no place in particular to go and plenty of time to get there.

Faia's foot went down into a fresh pile of droppings, and the redolent stink wafted up to her; she thought further malignant thoughts about cows. The greatest advantage cities offered over small villages seemed to her to be that the livestock stayed on the roads, while the people kept to the walkways—but this city had no walkways; the townsfolk had built out onto them, and men and beasts were forced to share the streets.

"Idiots," Faia grumbled.

She walked further, then stopped as she sensed a flicker of magic again. That way. She turned, following the tiny thread of power—and suddenly realized the tingle at the back of her neck had returned. She felt again what she'd felt in the mountains—that someone followed her. She felt eyes watching her, though of course that was ridiculous. No one knew she was out.

Then she thought, perhaps I should have been more careful where I walked. Perhaps this is not about the chalice—about magic. Perhaps this is simply a dangerous part of town.

She was so tall that with her hair tucked up into her hat and her heavy, baggy erda and sexless peasant clothes, she'd assumed most folk would mistake her for a man, and a big man at that. But even a lone, big man could be in danger. She loosened her knife in its sheath, and casually picked up her pace. She was still making her way up the same hill, though the road dipped and rose unevenly. She nodded to the rare passerby, who nodded back, and once stopped a woman in the street for the single reason that it gave her a chance to turn and look behind her.

She wasn't sure, looking back the way she'd come, that she'd seen anything real. She thought she'd noticed a bit of movement at the far edge of one building that jutted further into the street than the ones on either side of it. The woman answered Faia's question about a tanner with a vague shrug, then scurried off, and Faia headed up the hill again, moving even faster than she'd been before, but trying to make her increased pace look normal.

She listened. She could not hear anyone following her. The follower, if there was one, could be quiet if he wanted to badly enough.

Then the skies opened up, and what had been a miserable drizzle became a deluge that poured onto her head; rivers of rain sluiced off the roofs of the houses on both sides of the road and crashed and pounded against the cobblestones; the road became in an instant a river, and a fast, deadly one at that. Faia leapt for the stairs of the nearest house and clambered up them, then crouched, tucked back under the eaves where the storm couldn't quite reach her. She looked down the road. A bedraggled form pulled itself out of the torrent of the street onto another front stoop.

She studied the form. Male, she thought. The man was too far away for her to make out his features—and most of his face was hidden by beard anyway. He saw her looking in his direction and turned his back on her.

The man was dressed in the same sort of Bontonard foul-weather dress she'd seen on the local merchants and farmers—wide-skirted broidered black coat; rain hood; high, wax-treated boots. Most of the Bontonard men were clean-shaven, or sported dramatic, bushy mustaches; perhaps the beard would help her identify the man should she have to describe him. . . .

"*Hey,* tha'!" The woman of the house, plump and scowling, threw open her door; Faia jumped. "Hey, tha'! Get tha'self on, naow! Tha' cannot be sittin' on ma' stoop! I don' want tha' here!" She had a stick in her hands, which she brandished at Faia.

Faia had no desire to attack a woman at her own front door—not even to stay out of the deluge. The road was still a river, but Faia thought perhaps if she pressed herself to the steep side, where once the walkway had stood, the water would be shallower and she would be all right. She jumped down into the flood and the current caught her legs. She fought to keep her balance, and moved up as close to the housefront as she could. Then she inched her way along.

She fought for every footstep of progress she made, and worried with every slip that washed her backwards that she would end up captive to the man who followed her. She had no doubt anymore that he followed her. When she jumped off the stoop, he did the same thing though no screaming, stick-wielding matron had come out of the house where he had sat to chase him away.

Perhaps he was some street thug who'd decided she looked to be an easy mark. Or perhaps he was a pimp, or a slaver—she'd heard such men existed in the bad parts of towns. This could be a bad part of town, though the houses were pretty—brightly painted and well kept.

The rain let up again—became the faintest of drizzles. She heard voices ahead—a clamor of them, growing clearer and more shrill as she moved closer. A few moments later the river in the road shrank down until it roared only in the deep-angled center. Faia noted that the cow pies and other animal spoor were all washed away. She grinned. The stinking city had finally received the bath it so desperately needed. Faia ran the rest of the way up the hill to get away from the man who followed her—she thought she stood a good chance of losing him. Few were the people who could run for any distance uphill. She raced around a sharp curve, ducked down a narrow, dark alley, and ran out of that into a clearing, and almost into the center of disaster.

She threw herself back into the alley, behind the protruding wall of the nearest house, and prayed that she hadn't been seen. In the square ahead, battle raged. Men, blood-streaked and wild-eyed, fought three of the First Folk, who launched themselves in tandem from the roofs of the houses surrounding the square and attacked, then retreated to the roofs again, screeching.

"Kill 'em!" the men bellowed. "Set fire to 'em! Burn the houses they're sitting on!"

"Nay! They'll only fly away—then we'll have burned our own houses," one voice retorted. "Bring out their brother!"

The voices rose in assent.

"Aye, bring him out! Wheel him out!"

A storage door opened, and a handful of men pulled something forward—a statue, Faia thought at first—though if it were a statue, it had been carved by a genius. There were parts of it she realized were too perfect, though; the translucent wings, unfurled and arched, the delicate rilles spread around the face, the perfection of the nubby hide— those were nothing created by the hands of artists. The beast had been as much a living creature as the three who screamed in rage as the men wheeled it out—only now it was dead, stuffed and posed on a cart for display.

The three First Folk went into a frenzy, and Faia had a hard time remembering that they were thinking creatures, like her. They seemed no more than animals as they dove and shrieked and killed. Surely the men they fought believed them to be beasts, for no one would stuff and mount the skin of a dead enemy, unless he thought it a trophy.

She thought, however, that the existence of the stuffed Klaue must have been at least a part of the incitement for their enraged attack. She tried to imagine a stuffed human being rolled out into the street to taunt its fellow humans—surely humans would react much as the First Folk were reacting.

One of the First Folk flew in a high, tight circle over the alley in which Faia hid, and Faia froze. She prayed that it wouldn't see her; it screeched and plummeted to the ground just on the other side of the corner where she hid—so close she could make out the pebble-on-a-pebble texture and iridescent sheen of its skin. She held her breath, afraid the monster might hear even that slightest of sounds, and trembled.

The Klog crouched down with its nose pointed at its stuffed kin. The collar of rilles around its neck and face stood straight out and its body went rigid except for the heaving of its mammoth rib cage. It hissed. Then the Klog thrashed the ground with its tail—the tip of that tail whipped around the corner to within merest fingerbreadths of the place where Faia hid. Faia prayed to the Lady that the monster wouldn't note the warmth of her body the way some hunters could—and that it wouldn't smell her fear.

The Klog rose up on its long toes, listening and looking, and twisted around to sniff the air. Faia drew back to the place where she could no longer see any part of it—and where she hoped it could see nothing of her. She knew then, with horrible certainty, that it _did_ sense her presence, even if it hadn't pinpointed her location yet. She clenched her hands into tight fists, while her heart thudded in her chest so loudly she was certain its pounding would be audible over the sounds of fighting.

Suddenly one of the other First Folk howled.

The monster beside Faia roared and lunged forward, launching itself into the air with a thunderous flapping of wings, throwing itself back into the fight.

Faia breathed a deep sigh of relief.

"Enjoy that breath," a familiar voice whispered in her ear, "because unless you do exactly what I tell you to, it's going to be your last."

The cold, sharp edge of a knife pressed against the pulse point at her throat; she felt a flash of fire as the blade broke the skin. A rough hand yanked one of her arms behind her and up between her shoulder blades, pulling so tightly her shoulder became a blazing point of pain.

"One noise and you die—understand?"

She nodded, silent, wishing she could think of a way to escape. The man's voice was unmistakable, unforgettable. Thirk! *He* was the man on the stairs; he had followed her through the streets, had managed to locate the alley into which she'd run—but how could he have? She'd felt his magic, the magic of the chalice, ahead of her—she'd been following that magic. Had he doubled around? He must have. Somehow he had found her out and had used the magic of the chalice to come after her.

Thirk twisted her arm tighter, so that she had to rise on her toes. She closed her eyes and hissed; agony pulsed red behind her eyelids. The metal of the knife was both hot and cold against her throat.

"This is your fault," he whispered in her ear.

In the background, she could hear the screams as one of the Klaue caught a man and carried him, screaming, into the air; it dropped him from a great height down onto his comrades. Faia shuddered at the sound of his dying— she could think of herself making that same terrifying wail . . . and the same sickening thud.

"I ought to throw you out where they can see you," Thirk continued. "You've killed this world, and everything all of us held dear. You really ought to die in their claws. It would be appropriate if those evil animals killed you. You're the one who let them in."

Faia whispered, "You're the one who can fix it. Why haven't you?"

The knife tightened against her throat, nicking into the flesh again, and she cut off her protest.

Thirk dragged her further into the alley, where the overhang of the houses muffled the sounds of the fight in the square. "I ought to kill you," he said. "But unless you try to fight me, I'm not going to. Not yet, anyway. I want you to do something for me." He chuckled. Faia's stomach flipped at that sound.

"What?" she whispered.

"You're going to be my bait—so that the one who has it will have to bring it to me."

"Has what?" Faia was genuinely confused.

"The magic, stupid girl. The magic. The only thing that matters now. I've felt it—I know it's out there. But you don't have it, so one of them does."

"*You* have the chalice."

He laughed. "Don't try to fool me again. Edrouss Delmuirie made me think the chalice was the key, but I know better now."

"We followed you through the mountains—"

He slapped her then, hard. "Stupid girl! Why would you tell such an idiot lie? I followed you! I felt the magic ahead of me, and I followed you—though it near cost me my life." He stiffened his grip at her throat with his knife hand and dropped her wrist long enough to hold his left hand in front of her. The first and second fingers were nothing but stubs. "It did cost me these—frostbite. Some toes, too. I note that *you* came through unscathed."

He pulled the maimed hand out of her line of sight and caught her wrist again, and tugged it up between her shoulders.

"You don't matter, though," he told her. "I thought you did, at first. But I checked when I came into the camp. I felt for the magic—and it wasn't with you. It wasn't with any of you, nor in your packs. It was ahead. Still ahead. Now I know—the one that will come after you is the one that matters. So you're going to walk ahead of me, and you're going to walk slowly, so I don't have to cut your throat open. You understand?"

Faia nodded.

"Good. We're going to a place I know."

He marched her down the alley, then out into a busy street where people glanced at the two of them with curious eyes. A man looked to Thirk, and his eyebrows rose.

"Looter," Thirk said. "Caught her in my shop."

The man nodded, and his eyes, when they looked to Faia, were full of hatred. "They'll flay 'er."

"Sure will." Thirk chuckled. "Taking her to the square now."

"Come t' watch if I could," the man said. "Ain't got time."

"There'll be more."

"S'truth," the stranger said, his voice full of sad agreement, and turned away.

"They've had some trouble with looters," Thirk said softly. "Shops that depended on magical defenses were robbed the instant the town's criminals realized those defenses were gone. The *esteemed* Bontonard watch hasn't been able to keep up with all the looters *and* fight off the First Folk—" He chuckled softly. "So the good people of Bonton are taking care of the criminals themselves."

Faia shivered; justice had died within the city. No one would help her while Thirk spoke against her.

"You don't want to do anything to call attention to yourself," he murmured. "Truly you do not. You cannot begin to imagine the horrible ways I can make you die."

Faia considered Thirk, and decided she didn't want to give him an excuse to hurt her any worse. He would, she thought, and he would enjoy it. She made herself stay as quiet and meek as she could, and watched for an opportunity to escape. He never gave her one.

They arrived, mostly through alleys and backways, at a grubby, heavily reinforced back door set into a windowless wall in a dark, narrow cul-de-sac. The sign over the door said, in a handful of languages, "Rooms, Cheap—Inquire Within. Jarel Ronivet—Innkeep."

Faia imagined the rooms would be filthy, rat-infested, dank, and stinking—

"Let me go," she told Thirk. "I'll do what I can to help—"

Sudden, shocking pain flared at the base of her skull, and light exploded from everywhere around her, and the sound of a nonexistent sea roared in her ears. She heard herself cry out, and felt herself fall forward.

And the world went dark.

Chapter 24

What?

Pain——

The taste of old blood and vomit. Throbbing pain. Stench rising from somewhere nearby . . .

Under that the mold-and-punk odor of rotting wood, more smells . . . mildew, dirt, unwashed cloth, unwashed bodies.

More pain——

What?

Memory took tenebrous shape, flitted away.

Slight movement, terrible pain . . .

And overwhelming blackness.

Chapter 25

Faia woke feeling sick and weak, with her eyes gummed shut and a horrible taste in her mouth. She had vague memories of waking before, but no memories of the events that had brought her to this place of pain and darkness. She was facedown on damp, hard-packed earth. The air around her stank of old urine and decay. She could hear footsteps on wooden flooring above her.

The back of her head throbbed in rhythm with her heart. Her shoulders ached, her wrists ached, her knees ached, her ankles ached. She struggled to a kneeling position; both her ankles and her wrists were bound. Faia kept her movements as quiet as she could—she heard footsteps on the ceiling, and the dull murmur of voices.

Where *am* I?

She moved her wrists against each other, trying to loosen the bonds. The ropes rubbed her flesh raw, and her hands were already so swollen and numb she wasn't sure she'd be able to use them to help herself even if she worked them free.

She shook her head, trying to clear her thoughts—but that only made the pain worse.

The murmuring grew louder, and she heard heavy footsteps coming down wooden stairs. Through the wall, she heard voices.

She froze, listening.

"—naaaa. She hasn't moved the whole time. Y' might want to check on 'er—I know she's breathin' now, but if she's dyin', I don't want 'er in my place. The lairdlaw has been lively hereabouts since the Woes began."

"They check your cellars?"

"Aye. And my attics, and my closets. I suspect they'd check my britches if they thought I could hide a sick'un there. Innkeeps hereabouts were takin' in the injured and sick followin' the Woes—"

"For charity?" Thirk sounded astonished.

" 'Course not. For pay—families paid good money to keep their people from sleepin' on the street, or in the sick wards. Few of the families didn't visit regular—the 'keeps took care of the sicks, but sometimes forgot to let their families know of the ones who died."

"Of *course*. And the fact that the families kept paying made the innkeeps forget those deaths."

The other man laughed. "Poor fellows—you can't expect busy men to remember everything. Especially since they get stuck with a death tax and a body removal tax if they remember. Better to keep the bodies in the basement until y' can smuggle 'em out, fee the families, and save the taxes. 'Course, the lairdsmen don't like that at all."

"No—they wouldn't. I don't think she'll die, though—and I'll keep paying room-rate for the use of your cellar until I find the rest of what she stole from my shop. I've had some luck—I have an idea now of where she hid it." Thirk's voice sounded pleased. "And I'll take her to the square to be flayed when I'm sure I've got the last."

"Had a hard time makin' 'er talk?"

"She's a stubborn bitch."

They were just outside the door. Faia could hear their voices clearly. She didn't want them to know she'd awakened; she leaned to one side and tried to roll from her hip to her shoulder quietly, to drop to the floor so she could fake unconsciousness. With her hands and her feet bound, she couldn't control her fall; she toppled too fast, and in the wrong direction—she hit her head against something hard when she did, and whatever that was thudded solidly against something else and bonged. The fall brought the pain in her skull from merely terrible up to truly dreadful, but she was more concerned about the noise she'd made. Maybe, she prayed, Thirk and the innkeeper hadn't heard.

The voices outside the room stopped. She heard the rattle of a key against lockpins, and the lifting of a latch. She lay very still with her eyes closed, and worked to keep her breathing deep and regular.

A door near her head creaked open, and she could see flickers of light through her eyelids.

"She's moved," the innkeeper said.

"Of course she has, friend Jarel. I know you're awake, thief." Thirk's voice was cold, yet Faia could discern an undertone of pleasure—or perhaps amusement—in it. "You need not pretend otherwise. You might as well sit up so we can discuss what happens now." He waited a moment.

Faia didn't give any indication that she'd heard him.

"Or I can hurt you."

Faia considered that for only an instant. He would enjoy hurting her. She sat up.

Thirk sat on the broken frame of an old bedstead, staring down at her. He'd placed his lantern on the floor, and his face, illuminated from beneath, looked demonic in the dark room. He turned to the innkeep. "If you don't mind, I'd prefer to . . . talk . . . to her alone for a few moments."

The keep's teeth flashed. "Mind what I said about dead bodies."

Thirk nodded. "I want to keep her alive a bit longer, anyway." The keep, with a slow smile, backed out of the room.

"I've sent a message to your people," Thirk said. His

eyes glittered in the candlelight; that glittering was an unpleasant effect that made him look like a serpent.

Faia kept still, and concentrated on breathing slowly. She didn't want to give Thirk any excuse to hurt her more. She didn't think the keep would be inclined to believe anything she had to say in her own defense. And she doubted that Jarel Ronivet would be distressed if Thirk did kill her, no matter what he had said. The man hadn't sounded in the least uncomfortable about the idea of charging rent to the unsuspecting families of dead men, though he didn't sound like he wanted to get caught.

"I just thought you'd like to know we'll have this resolved soon." Thirk chuckled. "Or if we don't, I'll see you hang."

"I don't have anything you want."

He nodded and smiled. "I've come to believe that. I've come to suspect you even believed everything you told me this morning. You don't matter, though, you see— except as bait. One of the men who traveled with you has what I want, and whoever that is, he'll be along to get you soon."

"What if he isn't?"

Thirk laughed softly. "The same thing will happen to you if he doesn't come as if he does, dear girl. You'll die. I need you alive long enough for him to find you, and he'll have to use magic to do it. Once I feel the magic and know he's on his way, you become merely the first of a number of people with whom I have a score to settle."

"What do you want, Thirk?" Faia asked.

"I want to be a god." He stood to leave, and smiled down at her. "When Arhel's magic is mine alone, I will be."

He strolled out, taking his lantern, and closed the door behind him. She heard the bar drop into place with a depressingly solid thud. If she had harbored some hope before that someone might be able to reason with Thirk, she didn't have that hope any longer. The saje was crazy.

Obsessed, too. Faia tried to imagine Arhel if Thirk alone controlled its magic. She didn't like her thoughts.

Then she considered her own situation. Maybe *this* was the destiny her mother's ghost had hinted at—to stop Thirk. Perhaps she, and only she, could prevent him from becoming the god he wished to be. If that were the case, there had to be a way out of the cellar— a way to freedom.

Destiny couldn't be stopped by stone walls or iron-barred doors.

She hoped.

Chapter 26

Faia felt the rope around her wrists loosen at last. She worked first one hand, then the other, free of the coils. For perhaps a minute, they remained numb. Then pain flooded into her hands and fingertips, pain so searing she wanted to scream. She cradled her useless hands against her chest and briefly cried.

Pressure eased the pain somewhat—so did friction. She rubbed the hands together, hating the way her wooden fingers refused to move when she willed them to, and hating the flaring pain that streamed up from her wrists to her elbows and shoulders. An old woodcutter in Bright, whom she had known well when she was a child, had been pinned beneath a tree as it fell. The village men found him later, and cut the tree away, and took him back to Bright. Her mother—then the village healer—had soaked his hand and wrapped it and tried to massage the life back into it. The hand died anyway—one of the villagers had hacked it off with the woodcutter's own axe. The crude surgery hadn't been soon enough or complete enough to make a difference, however. The woodcutter had died not too long after.

Faia rubbed her own still-lifeless hands together and wondered if the same outcome awaited her.

Eventually the pain changed in quality—while her fingers

still throbbed and her wrists burned, the leaden, tingling sensation left. At last she could move her fingers and pick objects up, though her grasp was still weak.

She managed then to untie the rope around her ankles. That done, she rubbed the life back into her feet. Once she was able to move around the cellar, she made an inventory of the room. The walls were stone, the ceiling framed timber, the floor packed dirt. The room's contents consisted of the chamber pot on which she'd earlier hit her head, broken frames for two small beds, both lacking mattresses, and a long, high-backed settle with a missing seat. The settle's storage compartment was empty. The single door was locked—and it was sturdy, built of thick boards bound with metal. It opened out, so that she could not even work the hingepins free.

She saw no sense in calling for help—help would not come, though trouble certainly would. Her weapons were gone so she couldn't hope to fight her way to freedom, even if she could lure the innkeeper into the room with her. Her newfound brother might try to rescue her— but if he couldn't manage a rescue, she certainly couldn't hope for a ransom. There was nothing Bytoris could do to meet Thirk's demands. Gyels . . . well, Gyels was missing.

She sat down on the frame of one of the beds and rested her chin in her hands. She hadn't given Gyels much thought at all, other than to consider how best to turn down his advances without angering him.

But Gyels deserved consideration. How had he simply walked up to the guard and been admitted to the city? He wasn't a Bontonard. He'd said he was from Forst— and Forst and Bonton were bitterest enemies. He'd shown no identification. He'd said a word or two to the main guard at the gate and had gone in. She couldn't credit it to the guards' disorganization, or to the First Folk attack that had ended only moments before; those same guards had been only too willing to turn Edrouss and her away moments later.

Other strangenesses began to occur to her as she considered. Gyels had claimed Thirk used the magic of the chalice against him—yet Thirk was desperately trying to catch whomever had Arhel's magic. Gyels had tracked Thirk at an incredible pace across often rocky terrain, in darkness—he'd never backtracked, had never asked for help, had never expressed dismay or complained of the difficulty of tracking under such nearly impossible conditions. He'd goaded them on with fear of what Thirk would do with the chalice—and yet Thirk, in the cellar, had said the chalice was nothing. And Thirk insisted that he'd followed *them* through the mountains.

What if he had?

Every time Faia had felt a surge of magical energy, it had come from in front of the travelers. If Thirk had been behind them, that left only Gyels in front.

Which meant that Gyels either was, or had, the source of the magic.

Her stomach twisted. She had been right to distrust him, and wrong to let her fears of Thirk and his madness distract her from the evil that sat in front of her own eyes. Gyels had acted nothing like Witte; Faia had let the dissimilarities lull her into complacence. But what better way could Witte have found to win her trust than to "die," and let her rescue him yet again, disguised in another form? How he must have enjoyed his tricks at her expense—and seeing her drawn to him.

Thank the Lady she hadn't bedded him.

Out. She needed a way out—fast. Thirk wasn't the real problem after all, though Thirk would kill her when his plans didn't work out as he wished. Witte the Mocker was the problem and the real danger to Arhel—and Faia could only imagine what terrors he would cause if she didn't find a way to stop him.

She sat on the edge of one of the bedframes, frowning down into darkness, trying to think of a workable escape plan.

One of Faljon's sayings came to mind: "An innkeeper's heart / is deep as his pockets." She got up and paced in the blackness; her feet had learned the shape of the room well enough to let her walk without constant stumbling. She wondered—could the innkeep's greed be her path to freedom?

Thirk had accused her of stealing—and said he'd not yet found the things she'd stolen. He'd convinced the keep she was a looter. If *she* could convince the innkeep that she'd hidden some great treasure away, and that she alone knew where to find it . . . and that he could have half if he let her go, she might win her freedom. The keep was not an honest man.

She leaned against the cool stone wall and considered further—and she began to see the problems innate in the idea. At very best, the innkeep would want to go with her to be sure she didn't run away. At worst, he'd want her to tell him where this treasure was hidden, with her freedom as the prize if he found it. But she wouldn't trust him to go alone any more than he would trust her. So, assuming she could talk him into it, she would have to find some way to escape him in the streets.

No. He'd bind her to him in some manner, no doubt, so that she couldn't run. She had nothing with which to bribe him, nothing with which to fight him, no way to coerce him to set her free. And of course there was no treasure—because she wasn't a looter. If she led him to nothing, he'd simply give her back to Thirk, or have her taken to the city square and hanged as the thief he believed her to be.

She wanted her magic back. If she were able to reach the Lady's power, she would have some way to fight.

She sighed, and sat down on the broken bedframe again.

Arhel's survival depended on her and on what she had discovered—she held the lives of her daughter and her friends, and uncounted thousands of innocent people prisoner with her. She *had* to get out.

She stood again, desperate, and tugged at the stones that formed the cellar wall. They were mortared in place. If she had something to dig with and a hundred years, she could probably dig a tunnel through the dirt floor, under the wall, and . . . where? Out beneath a street? Faia had little time—rapidly becoming even less—and she dared not fail. Not if she ever wanted to see her daughter again.

She went back to pacing. She was sure her feet would wear a furrow in the dirt floor—when suddenly she lost track of her place in the room, and stumbled over one of the two bedframes. "Damnall," she snarled, and shoved the second frame against the first. She heaved and hoisted until she'd stacked them one on top of the other—she wanted clear room to walk and think.

She leaned against the bedframes when she'd finished, breathing hard. Footsteps rattled the floorboards over her head, then moved on. She looked up. Someone had walked overhead earlier—but there was no regular traffic in the place above her head. She nibbled on her lower lip, then shook the bedframes gently. They didn't wobble too badly.

Stacked as they were, they formed a platform that rose as high as her lower chest. If she lifted the settle onto the top of that platform, and laid it across the unbroken part of the upper bedframe, she would have a stable bit of homemade scaffolding that would allow her to sit comfortably just below the ceiling.

She grinned, and put thought to action.

She heard laughter and raised voices and snatches of drunken song above; the noise wasn't coming from directly overhead, though, but from a distance away. Certainly one room away, and perhaps two. Only rarely did footsteps pass directly above her now, and those always occurred in pairs, walking in quickly and lightly, and out slowly and with difficulty.

She guessed the innkeep stored his beer kegs in the room above, or something else heavy that only required infrequent replacement. If she were right, that would work well for her—it was nice to think *something* worked in her favor. If she could pry loose a few of the floorboards and climb into the beer-room, she could hide there until the inn's tavern closed, and its denizens slithered home. Provided, of course, she could keep out of the way of the bartenders.

Then, of course, she'd have to find Edrouss Delmuirie and Bytoris—and she'd have to figure out a way to fight Witte and a way to save Arhel.

She would have laughed at her plans had she been someone else looking on as she worked. Potential disasters and failures perched one on top of the other, waiting to topple onto her. She didn't let them stop her, though. The only way she would be certain to fail was if she didn't act—and if she acted, one step at a time, she believed she could conquer anything . . . even a malicious god.

One step at a time.

Freedom came first.

Chapter 27

She prized the nails of the third floorboard up, and stopped. She'd made the opening wide enough.

Thank the Lady for loud drunks. She'd dropped things and crashed and thumped enough to keep her heart constantly racing like a mouse in a boxtrap—but the drunks thumped and thundered and fought and sang—and covered the worst of her blunders. She'd tried to save her noisiest work for the tavern patrons' off-key renditions of "The Old Roxal Doxie"; they, in turn, had obliged her by singing all the verses.

Faia decided she would think kinder things about that song in the future.

She sat on the top of the settle and tied the ends of the two ropes together, then looped the resulting longer rope over the ceiling beam that lay beneath her escape hatch. She knotted that firmly, then climbed down her stacked furniture and pushed things back to their places as best she could. She tamped the dirt floor down as smoothly as she could manage while working by feel. She hoped she'd covered all her marks, though she had no way of telling. Then she shinnied up the rope—a painful process—and squirmed her way through to the next floor between the loosened boards.

She muttered curses on Thirk's head for stealing her

boots—she could have used the heel of one to hammer the floorboard nails back into place. Instead, she had to pocket the nails; she didn't want them lying around to point out how she'd gotten free. She wanted to leave as much confusion and mistrust in her wake as she could.

She found herself, as she'd deduced, in a room stacked floor to ceiling with beer barrels, cheap wine, and bagged potatoes. She stole two potatoes and one of the wine bottles and retired behind the kegs to wait for quiet.

Quiet wasn't what she got, though.

She'd devoured only half of the first potato when the door creaked open, and two people crept into the room and shoved the door shut.

"Are you sure they will not be in here for anything?" a boy's voice asked.

"Beer keg's full, and closing is within the hour. No one will bother us." A girl's voice, both confident and sly.

"What about your da?"

The girl laughed softly. "What about him?"

"He'll kill us both if he catches us."

"No. Only you," the girl said, then laughed again. Faia, huddled against the back wall, raised an eyebrow. For all the girl's laughter, Faia thought her words might not have been a joke. Poor foolish boy. On the other side of the beer kegs, clothes rustled softly to the ground.

"Marray, don't joke. Do you not think we should hide behind the kegs?"

Faia felt her heart rise into her throat—she nearly choked on her potato. No, she thought. You *don't* want to hide behind the kegs.

"We can if you want," the girl said. The tone of her voice implied that she considered this option one for craven cowards, however.

Faia heard the rustle of cloth again; then the boy said, "I think we'd better. I don't want your da to walk in and see us."

Marray huffed; then Faia heard the girl's bare feet pad across the floor, followed by the boy's heavier footsteps. Coming my way, she thought. She rose and listened, trying to guess which side of the kegs they were going to walk around so she could slip around the other side.

They went around the right, and she kept the barrels between them and went left, so that she found herself standing beside the two wine racks. She moved between those—she was hidden from the young lovers, but not well hidden at all from anyone who might come through the door.

The sounds of wet kisses and quiet little moans began to emanate from behind the kegs. Faia glowered in the lovers' direction—it had been long and longer since she had played "plow the field" with anyone. The little giggles and increasingly frantic thumping left her feeling even lonelier than she had before. She scowled at every gasp and whispered commentary.

"Oh . . . *do* that again!" The voice high and feminine and breathy.

"I am."

"Harder."

"I am."

"Oh, Joetz! Give me everything!"

"I *am*." A tinge of masculine annoyance then.

Thump. Thump. Squeal. Squeak.

"Ow, ow, ow! Your elbow is on my *hair*!"

Grumpily, "Well there's no place I can put them they *won't* be—it's all over the floor."

"I thought you liked my hair."

Sigh. "I do. I just don't have anyplace for my elbows."

"Then roll over, and I will too."

Thump, thump.

"*Watch your knees!*" This from Joetz, and in a panicky voice.

The thumping resumed, and Faia closed her eyes and

sighed quietly. She missed that—but she had come to realize she did not just want any man. She wanted one man, who would stay with her and . . . and *love* her. She had not wanted love when she was younger—she had wanted friendship and variety. Entertainment. Fun. She smiled slowly, listening to the young people on the other side of the barrels.

Let's be honest. Then I wanted sex, but not a bondmate. Life has changed me. Now I want a companion and a friend, someone I can count on. I want to wake up with the same man every morning, though I never did before. I will only be happy with that now.

When she closed her eyes, she saw a face—the plain, honest, caring face of an ordinary young man. Edrouss Delmuirie. She surprised herself—Delmuirie was not the sort of man who made women stop and stare. He was friendly and kind and willing to work to please—rather like a dog. She liked him enough to think that someone like him might be the person she was looking for. Perhaps handsomer, though.

The noises behind the kegs grew louder. Faia sat and rested her chin in her cupped hands and tried to pretend she heard nothing. She closed her eyes—she was weary, and her head was beginning to hurt again from where Thirk had hit her. She wanted to sleep, but she didn't dare.

Without warning, the door flew open, and two big men tromped into the room. Faia dug her fingers into the palms of her hands—her muscles went rigid. She prayed they would not look her way, and she could imagine the two youngsters behind the kegs were praying the same thing. The activity had stopped completely at the sound of the door slamming into the wall; Faia imagined Marray and Joetz crouched behind the kegs, round-eyed and sure the world was about to end. If her own situation had not been so desperate, she would have found some humor in theirs.

"He wants another of the dark brown, too," one of the men said.

"I wish he had to carry 'em. Thought he was goin' to close up."

"Said with that party what came in, he won't close 'til sunrise if they keep payin'."

"Just our luck." They picked up a cask between them and began to lug it out of the room.

The faintest of giggles drifted out from behind the kegs. Both men stopped.

"Did you hear anything?" the first asked.

"Yah. Back of the kegs."

The bartenders settled their keg on the floor.

Faia's heart rose to her throat, and she cursed both the young lovers in her thoughts. They were going to have to move if they wanted to stay hidden—and the only place they could move would be the place she already occupied. She looked around the room for someplace else to hide— the only remaining possible cover was directly behind the open door. She rocked to her feet silently, and began to edge toward it, as both men walked across the open floor to the false wall of kegs.

As she slipped behind the door, she saw the first shadow move around the far edge of the keg wall, followed by a second. The youngsters kept the barrier between them and their pursuers. Their naked skin seemed almost to glow in the tiny bit of light that seeped into the beer vault from the outer room. They edged between the two racks of wine, and crouched down, occupying the spot where she'd hidden an instant before.

They are not laughing now, Faia thought. *None* of us are laughing now.

"Anything?" the first man asked.

"I don't see anything, but I swear on Haddar's head I heard something."

"So did I. It was probably the cat."

"Didn't sound like no cat to me."

A thoughtful pause followed. "No. It didn't." Both men walked along the back of the keg wall; Faia could see the tops of their heads as tiny patches of moving darkness along the uneven row of kegs. The kids eyed each other, then moved out of their hiding place, crept within touching distance of Faia, and scooted across the little puddle of light to the far wall.

She saw their plan. They hoped to circle around and duck behind the kegs again as the two barkeeps came back out.

Faia was going to be right in line of sight of those self-same barkeeps—and unlike the kids, those two would be looking for someone, and so would probably catch her as she hid. She tried frantically to think of some diversion—

And then one of the kids stepped hard on one of the boards she'd loosened in her escape from the basement. One end of it flew up, then the board fell back into place with a slam as the kid lifted his foot. The sound seemed as loud as an explosion in the tense, forced quiet of the room. One barkeep came flying around the end of the kegs in front of her, but looking toward the noise, while the other doubled back and charged straight into them. The girl shrieked, "He tricked me!" The boy yelled, "I never!"

And the innkeep thundered into the keg room and roared, "Where in the sixteen blue hells of Fargorn is my bedamned beer?!" before he saw what his barkeeps had caught—his naked daughter and her equally naked swain.

The innkeep bellowed. Both kids howled.

Faia muttered, "Seize the moment," and slipped through the door, through the line of drunks that began trickling back to find out what all the excitement was about, and out into the cool, smoke-filled night air.

She found herself on a narrow, dark, nearly empty street—barefoot, without her pack or her weapons, lost, broke, weary, hurting, and hungry . . . though she did still have the other potato and the rest of the bottle of wine. She sighed, looked up the road, looked down the road, and saw nothing she recognized in either direction.

"Well, then." She lifted the wine to the sky. "Here's to adventures—may they happen only to other people from this day forward." She swigged the drink, tucked the bottle through her belt, and started off in a direction she picked at random, chewing on the second raw potato.

As she passed an alley, an arm reached out and dragged her in.

Chapter 28

She was too startled even to scream. She threw herself against the alley wall, pinning her captor's arm between her body and a stone building, and in one smooth movement pulled the wine bottle from her belt and shattered its base against the wall.

"Ow-ow-ow-ow-ow!" a familiar voice yelped as she spun to face her attacker, wielding the broken bottle as if it were a dagger.

Delmuirie cradled his arm against his side and backed away from her.

"Edrouss?" She lowered the bottle. She was amazed at how handsome he looked in the dark alley.

He winced. "I came to rescue you. Doesn't look like you needed me."

But Faia smiled at him. "I did, though. I have no idea where I am. How did you find me?"

"Thirk delivered his ransom note to your brother's house, and we followed him back here. We were amazed how simple it was to track him—Bytoris said he thinks Thirk was expecting a magical attack, and because of that, he wasn't watching for anything else. Once we found out where you were, I hid here to wait for the tavern to close so I could break in and get you out—your brother took off after Thirk. I haven't seen him since."

"What should we do, then?"

"We agreed that I would take you back to his house as soon as I rescued you. Not that you needed rescue." He rubbed his arm ruefully. "You're the least helpless person I think I've ever met." He pointed out a direction, and they started back toward her brother's house.

Faia smiled at him, but then her smile died. "We do need to get back as fast as we can. Thirk isn't really our problem." She told him what she'd discovered about Gyels.

Edrouss was horrified. "He's a *god*?"

"He's worse than just a god," Faia told him grimly. "He's the god of things that go wrong, the patron deity of disaster. He brings trouble with him because it's what he likes." She shoved her free hand in her pocket and picked up her pace. "He probably brought the Klogs back to Arhel because, to him, watching them eat people and destroy things would be funny."

Edrouss led her past a guardhouse at the corner of a street. The nightwatch called out and he stopped and showed his identification and hers. "My wife and I were at the tavern back there—but we're heading home now."

"Jarel's," Faia said helpfully.

One of the guards gave her an odd look—she studied him, but didn't recognize him. She wondered, though, if he might have been one of the guards who'd been at the gate, or if he somehow recognized her. She resolved to say nothing else.

"He's open late tonight," the other guard muttered. "That's going to get him in trouble with the lairdlaw if he's not careful." But both guards shrugged, and the one who'd been staring at Faia finally shook his head and said, "Straight home, then, both of you. It's not a good idea to be out this late, things bein' like they are."

"Yes, sir," Edrouss said. He put an arm around Faia's waist and the two of them hurried away from the guardhouse. "Some things don't change," he told her.

"Much of what I see in the world now, I don't understand—but I understand guards, always telling you 'straight home, now,'—as if it were their idea and not what you were already doing."

"Is it hard for you?" Faia noticed that even once they were out of sight of the guards, he left his arm around her. "I mean, seeing the way life is here, and knowing you can't go back?" As soon as the words were out of her mouth, she felt tactless.

But the man next to her only sighed. "It's terrible. More than anything else, I miss having a purpose. Thinking I was going to rescue you . . . that was the first time in a while since I felt someone needed me." His half-smile held little humor. "Then you didn't need my help after all—but for a bit I felt I mattered again." He sighed. "You probably can't imagine what it's like to feel that way."

Faia, though, remembered the three long months when everyone could do magic and no one in Omwimmee Trade needed her. "I do know how that feels," she told him. And she draped her own arm around his waist.

He smiled at her then, a sweet, hopeful smile that did wonderful things for his plain face. And for a while, as the two of them hurried through the streets, arms around each other, Faia felt truly happy.

Chapter 29

Faia snuggled beneath thick, downy covers, drifting. She became slowly aware of people talking nearby, but at first she didn't worry herself about what they were saying. After a while, though, their tone began to disturb her, and she began a gradual ascent to wakefulness.

The voices floated up through the floorboards in fits and starts—snatches of speech pushed into her woolly consciousness, leaving her with the oddest impression of what the men downstairs discussed.

". . . get away? . . . behind . . . has to be first priority!" That was Edrouss Delmuirie. She let her mind wander; she imagined his face, smiling. He had a good smile—and his arm around her had felt so nice. She rolled to her side and burrowed her head deeper into the feather pillow and tried to imagine what it would be like to kiss him.

". . . not important, and the Klogs . . ." Her brother's voice—so desperate. ". . . no sense . . . what about this god? . . . trouble . . ."

Faia stretched. Her head still throbbed, and she had the most horrible taste in her mouth. She opened one eye. She was back in the upstairs room. Pink-grey light crept through dusty slit windows and scattered little dapplings of color across the wall next to her. She watched dust motes drift upward through the bright lances of light, and entertained herself for a while by blowing gently and making them scatter.

So this was early morning. She was safe and warm in bed—the sheets felt clean and smelled good. She didn't have to concern herself with anything. She let her eyelids close again, and began to sink back into delicious lethargy.

". . . what if he tries to kill Faia?" Edrouss asked.

That carried well enough. Faia woke up completely, and sat up in the bed. The covers fell to the floor as she swung her legs over the side of the bed and eased herself up. Her head hurt worse when she moved—damn Thirk. She wasn't in any shape to be getting out of bed—but she didn't want to miss the discussion downstairs.

She threw her clothes on—wondered briefly how they'd gotten off in the first place; she didn't remember undressing, or even getting as far as the bedroom, for that matter—and headed down the narrow stairs as fast as she could. She found Bytoris and Edrouss sitting at the morning table, eating dreary *antis*-fare and looking worried. Both nodded to her as she came in. She attempted a smile, but gave it up as a bad idea. Her head felt like it was going to come off, and she began to wish it would. She could hear the youngest of her nieces and nephews playing quietly in another room. One of the older girls was singing while she worked out in the walled yard, cleaning the birds they would eat for *nondes*.

Faia pulled up a chair and settled across from the two men and ladled some of the grey paste and spiced gravy into her dish. It looked disgusting, but didn't smell too bad. She took a tentative nibble, and decided, glumly, that its smell was deceiving but its appearance wasn't. She poured herself a little glass of the ale that sat opened on the table, then made a face at the taste of that, too—it was too strong for breakfast. She would have preferred water, if only Bonton still had a safe supply.

Edrouss studied her and his expression became concerned. He touched her hand. "Are you not well?"

"My head hurts," she muttered. "Where Thirk hit me when he knocked me out."

Delmuirie's lips thinned to a tight line. "Hit you?"

Faia shoved her sleeves up her arms. Her wrists were purpled with bruises and swollen. She held her hands in front of her and turned them so both men could see the marks. "He did this, too."

Bytoris frowned.

Faia saw Delmuirie pale, though. "He's going to hurt for that," the man whispered.

Bytoris said, "I wish I could have caught him last night."

"He got away?" Faia pushed her bowl back. The headache was destroying her appetite. She thought perhaps she would go back to bed and wait until it went away.

"He ran straight through the middle of a street fight and apparently went down an alley while I was trying to get past the fight without getting killed. I looked for hours, but it became obvious after a while that I had an Arisser's chance in a wit battle of finding him."

The front door slammed, and Bytoris's wife Renina appeared in the doorway, soot-streaked and breathing hard. "They attacked the district marketplace," she shouted. "They were dropping fireballs into the stalls—the market is ablaze—fire jumping from house to house, and the roofs burning, and the beasts eating up the fire brigade!"

No one needed to ask who "they" were.

Edrouss asked, "Should we get out of here, then?"

Bytoris told him, "The marketplace is not near here, but all the houses are very close—this house will likely burn with the rest." He frowned, then told his wife, "Gather the children; have them bring a few clothes. I'll pull out the cart—we can carry more in that than in our arms."

Faia looked at the grim, frightened faces around her. "You're going to run."

"Better to run than to burn."

Edrouss said, "Show me where I can be of service. I'll carry what I can for you."

Faia nodded. "Me, too." All of them rose from the table; then a surge of magical energy blanketed the city. For an instant, the room, the people around her, sights and sounds and smells—all ceased to exist in her awareness. She felt magic shaped and aimed and fired; the power of the blast was so great she could feel the forms of the buildings it touched as clearly as if she stood among them.

Then it was gone, and sight and sound came back— she found herself sprawled on the floor of the morning room with Edrouss, Bytoris, and Renina around her, staring down.

"No fire," she said slowly. The room still spun, an odd aftereffect that she thought might have been a result of the sudden magical blast but was more likely the result of Thirk's whack on the back of her skull. She sat up slowly, discovering new levels of pain in her head as she did. "Gyels—I mean Witte—put the fire out. He was somewhere near the market when he did it, but he's stopped using magic again, and I can't find him."

"I thought you said he only did evil things," Bytoris said.

"He had some ulterior motive for putting the fire out," Faia told him. She rubbed the back of her head, wishing the pain would stop.

Sounds seeped from outside: shouts, joyous cheering, applause.

"Oh. How foolish of me. I forgot how much he enjoys playing the hero," Faia muttered.

She staggered to her feet, and without even excusing herself, returned to bed.

Chapter 30

Faia's next few days passed in a fog. The pain in her head grew worse instead of better. She was endlessly sick—retching to the point of dry heaves, hearing voices she knew didn't exist, all while the world pitched and rolled beneath her. Her vision blurred; at first she saw a ring of fuzzy light surrounding everything she looked at—then the images grew darker, and she realized she was going blind.

Edrouss Delmuirie stayed with her, holding her hand, putting cool cloths on her forehead, talking to her. His calm, reassuring voice was always there when she woke, frightened from worsening nightmares. He encouraged her, he sang to her—and finally, as days passed and she got only worse, ever worse, when he was afraid she was dying, he told her he loved her and implored her to hang on.

At last a healer came—a woman with a bag of herbs in hand and a gloomy prognosis.

"I couldn't get here any faster. Others worse who need help right away—and she hung on, then, didn't she? For what good that will do in the long run. Blow to the head, was it?" The woman's voice was weary, and offered little hope. She was talking with Edrouss and Bytoris outside the door, but Faia could hear what she said well enough.

"I can tell you exactly what's the matter with her. She's bleeding into her brain—slowly, or she'd be dead already. There's a pool of blood pressing into the grey matter of the brain—that's why she can't see, why she can't stand up, why she vomits all the time. I'll tell you, she's likely to lose movement on one or the other side of her body, too. This is a bad, bad situation. If the magic weren't gone, I could fix it ready enough, just heal the bleeder and release the pressure on her brain—but as it stands now, she'll either stop bleeding soon, and gradually get better as her body absorbs the blood back, or she'll die."

"Couldn't you drill a hole in her head to let the pressure off?" Edrouss asked.

"Could," the healer answered. "If I knew where in hell to put the drill. But without magic, I can't see the bleeder, I can't see the pressure spot, and I can't tell how far in to drill or what tissue is healthy and what is dying."

"There's no hope, then." Bytoris said that.

"I didn't say *no* hope. There isn't much."

Faia heard a rustle in the hall—it sounded as though the woman was getting ready to leave. "Keep fluids in her if you can—don't worry about solid food at this point." A sigh. "There's one other thing you might try. I've heard, in the past few days, of a priest who can do miracles— he's brought back the magic water-fresher in the Sookanje district, and kept the flying nightmares from attacking the wall just yesterday. If he's doing miracles, he might be your man. Your friend in there could use a miracle."

Silence. To Faia, it felt wary.

"Is his name Gyelstom ArForst?" Edrouss asked her.

There was a pause. "No . . . that isn't it. This is an Arisser name. Calls himself Holy Perabene Hannisonne . . . Heralsonne . . ."

"Huddsonne?" Bytoris's voice then, with strain evident in those two syllables.

"Yes! That's it. You know him, then?"

"Of him. He's . . . not a friend."

"Too bad. He'd be a good man to be friends with." The shuffle again, then, "Good luck. If she's still alive in the next few days, call me and I'll stop by to take a look at her again." The sound of feet, hurrying downstairs, muffled voices from below, a door slamming.

Another long silence. Then Bytoris's voice, sad. "So he lied to her. The chalice was the source of magic after all."

"I don't think so," Edrouss answered slowly. "I would guess . . . well, I would guess this is worse even than that. Imagine if Thirk found Gyels—er, Witte—and enlisted as Witte's priest. Then we would have the God of Mischief and a madman as his chief worshiper and servant."

"Yes. I can see that—but what would be in it for the god? Why would he accept Thirk, or give him power?"

"What could a god desire? If you know that, then you know the rest." Edrouss sounded thoughtful when he continued. "Faia said Witte told her he liked to stir up trouble. How better could he stir up trouble than to give a madman magical power, then turn him loose to use it?" He fell silent, then, after an instant added, "Gods always want worshipers, too, don't they? It will be a simple thing for him to gain worshipers in a city without magic if he offers them what they've lost."

"Then disaster is coming."

"As clearly as thunderheads on a horizon."

Bytoris swore softly. "How do we avert it?"

Faia thought, I think I know the way. She tried to call to them, but her voice wouldn't work as she wished. She tried to get out of the bed, then, to go and tell them, but when she sat up, she lost her balance and heard her pulse roaring in her ears.

And for a while, she knew nothing at all.

Chapter 31

"Faia, can you hear me?" A gentle voice, the warmth of a touch on her shoulder.

Faia opened her eyes. She saw light, and a blurry form in front of her. "Yes." Her voice came out as a croak. "I can see you, too." She blinked, but her vision didn't clear. "A little, anyway."

"You can *see*?" The voice belonged to Edrouss, though her vision was too blurred for her to identify his face.

Faia rubbed her eyes. She was amazed at how much effort it took to move her arms. "Everything is fuzzy," she complained. "I'm starving. Can you get me something to eat?"

"You're *hungry*?" He sounded overjoyed. He shouted through the house, "Bytoris! Faia's awake—and she can see! And she's hungry!"

The shout was loud enough that it made her head hurt. "I'm hungry. I don't see where that requires you to scream in my ear."

"You haven't responded to anyone or anything for almost a week now. You wouldn't eat, you wouldn't drink, you wouldn't move. When the healer returned, she put a tube down your nose into your stomach, and we've been giving you sugared wine through that."

"A week?"

"A week. You've done nothing but breathe in all that time—until a few minutes ago. You seemed to be having a nightmare—you were talking about Witte."

"The little god. There's something about him that I needed to remember."

"He's become God of Bonton. The Bontonards have embraced him as the god of the city—and Thirk is his priest."

Yes . . . that was it. Faia tried to sit up. She was weak, but she didn't feel too badly otherwise. Now that Edrouss wasn't shouting in her ear, her head didn't hurt. She didn't feel sick. The tube in her nose itched; she pulled it out—though that made her stomach twist. She coughed and gagged—and then she felt better.

Then Edrouss Delmuirie hugged her, and kissed her on the cheek, and she felt even better. She smiled and asked him, "What was that for?"

"That was because you're going to live. The healer said when she came last time that if you ever woke up again, it meant you would get better."

Faia snorted. "I've always heard that people get better just before they die."

"That isn't what *she* said. And right now, I'd rather listen to her than you."

Faia lay back on the pillows. "Me too."

Bytoris came up carrying a steaming bowl of soup and a glass of water. He put them on the little table beside the bed, then sprawled in a chair across the room. "Are you awake enough for company?"

She sniffed the soup—thin broth, but it smelled wonderful. She tried a spoonful—it tasted wonderful, too. "I'm tired," she told her brother, "but company would be nice."

"You've missed a lot," he told her.

Edrouss said, "I already told her about Thirk and Gyels."

"Witte," Faia corrected.

"I only knew him as Gyels," Edrouss said. "It's easier for me t' think of him that way."

"Did you tell her about the First Folk?"

Edrouss shook his head.

"Thirk is making the First Folk behave like trained dogs," her brother said. "They attacked not too long after you . . . um, stopped answering us—came in at the wall with their stones and Thirk was waiting for them. From what I hear, he was up on the wall, dressed in gold and white robes, holding a staff in one hand and a book or something in the other, and when they swooped down for the kill, he prayed for the hand of the One True God to touch him, then forced the First Folk to land on the parapet one by one and kneel at his feet." Bytoris sighed. "It was all very dramatic. He and his One True God have been getting followers by droves ever since."

"So the First Folk are tame now?"

"That's the funny thing," Edrouss said. "They aren't. They've attacked other parts of the city, killed people, and done a lot of damage. They haven't been able to attack any place that was under Thirk's protection, though—and I suspect Thirk has let them attack because the fear brings him and his god more followers."

"That's ugly," Faia said softly.

"Yes. But effective."

"Does anyone realize that the First Folk are people, too?" Faia asked. "Has anyone tried to communicate with them, to find out why they're attacking?"

Both men shook their heads. "I haven't heard of anyone doing that," Bytoris said.

"They're hard to talk to," Edrouss added. "You have to know how to address them—you have to understand their culture, which isn't at all like human culture. It's easy to make mistakes dealing with them, and if you make mistakes, they kill you."

"But you know how to talk with them, don't you?" Faia asked.

"Well, yes—"

She smiled, suddenly excited. "Could you negotiate with them and convince them to leave the city alone? Find out why they're attacking, perhaps?" She began to feel excited. "Think of what it would do to Thirk if the First Folk stopped attacking. People wouldn't be so afraid— they wouldn't flock to his religion anymore."

"He's giving them magic, Faia," Bytoris said. "They'll follow him even without his protection from the Klogs."

Faia wasn't deterred from her idea. "Not if we could prove he let the Klogs attack people so he would have something to save them from," she argued. "People in Bonton have died, Bytoris. If we can convince the Klogs to stop attacking and stop killing, and show them that Thirk could have made them stop killing at any time, they won't follow him anymore."

"Maybe." Bytoris sounded doubtful.

"It's worth a try," Edrouss said. "Your wife said Thirk and his followers have started rounding up and forcibly converting nonbelievers. If we don't do something now, we may not have a chance to do it later."

Faia leaned back, picked up her soup, and sipped it from the bowl. She found she was too tired to use a spoon; that she was, in fact, becoming too tired to do anything at all. She listened as her brother and Edrouss discussed Thirk and his repressive new religion. Thirk was using the Bontonards' desperate need for working magic to strip them of their independence.

She finished her soup and her water and lay down. She wanted to sleep, and was just about to ask both men to leave when Bytoris brought up an objection. "It's all very well for us to say you're going to talk to the Klogs, Delmuirie—but you can't just walk up to them when they're attacking and say, 'Excuse me, but

I'd like to talk with you for a moment.' They'll eat you alive."

Edrouss sighed. "That isn't as difficult as some things. We'll make a roarer—it's what we used before when we needed t' call the Klogs. Such things aren't difficult t' make. We can carry ours outside the city walls to the top of a hill and use it to call them from there. I suppose they'll still come to a roarer."

Faia fell asleep wondering what a roarer was.

Chapter 32

Faia woke to darkness, and the sound of someone breathing nearby. Her heart caught in her throat, and she felt around on the floor for something to use as a weapon.

"Are you awake?" Edrouss whispered. "Do you need anything?"

Faia relaxed. "I didn't know that was you in here."

"I've been in here every night since you wouldn't wake up the first time. I wanted to be here. . . ." His voice trailed off, and Faia could imagine the dire eventualities he'd considered.

"Thank you." She sat up. "You've been very good to me."

Edrouss said nothing at all for a long time. Then he whispered, "Faia?"

"Yes?"

"As far as I can tell, you have neither husband nor lover."

Faia waited for him to continue, but he didn't, so she said, "You're right. I'm alone, and have been for a very long time."

"Yes. Well." He cleared his throat, then sighed deeply. "Do you feel like talking, or would you rather go back to sleep? I know you still feel terrible." He sounded like he almost hoped she didn't want to talk.

But she did. She hoped she knew what he wanted to say—and if she was right, she didn't want to wait to hear him say it. "I feel quite well, actually. And very awake. I think I've had more than enough sleep for a while." She smiled in the darkness.

"I, ah. Yes. Good. I'm glad you're feeling better."

"Edrouss, what did you want to ask me?"

"Oh. That." He sounded so nervous. "Faia, I am neither rich nor handsome—but I remember how things were done when no one had magic. I think I'll be able to make a place for myself in this world—I have nothing now, but I think I will."

Poor man. He stuttered and paused—she hadn't heard anyone so nervous when speaking to her in years.

"I think you will, too," Faia told him. "I think you're very smart, and very talented, and even rather nice-looking—at least you have a wonderful smile . . . and nice eyes—and I think you will do well here." She grinned. "But what does that have to do with anything at all?"

There was a pause. "You think I'm nice-looking?"

"Rather."

"Oh." His voice was much happier. "Well, thank you. I think you're the most beautiful woman I've ever seen."

Faia's cheeks burned. "Thank you," she whispered. Suddenly she didn't feel so completely sure of herself.

"And I do love you," he added. "I didn't want you t' think I would propose marriage if I didn't have something to offer you. And your little girl."

Faia knew she was well on her way to recovery—had anything shocked her that much a day or two earlier, she was sure she would have fainted. "Marriage?" She stared at the dark silhouette in the chair next to her bed, dumbfounded. "But, we haven't even kissed each other yet. Much less bedded together."

"Bedded?" It was Edrouss's turn to sound stunned.

"I was raised that before either a man or a woman proposed public bonding, they had to know each other well first. And no woman can know a man she hasn't bedded."

Edrouss gave a low whistle. "I was raised believing marriage was for virgins."

"Are you a virgin?" Faia found this possibility intensely interesting.

Edrouss sounded like he was choking. "No," he said after a moment. "Though I don't miss being one by much. A girl and I . . . well, once we, um . . . It didn't go very well. The girl she shared her quarters with came in while we were . . . um . . . which ruined things."

"I can imagine."

"That was my one great opportunity—and then I had to go do my service for the Klogs, and no woman would take a chance on me again until she could be sure I survived that."

Faia lay back. "Why don't you undress and get in bed with me?" she suggested.

"You aren't feeling well enough for *that*, are you?"

"Maybe. But even if I'm not, we can still sleep together. You won't have to spend the night sitting in an uncomfortable chair, and I will have the pleasure of your company."

"I would like that." He paused. "But you won't say whether you'll marry me?"

She liked the sound of his voice, and she liked his smile. She trusted him, she found comfort and pleasure in his company—and if he were not wonderful in bed to begin with, well, she'd found those skills came with practice anyway. She considered the entries in his diary bragging about all the women he'd had—he was a man who was certain he was going to like sex, at least, whether he'd actually had the chance to try it out or not.

More than that, she realized she loved him. If she woke up every day for the rest of her life to find him beside her in the bed, she would be happy.

"I'll marry you," she agreed.

Chapter 33

She sat in Renina's kitchen peeling tubers several days later. Faia was happy to be up and moving again—and was pleased her eyesight had returned to normal. Her appetite had returned, too, though she was still very thin and weak.

"We could hold the wedding here," Renina said.

"No—Kirtha has to be there. I don't want to surprise her by bringing home a husband."

Renina nodded. "True." She smiled, while her knife whisked the rough skins off the vegetables. "You two look so happy."

"I've waited a long time to find someone I could love," Faia told her. "I *am* happy. I feel like my life has started over." She threw her cleaned tuber into the bowl and picked up another one. In the walled garden, she could hear Bytoris and Edrouss hammering on the roarer they were building.

"I still have some promises to keep before I can really start my new life, though," she added. "After Edrouss talks to the First Folk, I have to find a way of convincing Witte the Mocker to give Arhel back its magic. If we can discredit Thirk, that may be possible."

"What if you can't convince him?"

Faia frowned. "I have to. Somehow, I just have to. Medwind Song will die if I don't—and perhaps a lot of

other people will, too." She smiled then. "It will work
out somehow. My mother told me it would. I just have to
not give up."

Someone pounded on the front door.

Renina jumped at the sound; Faia could see fear in her
eyes.

"Were you expecting someone?"

Renina pursed her lips. "Maybe. The People of the One
True God were stoning heretics in market square this
morning," she said. "They were also announcing that
anyone who refused to pay tithe was a heretic."

Faia put down her tuber and looked at the little paring
knife. It would be almost useless in a fight, and she was
weak anyway. "You think they've come for us?"

"I think they've come for their tithe."

"Oh, Lady. It *could* be someone else."

"It could be." Renina didn't look like she thought
that was a possibility, though. "I'll handle it," she said.
She ran for the front door, yelling, "Wait! I'll be right
there."

Faia waited. The noise in the backyard had stopped
completely. The children, who had been running through
the house arguing, fell silent, too. Low voices talked at
the front door, then footsteps echoed through the hall.
Renina stalked back into the kitchen, her face a study
in fury. "Hembult Chemmerd," she muttered. "He used
to be the taxman for the lairdlaw—now the lairdlaw has
converted and damned Hembult is back on my doorstep,
stealing rits for God." She stood on a chair and reached
into a cubbyhole at the top of her pantry shelves.

Renina brought out a leather bag and rummaged
through it, then pulled out a gold coin, looked thoughtfully
at the ceiling, and shook her head. Faia could see her
lips forming silent curses. The woman began fishing out
coppers and split silvers and placing them on a lower
pantry shelf, until, by Faia's calculation, she had the same

amount the single gold piece would have given her. Then Renina carried the handful of coins to the front door.

This time the voice carried well. "Blessings and benedictions of the One True God on you and your house," a man said. The thud of metal on wood rattled the pottery on the shelves, and he added, "I have affixed to your house the Mark of God. Now all will know you are a believer, and not a damned heretic."

Renina asked, "I hear the priest is fixing believers' water, Hembult. Will my water be back on soon?"

"It's *Brother* Hembult, now. The Holy Perabene beseeches the One True God on your behalf daily, sister, and speaks for the rest of the righteous of Bonton, too. But there are many prayers that must be answered. Meanwhile, God will meet your needs as he sees fit. Pray and wait upon the will of God, sister—and remember that patience is a virtue."

Faia heard the door shut.

Renina came back into the kitchen, scowling. "Patience may be a virtue, but you'll notice the One True God doesn't patiently wait for his tithe," she snarled.

Faia nodded. "We're doing what we can about that. It may take time, but I'm sure we'll win eventually." She picked the tuber back up and began peeling. "Why didn't you give the collector the gold coin? It was the same amount of money as all the smaller coins, and would have been faster."

"They write down how you pay," Renina said. "If you have gold, it goes into the book—and those who have gold also have silver and copper." The woman smiled slyly. "Those who have silver and copper, however, don't necessarily have gold. I'd rather leave the matter in doubt where this god and his vile followers are concerned. We've sold none of our relics in weeks. We need every rit we have to live on—and I haven't budgeted for mandatory tithes to a god who has done nothing for me."

"I have some money with me—primarily Arissonese coin, but that still spends," Faia told her. "You can have that to add to your budget. After all you and Bytoris have done for me . . ."

Renina nodded. "I thank you. I don't know how much longer we're going to be able to survive if things don't improve—but that will help."

Bytoris came in from the walled-in garden at the back of the house, with Edrouss Delmuirie right behind. Both looked serious.

"The roarer is done," Bytoris said.

Edrouss lifted Faia to her feet, pulled her tightly against him, and kissed her. "We can take it out tonight or tomorrow. We even thought of a way to get it past the guards. We can't test it to be sure it will work until we have it outside the city—I can just imagine what would happen to us if the Klogs answered the roarer's call while we were inside the city walls."

Faia said, "I don't want to wait until tomorrow. I want to get this over with—if we can bring Thirk down tonight, so much the better."

"Fine," Bytoris said. "But Delmuirie and I will go. You're not well enough to make the trip yet."

"I want to be there."

Edrouss looked from Bytoris to her, then back to Bytoris. "I think she should be there, too. I want her with us."

"We can take her, I suppose. We'll be traveling most of the way in the wagon."

"Good." Edrouss put an arm around Faia's waist and kissed her cheek. "Then it's settled. We'll call them tonight."

Chapter 34

Everyone packed the little goat wagon in silence. Faia helped Edrouss and her brother hide the disassembled pieces of the roarer in clay pots. Then they filled the rest of the goat wagon with empty pots. As an afterthought, Edrouss picked up one of the reproductions of the Klaue-Annin treaty Bytoris had set his children to work on.

"You don't have the texture of the tablet right," he said, studying it. "I'll tell you—you aren't going to get it right, either. The Klogs used ground bone in their slip—"

"Human?" Faia asked. The idea horrified her.

"No. Klog. They did not bury their dead. The librarians and other 'great' Klaue went down into the catacombs when they were ready to die. The rest died in their homes, and their bodies were dragged off by the living and used to make tablet-clay." He shook his head, and put the tablet along one side of the cart. "You might fool people who have never seen the real thing with this," he told Bytoris, "but do not try selling it to anyone who has ever seen the real thing."

They hooked the goat to the cart, and Bytoris hugged his wife. "We'll be back as soon as we can. Wish us luck."

"Luck." She and their children stood by the gate, identical worried expressions on their faces.

The children's whispery voices called, "Luck, Papa!"

and "Hurry back!" and then Bytoris clucked to the goat and tugged at the bridle. The cart lurched forward, the goat's hooves clicked across the paving stones, the wooden wheels clattered, the pots rattled together, and they were on their way.

Faia rode atop the cart seat, with Edrouss and Bytoris walking to either side. Cool twilight brought out the worst of the city stink, a nearly visible miasma born of garbage and excrement and stagnant water and acrid smoke. Disease could not help but follow such a stink, Faia thought. The healer had mentioned some sickness—but it would only get worse.

Cookfires burned in homes throughout a city that had not needed wood fires in hundreds of years. She wondered where a city full of people got enough wood to burn. From their furniture, perhaps; that wouldn't last long. Certainly from the trees that had once lined the larger avenues—the stumps of those stood up like broken teeth in a battered mouth on either side of roads they rattled down.

The city was quiet far too early—in twilight, the streets should have been full of neighbors on front steps, talking, and children running and playing. But hardly anyone shared the streets of Bonton with her and her brother and her betrothed. Faia saw only shave-headed men in white robes—Servants of the One True God—walking; and a man or two on horseback; and the few people who burned trash in the alleys beside their houses, adding to the stink.

I suppose everyone else is inside because of the smell, she decided.

Further along the road, she discovered how wrong she was. Three Servants stepped into the street from a corner, and held up their hands. Bytoris brought the cart to a halt.

"The One True God has declared the hours between sunset and sunrise a time for fasting and prayer," one of the men said. "Who are you to ignore his decree?"

Bytoris clasped his hands and hung his head. "We are followers of the One True God who must find a place to sell our wares or we will have no money to pay our tithes. We plan to travel all night so that tomorrow we can, perhaps, begin to sell our pots and jars in the nearby villages."

The Servants conferred for a moment; then the one who had spoken before spoke again. "To travel during the time of prayer and fasting with the blessing of God, you must carry the mark of God upon you." He cleared his throat. "If you have three—"

"Five," one of the men behind him whispered.

"—five rits, we will stamp your cart with the mark of the One True God, and you may proceed. Otherwise, you will have to wait until morning to travel."

Both men began digging through their pockets for coins. Faia knew she had none; she'd given every bit of cash she had to Renina. Still, she made a show of looking. She didn't want the three Servants of miserable Witte to think she wasn't cooperating.

"Here's one," Edrouss said.

"I've a half-rit here."

"And I found a half—that makes two."

Bytoris pulled his pockets out. "And here is a two-rit silver. For the glory of God, brethren, would you give us our mark for four rits? We have no more money."

The men took what Bytoris offered, then conferred; at last the man who had suggested five rits instead of three said, "We can mark your name in our book, and note that you owe an additional rit. Realize, though, that if you proceed and do not pay this money at our next asking, you will be branded as a heretic and stoned."

Bytoris turned to Edrouss and Faia. "Do we really need to travel tonight? I've no real wish to die over a single rit."

"Nor do I," Faia said. "Perhaps we could begin our journey in the morning."

Edrouss nodded agreement.

Bytoris held out his hand to the man who'd accepted their money, and said, "We've decided we'll travel by day."

The Servant, though, didn't give the money back. "For the traveling you have already done tonight, we'll keep this money."

Bytoris said, "Then we might as well go on."

The Servants conferred, and the first said, "For five rits, we will mark your cart with the mark of the One True God, and you may pass freely."

"We don't have any more money. You said you would stamp our cart anyway, and we could owe you the extra rit."

"No. For five rits, we will stamp your cart."

"But we already gave you four!" Bytoris yelped.

"That was an earlier decision. Following our generous offer, you decided not to travel the roads at night in counter to the wishes of the One True God—for which your eternal souls surely thank you—and you donated your money to God. If you wish, now, to change your better decision to a worse one, you must pay five rits."

Edrouss started to step forward, anger clearly written on his face.

Faia grabbed his shoulder before he could get out of reach, and nodded to the Servants. "Our blessings, then, brethren. We will return home and travel in the morning. Have a good night."

Bytoris took his cue from her and turned the goat cart around, and the three of them returned home before their situation got worse.

Chapter 35

"You have money with you?" Edrouss asked Bytoris. The goat was back in harness and trotting toward the Timnett Merchanter gate, with the newly risen sun glaring in their eyes. Faia once again sat in the seat, while the two men ran alongside.

"I have coins hidden all over me," Bytoris told him. "I won't take a chance on running afoul of the Servants again."

"There are a lot of them," Faia said. She looked over the crowd that thronged in the streets; nearly a quarter were shave-headed men in white robes.

"Bonton had more tax collectors even than guards, before the Woes began. And the lairdlaw had petty officials to plague every other segment of our lives, too. From all appearances, every cursed government official has 'converted' to Witte's new religion."

Edrouss wrinkled his nose. "They haven't been improved by their conversion. Where do you suppose they get all those robes?"

"Gift of the god?" Faia suggested.

Bytoris nodded.

"Yes. I suppose so." Edrouss frowned. "I'm not used to thinking of a god in concrete terms. We had the religious among us in my time, but their religions were ones of true faith. Which meant, of course, that they had no proof. I wasn't a believer."

"How very strange to have neither magic nor gods who proved their existence; I cannot actually imagine it," Bytoris said. "What an uncomfortable world it must have been."

"I liked it considerably better than what I've seen of this one," Edrouss told him mildly.

Bytoris laughed—a short, sharp bark. "I suppose you would," he conceded, "though you find us at our worst right now. When things are as they should be, Bonton is truly the city of the gods."

Edrouss gave him a sidelong look. "I wouldn't consider that a recommendation."

"Oh, no." Faia nodded toward the gate, trying to keep her movements covert. "Look ahead."

As they drew nearer the gate, the crowd had thinned— and what Faia saw there chilled her. The Servants waited next to the guards, taking tithes, questioning people, checking identifications against a roster.

"This might be bad," Bytoris said. "You still have your identity voucher with you, Edrouss—er, Geos?"

"I have mine and Faia's."

"What did we name her? It was one of those Fisher names."

Edrouss pulled out the paper Bytoris had forged. "Reeluu."

"Of course. And since you two are married, that will make her Reeluu ea Rull. She still can't speak, either."

"I did last night, to the Servants. What if some of them are the same men?"

"What if some of the guards are the same? They might remember her." Edrouss nibbled on his lower lip.

The men held their identification tags out as they reached the Servant who stood in front of the guards. The man looked over each of them and nodded curtly, then studied Faia's forged paper.

"This won't do," he said, handing the paper back to Edrouss. "The One True God does not recognize a bought wife as a true wife. We'll have to take her."

Faia's stomach knotted, though she tried to keep her expression impassive.

"Take her?" Edrouss asked.

"Brother Rull, you are committing an unchaste and immoral act by associating with a woman not your wife— to the detriment of your soul and hers. We cannot permit you to do that, so we'll take her and send her to the Hall of Sisters with other women we have saved."

Edrouss went pale. "I don't want to be rid of her. What can I do to keep her?"

The Servant frowned. "It is a bad sign that you are more concerned about matters of the flesh than about your immortal soul, brother."

"I love her," Edrouss snarled. "This isn't *about* matters of the flesh."

Faia rested her hand on his shoulder and prayed to the Lady that he wouldn't lose his temper. If he did, there was no telling what punishment the Servants would exact.

"You *love* her." The Servant glowered. "Committing not only immorality but also putting others before the One True God. Your soul teeters on the brink of annihilation, brother."

Bytoris sighed. "What can we do to keep my friend's wife with us?"

"She isn't his wife," the Servant snapped.

The line behind them was growing—and growing restless, Faia noted. She wished she had been content to sit at home, waiting, but she didn't think the Servant would let her return home—she remembered the coins from the night before, and thought no matter what happened, she and Edrouss dared not back up or appear to change their minds.

"What can we do?" Edrouss repeated.

"If you want to make her your wife, you will have to fill out a form at the Sanctuary of the One True God—and you will have fees. A fee for living with a woman not your wife, a fee for prayer for indulgence, a fee for filing the paperwork for your request, and a fee for the Servant of the One True God who will perform the ceremony to unite you in true marriage. Plus a cleansing fee for each of you." The Servant shook his head. "Honestly, you could save an enormous amount of money by going through the Sanctuary and having the Perabene pick out a wife for you."

"I'll pay the money," Edrouss said. "When we get back from selling our pots, I'll go to the Sanctuary first and fill out the papers and pay the money."

"Very well." The Servant shrugged, then pointed to Faia. "You. Reeluu? Off the cart and come with me."

Faia looked at Edrouss, and Edrouss turned to the Servant. "Wait! I need her to go with me, so she can help me sell the pots for our tithes. I just said I'd take care of the other things—"

"You thought you could take her with you—a woman with whom you've lived in violation of the laws of God?"

"I thought I could take her with me."

The Servant turned and called another of his kind to his side. He explained his "problem" and the fact that the man wished to take his sinful not-wife with him and not leave her in the care of the Servants until he could legalize the union.

The second Servant tipped his head to one side and rested his chin in his hand. He stared off thoughtfully into space for a moment, then smiled. "Twenty rits," he said calmly. "Dispensation from the One True God for traveling in amoral circumstances."

Twenty rits? That was a terrible amount of money. The bastards were determined not to let her go, weren't they? Or else they figured they had found two men who would pay whatever was demanded of them.

Edrouss looked at Bytoris, Bytoris looked at Edrouss—then both of them looked at her where she sat on the seat atop the goat cart. Edrouss had no money, Faia knew. Everything he had he'd given to the Servants the night before. Bytoris had some . . . but twenty rits . . .

Faia watched him begin pulling out coins, slowly—half and quarter coppers, split silvers, more copper—and handing them slowly to Edrouss. Neither man handed a single one of the coins to the Servants, though both of the god's hoodlums stood there with their hands out.

"I count twenty," Edrouss said at last. He looked to the Servant. "Please fill out the receipt that shows I paid this."

The second Servant frowned, then walked back to the guardhouse and came back a moment later with a slip of drypress which he handed to Edrouss. "If you're still with her after the date on the bottom and you haven't made the union legal, you'll be stoned for your heresy."

Edrouss nodded and pocketed the sheet of drypress. His eyes narrowed, but he said nothing.

Faia considered the pending threat of stoning. It seemed to be the Servants' answer to everything.

The Servants went over the cargo, too, and counted each pot—but finally Bytoris, Edrouss, and Faia had their first piece of luck. The line behind them had continued to grow, and people in the back began getting restless. They started complaining, and edging forward, and shouting that they needed to get through the gates—so the Servants' inspection of the pots was only cursory.

"Anticipated sale value?"

Bytoris shrugged. "No more than forty rits, if we're lucky."

"We will assume you're going to be lucky." The Servant smiled a most unpleasant smile. "You owe ten percent of that now—here's a credit chit. Bring that back, and completed receipts of all your sales. If you make over forty rits profit, you will owe ten percent on the extra, plus five percent in punitive tithes—for lying. You have one hundred fifteen pots in the back. Are you sure you won't make more than forty rits total?"

"I'm absolutely certain," Bytoris said.

"We'll count pots against receipts when you return, then. If you claim breakage, you'd better have the shards to prove it." The Servant waved his arm. "Move along."

The guards stopped them next. Behind, Faia could hear the Servants beginning to grill the next people in line.

The guard at the table nodded and only glanced at the identification papers. "I figure you folks have had enough trouble for one day." He glanced at the Servants and kept his voice down. "I hear a lot of people are settling out in the villages."

Bytoris nodded. "I can see why. Is mail getting through unread?"

"You have family still inside, eh?"

"Yes."

The guard kept his head down and wrote something in his log. "You have to be careful who you give it to, but mail still goes through safely." He looked up and handed a slip of drypress to Bytoris. "Though even that might not last much longer. You want to send any letters, I recommend doing it quickly."

"Thanks, then." Bytoris glanced at the drypress, smiled briefly, then turned and clucked to the goat.

Chapter 36

"I don't ever want to go inside that city again," Faia said.

"I don't know that we dare to." Bytoris frowned. "The captain of the guards gave me a list of his people that I could trust to get a message through to Renina; after we've talked with the Klogs, I may go back to the gate and try to do that." He glared down at the dusty road, and kicked at a clod of dirt. "We'll lose everything," he said. "Our house, our business, all the things we've worked for—but that will be better than living with the Servants and their One True God."

Edrouss held Faia's hand. "I won't take a chance on losing you to those people again. We won't go back."

Faia sighed. "I may have to. We'll see what happens, but I will do what I have to do to take magic out of Thirk's hands and give it back to all of Arhel, the way it's supposed to be." She shivered. "Though I really don't want to go back there. I thought for sure they were going to drag me off to their Hall of Sisters—and if they had, I don't know that you would have ever found me again." She squeezed Edrouss's hand and closed her eyes. "I hate feeling helpless."

"You won't be helpless forever." Edrouss looked over at her and touched her cheek.

Love really does make the world a bearable place, she thought.

Men and women worked in the fields on either side of the road. The irrigation pumps were working again—evidently, Thirk had decided he didn't want to do without food. Faia noted a few of the Servants scattered around the fields, though none of them appeared to be working. They stood and watched, and jotted things down on their drypress pads from time to time.

"How far out do the cultivated fields go?" Edrouss glanced at the workers, then at the fields that covered the hillside before them.

"The other side of town has better water and better soil. This side goes to woods quickly. We'll be past all this in another hour."

Bytoris was right, too. An hour of steady travel eastward took them to the edge of thick forest.

Edrouss studied the terrain and frowned. "These are the hills you meant? I thought you meant meadow hills like the ones we crossed to get to Bonton."

"People work on that ground. Here, we'll be safe."

"The Klogs hate trees. Their wings foul and tear in the branches. We're going to have to clear a hilltop for them before we can even begin to call."

Faia saw Bytoris's brows draw together, and his shoulders set. "Then that's what we'll do. We can't use the cleared land."

They found a narrow animal path, and followed it into the woods as far as they could—when it ran out, they tied the goat to a tree, lifted the pieces of the roarer out of the jars where they'd been hidden, and continued on foot. Faia carried what little food they'd brought, and Bytoris's forged First Folk tablet.

They found a likely hilltop, and Bytoris and Edrouss began felling and dragging off trees. Faia helped as much as she could—the first day by carrying water from the

stream at the foot of the hill, and the second, by foraging
for food from the woods. She found some tubers, but not
enough for a meal. So she fashioned a sling out of leather
from the hems of her breeches and gathered rocks; she
brought down enough hovies and chervies that by evening
of the second day, all three of them rested with full
stomachs.

She slept both nights curled against Edrouss, and both
nights fell asleep happy.

The third day at about midday, Edrouss declared the
hilltop clear enough to serve as a landing spot for the
First Folk.

They set up the roarer at the edge of the clearing—it
was a bizarre-looking device, with a giant funnel at one
end and a crank at the other.

"Shall we call them now?—or would it be better to wait
until dark?" Bytoris squinted into the sun—he'd spotted
Klogs flying over the day before, heading for the city in
a flock.

"They aren't any more nocturnal than we are," Edrouss
said. "A few of them like the darkness, but not many care
to fly in it. We'll call them now."

He turned the crank. It grumbled and muttered and
moaned softly, but didn't roar.

Faia held her breath, with her fingernails digging into
the palms of her hands, and prayed to the Lady, and waited.

Bytoris paled. "Please don't say it doesn't work."

Edrouss swore, stopped cranking, and pulled the funnel
away from the body of the roarer. He began twisting pegs
that Faia could see tightened a rawhide drumskin stretched
over the narrow end of the funnel.

He shoved the pieces back together and cranked again.
The noise it made was louder—but still no roar.

"Damnall," he growled, and repeated the tightening
process. He stopped at one peg, and ran his finger along
the rawhide adjustment cords. "This one is fraying already.

God send to perdition a world that doesn't have decent mechanical equipment available!" He looked up from his roarer and gave Faia a slow, doubtful shake of the head. "We'll be more than just lucky if this lasts long enough to draw Klogs here."

"Maybe we should wait and see if they fly over," Faia suggested.

Edrouss pursed his lips. "That might work—though you're always better off to engage their curiosity beforehand, so they come looking for you. Surprising a flock of Klogs can be very, very dangerous." He tightened the rest of the cords, and sighed. "That's the best we can do." He gave his roarer a quarter crank—this time it roared with a sound like the earth splitting open.

"At least it works," Faia said.

They waited, sitting in the shade of the trees at the edge of the clearing, watching the sky.

"I should have left a message for Renina to take the children and get out of the city while she could," Bytoris muttered at one point.

Later, Edrouss said, "I wish I had an idea of what we could do if the Klogs won't negotiate." Then he laughed. "I've been away from this for too long. I've forgotten—if they won't negotiate with us, *we* won't do anything else. They'll rip us into little pieces and feed us to their young."

And later than that, Faia pointed at the sky and said, "There." Nine winged shapes soared overhead in arrow formation, heading toward Bonton.

"Right," Edrouss said, and ran for the crank.

The roarer bellowed. Edrouss turned the crank in a pattern of long and short roars—Faia watched the specks high overhead that had been soaring toward the city suddenly loop and circle back.

"Yes!" Faia shouted. "They heard!"

Then, in midroar, one of the cords snapped, and Edrouss's machine fell silent.

"No!" he shouted. "Not yet!" He yelled at Faia and Bytoris, "Quick, into the clearing and wave your arms. Yell. Jump up and down. Maybe they'll see you."

He was pulling the funnel away from the main body of the roarer when Faia and Bytoris ran out to try to catch the attention of the Klaue.

Faia pulled her overtunic off and waved it in the air; Bytoris followed her lead with his shirt. The Klaue were circling, but not coming closer—they seemed to be trying to find the source of the noise, but they weren't having any success.

"Don't quit," Edrouss shouted. "I think I've almost got this—"

Faia and Bytoris kept swinging their clothing and jumping and shouting. Then their shouts were drowned out by the bellow of the roarer—and the Klaue homed in on them with swift, terrifying precision.

"Get back into the trees," Edrouss yelled.

They ran for cover, and succeeded in ducking behind two sturdy *banims* just as the ground shook with the impact of the first Klaue's arrival.

Faia looked around her tree at that first nightmare creature, and found to her horror that it was studying her with a steady, curious gaze—its bright black eyes gleamed exactly as the stone eyes inset into the whitestone First Folk statues in the ruins had. These eyes, though, blinked occasionally. And this face, rich coppery gold with dun stripes, grinned at her with a mouthful of teeth like daggers. Then the creature made a chuckling, gargling sound and looked back over its shoulder as its fellows landed.

They thudded to the ground one after the other, each moving out of the cleared center with neat efficiency so the next could follow. When all of them had landed, the coppery-brown one settled onto its haunches much as a cat would, and shook its wings, pulling them in with a finicky-looking movement, and curled its tail around its legs. Paws? Feet? Faia thought its forelimbs looked very much like hands, except for the long, sharp, flat black claws. The rest of the Klaue—red and black, rich iridescent blue-green, grey, solid black, brilliant yellow, gauded out in hovie patterns and hovie colors but only as much like hovies as a hawk would be like a hummingbird—found various positions of repose. Then they sat and watched.

Edrouss stepped out of the woods and faced the Klaue leader.

He squatted and rested his arms straight to the ground; frank imitation of the Klaue leader's position. Then he growled and hissed and whistled. All of the Klaue had been watching him calmly, but as Edrouss talked, a transformation overcame them. The long-spined rilles that draped like curtains to either side of their faces began to stand out. Their colors grew darker and richer, their muscles tensed; then one by one they leaned forward, stretching their long necks toward Edrouss, and one by one they bared their teeth.

Faia watched the transformation with increasing unease. "Bytoris, do you suppose that's the way he wants them to act?" Faia asked.

Bytoris said, "I don't think so."

"Can we help him?"

Bytoris stared at her and his eyebrows slid up his forehead. "You jest. Unless you speak whatever . . . language . . . they speak, I don't see any way we can help."

"I don't either," Faia agreed.

Edrouss Delmuirie's speech had faltered, and he stood staring at the monsters before him, silent.

One of them answered, a soft trill, two short whistles—first a rising tone, then a falling tone—another trill, a hiss, a cough.

Edrouss seemed to freeze. He hissed and whistled again, but the sounds were slower, and less sure.

The coppery-gold Klaue trilled and chirped and whistled.

Faia could see the tension across Edrouss's shoulders, and the way they sagged and his head dropped forward after a moment—in despair, or defeat. She could not be sure.

The Klaue growled, a deep falling tone that grew louder and rougher—and that didn't sound to Faia like any possible part of speech. It was a threat—no doubt about it. The Klaue bared its teeth and lowered its muzzle until it was face-to-face with Edrouss.

Do *something*, Faia thought.

She ran to the tablet they had left leaning against a tree, snatched it up, and raced out to face the Klaue.

"Faia! Get back! Stay in the trees!" Edrouss shouted.

"Don't growl at him," she shouted at the giant Klog, and threw the tablet at it.

The Klaue caught the tablet with one hand, its reflexes predator-quick, predator-sure. It hissed at her, and whipped around to face her. Then, almost as an afterthought, it looked at what she'd thrown.

It gasped—the same quick intake of air a human would make—and turned and shouted to its companions. The shout was loud enough Faia felt it shake the ground beneath her feet. One of the Klogs stood and trotted over—it was a gorgeous scarlet creature with legs and wings and rilles darkening to black at the tips. Both the gold-and-dun and the black-and-red studied the tablet, and trilled and chirruped at each other.

Faia crouched next to Edrouss and whispered, "What happened? What are they saying now?"

"I don't know. Either they're from a branch of the Klaue that doesn't use Air Tongue, or the language has completely changed since I last used it." He frowned. "I caught one or two words, though, so I would assume the latter."

"They seem to know what that is."

"Well, yes. It's Stone Tongue—which is probably unchanged."

"You mean there's another language you can use? One you know?"

Edrouss Delmuirie sighed, and stood, and stretched his legs. Then he dropped back into a crouch and looked over at Faia. "There are—or were—four languages—I know all of them. The problem is, the correct language to use for working out concepts and entering into nonbinding discussion is Air Tongue. The trouble I could get us and everyone in Arhel into by using Stone Tongue defies belief. Stone Tongue is the language of things that are decided, unchangeable, and nonnegotiable."

Faia didn't see the problem. "Then use one of the others."

"I can't. Water Tongue is the Klaue spiritual language. Words for negotiation and discussion that we would need do not even exist in Water Tongue. And as for the fourth . . . if I uttered a word in Blood Tongue, yon big fellow and his friends would eat me before you could blink."

"A entire language for war?" Faia found the idea dreadful.

"War and sex." Edrouss gave her a wry grin. "Apparently the Klogs see connections between the two activities that humans do not—or do not admit to."

"You haven't met the Hoos."

Edrouss raised an eyebrow, but Faia didn't elaborate.

Instead, she said, "You have to find some way to talk to them."

Edrouss nodded. "I know."

"Can you write?" Faia considered the fact that she had learned to read Old Arhelan, though she would have no idea how to speak it. She told Edrouss this, and suggested that perhaps Air Tongue would work the same way.

Edrouss grinned at her. "That might work, love of my life. You might save us yet. Find me a stick, would you? Since I called them here, I do not dare leave or make any sign that my attention is lapsing. It would be an unforgivable—and fatal—rudeness."

Faia nodded, ran into the woods, and cut a long, thin branch from a sapling, then shaved the branchlets from it and took it back to Edrouss.

He smoothed a square of dirt to one side of himself, then made a rattling noise in the back of his throat Faia didn't think she could reproduce if she tried for the rest of her life. Nine Klaüe heads snapped around and nine pairs of cold black Klaüe eyes narrowed.

Edrouss turned to face his smoothed square, then held up one hand while he scratched marks in the dirt with the other. He spoke in the whistling, trilling Air Tongue again while he wrote. The leader's rilles stood out, and after an instant's hesitation, the gold-and-dun snaked his neck out, tucked his rilles back, and poked his massive head over Edrouss's shoulder so he could see what the man was doing.

One of the other Klaüe made a questioning sound, and the leader looked back and snapped a reply that sounded rude to Faia—and apparently to the Klaüe thus spoken to, for the creature tucked its head under its wing and snorted. It sulked as obviously as Kirtha when Faia told her to behave. Faia felt a thin tendril of hope grow inside her. It might be possible to understand the monstrous First Folk after all, and negotiate a peace between them and Bonton.

It might be possible to win.

In front of her, the Klaüe flicked its tail over the message Edrouss had written, obliterating it. It nibbled thoughtfully at one knuckle on its huge fist, then began pressing shapes into the dirt with its claws. It spoke at the same time as it wrote—and Edrouss gasped.

"Faia," he almost shouted, "this is going to work! The sounds have changed, but the written words are still almost the same."

Faia was elated. "What is it saying?"

"He. This flirt is definitely male. The red hussy over there is his intended mate, too, I'd bet you." He glanced up at her. "These are young Klaue, the whole bunch of them. They're the Klog equivalent of human adolescents— too young to marry, but too old to stay home."

"What is *he* saying, then?"

"He says they were out flying when a storm came up— it blew them off course, and they landed here."

"The storm that blew up when the Barrier came down?"

"Probably." Edrouss wiped the ground smooth with his stick, and wrote something else. Then he read the Klaue's reply to Faia and Bytoris, who had walked over to join them. "He says, 'We attack the city because there are no true-men there.' "

He wrote again. "I asked him what he meant."

Edrouss watched the reply, then hissed. "They landed in the center of Bonton, wanting to get directions and perhaps buy drinks—and the people there killed his sister and some of his friends. These nine flew off, but when they went back to get the bodies . . ." He paused while the Klaue erased the first part of his message and continued writing. "Oh, no! He says they skinned and stuffed his sister, as if she were a trophy bletch!" Edrouss looked at Faia, his eyes wide. "No wonder these youngsters keep attacking. That isn't just a terrible thing t' do—that's sacrilege of the very worst kind. They never leave their bodies to the open air—never. They burn them or bury them in catacombs."

"I saw a stuffed Klaue," Faia said. "The fighting men dragged it out on a wheeled cart and taunted the rest of the Klaue with it—just seeing it seemed to drive them into a rage."

"Why would they do such a thing?"

Bytoris said softly, "It is a custom among the Bontonards that a hunter, having killed a dangerous beast, and one that could as easily have killed him, will stuff the beast's skin and keep it in his home as proof of his feat."

Edrouss turned on him and shouted, "But these are not beasts!"

"But how were the common Bontonards to know that?" Bytoris held his hands wide. "Klogs do not look like people, and they do not speak like people, and only within the last year have even the *scholars* come to accept that those who built the ancient cities were not humans. . . ."

Edrouss nodded. "True." He turned and wrote in the dirt again, and at the same time said, "I'm telling them how this mistake happened. I'll see if they'll agree to a truce, to allow us to barter for the release of this one's sister's body."

When the Klaue replied, he said, "He agrees. He says they will not attack the city again if we can do that, and they will leave this place and never return."

The Klaue flicked his tail over the words, then began writing again in the dirt. "He says this place shouldn't even be here, that it is, he thinks, the . . . this doesn't translate well . . . ghostland would be the best I can manage. The word has a second meaning, of something that has been cursed."

"I can imagine how he would feel that way."

Suddenly Faia smelled smoke. She looked up from the dirt, and saw that Thirk had appeared, and was watching her from just beneath the canopy of trees—and with him were perhaps fifteen Servants, and half a hundred townspeople. The people pointed at the Klaue and whispered.

Thirk stepped into the circle and raised his arms above him and waved his fingers at the Klaue. Fire appeared in the air, racing around the First Folk without touching them.

They bellowed, then leapt into the sky, their wings thundering in the air—and within an instant they were high above, and sailing away from Bonton.

Thirk's Servants and the townsfolk stepped into the clearing behind him, surrounding Faia and Bytoris and Edrouss.

Faia felt her heart sink. This was the confrontation she had not wanted.

Edrouss stood, and faced Thirk and the majority of the Servants. "The Klaue agreed to a truce," he said. "They agreed to peace! Why did you chase them away? If you release the body of their sister to be burned, they will not attack Bonton anymore, and they will leave Arhel."

"Will they?" Thirk asked softly. "They'll leave?"

"Yes," Edrouss said. "At least, they said they would before you . . . before you shot fire at them. I explained how the people of Bonton misunderstood who they were, and I negotiated a truce with them. They intend you no harm anymore. If you just give them their sister back, they will leave you alone."

Thirk turned to his followers, and in that same flat, quiet voice, he said, "With your own eyes, you see this. These are the people who have spoken to those monsters. They say now that the monsters will not attack you . . . *anymore*; will not kill your husbands and wives and children . . . *anymore*; will not destroy your homes and businesses . . . *anymore*. That should be a good thing, shouldn't it?"

His people watched him silently, waiting for a cue.

"I say, *no! Anymore* . . . that is nothing. The monsters have already attacked, have already maimed and killed and destroyed. These three have done you no kindness today! Where were they when the monsters attacked the first time?" Thirk smiled and looked at his followers one at a time. "How did they learn to speak with the beasts? Think of that. How did they learn this cursed beast tongue? I'll tell you—they are in league with the monsters. When they flew against you and your loved ones, these are the people who commanded them. They brought the monsters to Bonton, and set them against you. Now you understand the depths of evil that I have been protecting you from."

"That's a lie, Thirk, and by the Lady, you know it!" Faia shouted. "You know who Edrouss Delmuirie is, and how he knows First Folk speech! You know perfectly well that we had nothing to do with the attacks! It was their own stupid fault!" She pointed at the townsfolk. "If they hadn't skinned one of the First Folk and stuffed her, you wouldn't have the problems you have."

"By the *Lady*, indeed. The heretic speaks," Thirk said. "This same heretic brought down the Delmuirie Barrier. She killed Edrouss Delmuirie, and destroyed Arhel's magic. It is only by the grace of the One True God that we are not bereft of all magic."

The murmurs in the crowd grew louder, and the men and women moved closer. Faia felt doom closing in on her.

"I didn't kill Edrouss Delmuirie!" she shouted. "He's Edrouss Delmuirie."

"The records at the gate say he's Geos Rull," Thirk said.

"I'm Edrouss Delmuirie."

Thirk smiled. "So you came into the city under false identity? Tsk, tsk. Normally, that would be a stoning offense—but the world needs Edrouss Delmuirie. If you *are* Edrouss Delmuirie, I'm sure you can prove it."

"Of course I can prove it," Edrouss shouted. "Ask me anything."

"Fine. Edrouss, if you are Edrouss—put the Delmuirie Barrier back up. Give Arhel back its magic."

"Let's see some magic!" a man shouted.

"He can't do magic! He's a liar!"

"Stone him!"

"Stone *her*!"

And someone else yelled, "Stone them all."

Thirk crossed his arms over his chest. "What, Edrouss,

Faia—no magic? Can it be that you lied to all of us?"
He waited.

Faia took Edrouss's hand in her own. She could think
of nothing that might save them. She looked into Thirk's
eyes, and saw her own fear reflected. In her brother's face,
she saw more of the same fear. She had no magic, no
power—and no hope.

All around them, the people still called for their deaths.

"No magic for us—it must mean you lied to us after
all. What a pity." Thirk shook his head slowly, then turned
mournful eyes on his followers, who cried out for stoning.
As if saddened by the reactions of his followers, he said,
"Children, children, I have taught you time and again that
punishment must always fit the crime. Common heretics
are stoned—but these are no common heretics. These
people are a veritable wellspring of evil." He smiled slowly.
"They wanted you to burn the body of the monster you
killed. I say we burn these three instead."

"Burn them," the mob replied.

"Yes, *burn* them!"

And the crowd moved in around Faia and her lover
and her brother.

Chapter 37

Thirk transported everyone back to town—his three captives, the Servants, the townsfolk. They arrived in a billow of smoke, in the town square.

"Ring the bells," Thirk shouted.

Men ran to do as he commanded, and within an instant, the town bells rang through the gathering night.

"Tie them to the pillars!"

In the center of the square, long ago, the Bontonards had erected a stone pavilion with graceful stone pillars that supported a delicately carved stone roof. The structure still stood, moss-etched and worn, testament to a better age.

Faia fought against the two men who held her—both brawny Servants—but she was no match for their strength or determination. They dragged her to one of the pillars, and within an instant, townsfolk ran up, offering rope to bind her. The Servants tied her tightly, with Edrouss on the pillar next to hers and Bytoris on the other side of him.

The bells rang on, and the square filled with more people; people who ran back home to bring bits of wood, who threw pieces of their furniture, bits of carts, and even the doors of their homes, smashed and reduced to kindling, at the feet of their victims.

The piles of wood grew until they reached waist-high around Bytoris, Faia, and Edrouss.

Then men lit torches, and brought them to the pyres.

"I love you," Edrouss called to Faia.

"I love you, too." Faia felt tears running down her cheeks. "And you, too, Bytoris. I'm glad I had a brother again, even just for a little while."

Thirk floated into the air, and illuminated himself with magic. He magically amplified his voice, too, so that when he spoke to the crowd gathered beneath him, it was in gentle, kindly tones, and yet all could hear him.

"My beloved children," he said. "At last the causes of our many griefs are brought to justice. The men and woman you see before you destroyed Arhel's magic. They summoned the murderous monsters who fly against our city, maiming and murdering those you love. These three have, by their every action, brought horror and pain to you who have done nothing to them. They are heretics, despisers of the One True God, and for their many evils, their sentence must be death."

"Death!" the crowd shouted.

"Burn them!"

"Watch them burn!"

"Children. Oh, my children. We cannot rejoice in their deaths, for the three of them cannot repay you for the hundreds—nay, the thousands—who have died by their actions. There is no joy in this little justice."

The crowd stilled.

I want my daughter, Faia thought. I want Edrouss. I want to live!

"But, joy or no joy, there will be justice." Thirk waved a hand, and the people began to throw their burning brands against the bases of the pyres.

Some of the wood was green, and resisted the flames— but more of it caught. Smoke began to curl up into Faia's eyes, and little tongues of flame licked along the wood at her feet; the flames grew, leaping from stick to board. Bytoris coughed. Edrouss struggled with his bonds, trying to the last to break free.

"Burn! Burn!" the mob screamed.

Faia felt a cool breeze blow against her cheek, and the roar of the crowd dulled to a whisper.

I'm dying already, she thought.

No. I don't want you to die, Faia. You can set the men free, you can give Arhel back its magic—and you can live.

She saw a hazy shape form in the smoke in front of her. Gyels—Witte.

"What do you want from me, Witte?" she snarled. "What do you demand in exchange for your favors?"

I'm not Witte. I've never been Witte. I am that which you know as the Dreaming God—and all I want for my favors is you, Faia. I have been too long alone. If you will agree to come with me, I will save your friends. I will save your Arhel.

He wasn't Witte? She was shaken—she had been so sure. Gyels was not Witte. He was the Dreaming God— and the Dreaming God was not, and had never been, Edrouss Delmuirie. She wished with her whole heart that he were, that she could give herself to the Dreaming God, and by doing so have Edrouss, too.

Instead, she would have nothing. Not her daughter, not her lover, not her life.

But the people she loved would live.

At that instant, Bytoris's clothing caught fire. The flames licked along his body, and caught his hair, and all the while he screamed, and screamed, the screams clear and loud in Faia's ears. And Edrouss began to writhe as one tongue of flame danced along the tip of a board that touched his side, burning ever nearer his shirt.

Hurry, Faia, or they die.

"Take me," Faia said, "but save them. Not just from the fire—get them safely away from these madmen. And give Arhel back its magic."

Gyels smiled at her, and suddenly she was far away, in a universe of light and the music of the infinite.

Chapter 38

Faia was in the emeshest again—but this time she was all the way in; committed both body and soul. Her spirit would not be able to effect a careful retreat this time.

The presence of the Dreaming God surrounded her, pushing his unwanted love and happiness at her.

Let me see! she demanded. *Let me see what happened to them.*

Why must you see them? I told you I would send them to safety.

Let me see. Faia fought off his attempts to soothe her.

Very well. Look here—see whatever you would see.

In the light of the emeshest, a window opened onto Arhel, a flat circle of dullness and dreariness in the center of the infinite reaches of light and joyousness in which Faia was trapped. She stared hungrily into that plain little window. *Show me Edrouss.*

The flames touched his shirt, and his face contorted in agony. But at that instant, he began to glow brilliantly, illuminated from the inside as if he were a suddenly transparent magelight. Bytoris, tied to the pillar beside him, also lit up with that same radiant light—and Faia saw the same thing happen to her own body.

This was just before now, the Dreaming God told her.

And then the three bodies vanished from the pillars to which they were bound. Faia willed the window to focus on Edrouss Delmuirie; it followed him to the place where he reappeared, a little town nestled in the southern mountains. He fell to the ground, unharmed, and crawled into a barn, and found a place to sleep. Celebrations in the street woke him the next morning—Arhel's magic had returned. Pure fresh water once again flowed from taps, airboxes flew in the skies above the village, mages and sajes practiced their trades.

Edrouss looked for a place where he could be of use— but he was far from the ruins and the scholars. Magicless, moneyless, without skills, without *her*, he fell into despair. He began taking whatever odd jobs he could find, and with the little money he earned, he bought cheap wine. He drank himself to sleep nights, and ate nothing. The first cold night of winter found him out, in thin clothes, too drunk to seek shelter.

And he died.

No! Faia wailed. She pulled back from the Dreaming God's window, away from the world and the man she loved, and let the brightness of the emeshest wear away at the edges of her pain.

Time passes, my beloved, and you busy yourself with the world. We have all of eternity, but I desire your company now. I have waited so long.

Faia turned her attention to the Dreaming God. *Another moment*, she demanded. *There are things I must see.*

She looked through the window again, searching for Bytoris, and found him separated from Renina and their children. The Dreaming God had moved him to a safe place outside the city, but had left his wife and children behind. Bytoris went back to Bonton to rescue them, but the Servants caught him trying to smuggle them out of the city, and arrested him. Her brother was branded and given to Thirk as a personal slave, while the Servants branded Renina and all the children as heretics and kept them for their own uses. Thirk delighted in torturing Faia's brother.

If she had been able to, Faia would have wept.

So magic had not freed Bonton of Thirk and his evil religion. Somehow the madman had managed to hang on to his power. Faia shifted her attention to Thirk, and followed him as he went about his life of luxury, waited on by multitudes—commanding them with a snap of his fingers. His religion had spread, until not only Bonton but much of Arhel was infected with it.

Why?

She searched from person to person through the believers, until she found the truth. Arhel's magic had returned the instant she and Edrouss and Bytoris had vanished from the burning pyres—and Thirk, ever crafty, had claimed the magic's return as his own doing. There was no one to naysay him—and he had taken the grateful adoration of the multitudes, and turned it into even more power.

She turned away from Thirk in disgust.

She found her own body, frozen in a pillar of light.

Why? she asked.

Only when I embrace the mind of one human can I touch all humans. That is the source of the world's magic, beloved—the embrace of my mind and yours.

Then in a way, Edrouss was the source of Arhel's magic.

He called upon me in a moment of dire need—and for that moment, his mind was open, and met mine. I thought he was the one I had waited so long to find, and I embraced him as I now embrace you—but he had no capacity for the easy speech you and I share. My touch over the many years changed him, but never enough that he could see me for what I am, or hear my voice. Never enough that he could be the companion I yearn

*for. He gave me a conduit to the rest of Arhel, and finally
brought me you.*

The Dreaming God paused, and when he resumed, his
desire burned in the emeshest like the fires of a sun.

*Time passes, heart of my heart. Come be with me.
Rejoice with me in our togetherness. Take joy in the magic
we make.*

Faia ached—for her lover, for her brother, for her world.
Wordless, she turned her back on the Dreaming God and
stared into the window to the world.

She willed the window to show her Kirtha.

Her little girl had grown while she watched the others.
Kirtha was tall and beautiful, already as old as Faia had
been when Faia and Kirgen had conceived her. Kirtha
had long red hair that blazed in the sunlight, a wonderful
smile, beautiful brown eyes.

But she was unhappy. She fought with her father
and stepmother, she hated her twin half-brothers and
their younger sisters. She used her magic angrily—Faia
came to discover that she blamed Kirgen, Medwind,
Roba, and the twin boys with whom Roba had been
pregnant for her mother's disappearance and presumed
death. She was sure Faia would have stayed behind
and Kirgen would have gone if Roba had not been
pregnant. She refused to train with Medwind, so her
magic was wild and uncertain, and more dangerous
than Faia's had ever been; and she used it for any reason,
at any time.

As Faia watched, she left Roba and Kirgen and went
off on her own. She traveled around Arhel, looking for
trouble and invariably finding it. She took lovers carelessly,
and each one left her more unhappy than the one before.
She grew old before her mother's eyes—old and bitter
and lonely and unloved, with no children or grandchildren,
no real home, nothing she cared about. The magic borne
of her mother's body and a god's desire she abused—

and it in turn abused her, causing Kirtha nothing but pain and grief.

Distraught, Faia turned away for an instant, and when she looked back, it was to see her daughter as an old woman, sick and alone and dying. And then dead.

No! Faia wailed. *Not my daughter! Not my beautiful daughter! This is not the way things should have been. I gave up my life so I could save them, but nothing good has come of this.*

She turned her attention back to the Dreaming God.

Why? she demanded of him. *Why have their lives been so terrible?*

Life is short and full of pain, he told her. *You have eternity with me. Forget about life. Forget the pain— there is no pain here. Rejoice with me. Love me.*

Must things be as the window showed them to me? Faia railed against the horror and the despair she had seen. *Must the future hold the endless pain I saw?*

You did not see the future, beloved. You watched the present as it unfolded. You followed time; the things you saw happened not in a seeing, but in truth.

Then the people I loved are all dead?

Everyone dies, Faia. Everyone but you and me.

Faia pulled back from him. Neither the soothing brightness and warmth of the emeshest nor the glorious music of eternity could soothe her pain. At last she said, *Then let me die.*

You are my love, my soul, my heart. You are the embodiment of my only dream. I love you. I waited an eternity for you.

Inside of Faia, something snapped. *Don't you understand? I don't love you! I love my daughter. I love my brother. I love Edrouss!*

The Dreaming God did not react to Faia's explosion. He maintained a calm, reasoning tone. *Edrouss was mortal—human. Now he is dead, and his spirit is elsewhere, seeking another place. Whereas I am not mortal, not a man. I am the greatest of the gods; I am the Dreaming God. If a man is worthy of your love, how much more worthy am I?*

Without a body, Faia could not weep physical tears. But her soul wept. *I cannot make myself love you. Can you not understand that love is not something I can just make appear because you want it to be there? I will talk with you if you are lonely—because I must. I am here of my own choice, because I wanted to protect the people I loved—though I did them little good. But I cannot love you. I do not have whatever secret thing my heart would have to hold to make that love be there. And I can never forget that the people I loved with all my heart died unhappy and alone without me, because of you.*

Then everything I have done has been in vain. I was wrong to lie to you, to trick you, to use my power to make you desire my human form, to use your enemy Thirk to bring you to me. Had I not done those things, would you love me?

Faia thought of Gyels as she first saw him, as she first knew him. When he was a simple hunter, she had thought she might come to love him. But he had become a jealous man, and a jealous god.

Perhaps, she told him. *We cannot know that now. Jealousy kills the thing it most desires; love not freely given is not love, but fear.*

The Dreaming God was silent for a long time—so long that Faia could not help but wonder how many thousands were born, lived out their lives, and died in the faraway mortal world she yearned for.

At long last the Dreaming God stirred. *Through you, I have discovered love—I loved you as a god before I was a man; I loved you as a man; and once again a god, I love you still. For all of eternity, I desired someone*

*would could be my companion and my equal—someone
who could share eternity with me. If my love was not
free from jealousy, it was still the only love I knew. I
will learn another love.*

*I moved worlds and shaped the lives of countless
humans, as well as the lives of creatures of my own making
and design, so that the day would come when someone
who could talk with me would be born. There were others
with your abilities, soul of my soul, but they never came
to me. Only you came to me. Surely you were the one
for whom I have waited.*

*My love is not the love of mortals; yet having once
been mortal, I can feel within me the strong, hot stirrings
of what you feel. Faia, I cannot make myself not love
you. Yet I cannot bear to see you as you are, deep in
your human misery, outside of the reach of my caring
and my desire. You gave up everything to save the people
you loved.*

The god paused, then added, *Love accepts pain. I
think, though, that love does not willingly cause pain. I
will not keep you with me. In this way, I will love you
without jealousy.*

Faia felt hope flare inside of her, then gutter and die.
*Everyone I ever cared about is gone now. Dead. Your
realization and your kindness come too late.*

She felt amusement in his response. *They are dead
now. But what is* now, *Faia? What is time to me? I am
eternal. I exist in all places and at all times, forever.
Because I love you, I will set you free to live as a mortal
with those you love. Remake the world as you would,
Faia. Time is fluid, changeable—if you can bring joy to
your daughter, your friends, and your lover, do so. I
hope you find happiness.*

Faia felt both the Dreaming God's pain and a tendril
of his hope wash over her.

Maybe you will discover that mortality, with its pain

and suffering and certain death, is not what you wish after all. If that happens, or if someday you discover that you can love me as I love you, ask, and I will bring you back to my side.

How shall I call you? Faia asked. *I don't know your name.*

I have never had a name. But I will take one. When you call me— The Dreaming God paused.

—Call me Sorrow.

Chapter 39

At that instant, Bytoris's clothing caught fire. The flames licked along his body, and caught his hair, and all the while he screamed, and screamed, the screams clear and loud in Faia's ears. And Edrouss began to writhe as one tongue of flame danced along the tip of a board that touched his side, burning ever nearer his shirt.

Then she felt it—the mind of the Dreaming God, of the god Sorrow.

Would you still have magic in Arhel? he asked.

"Yes!" she shouted above the roar of the flames. Her own clothing caught fire, and she felt heat, and searing pain. Smoke stung her eyes and filled her nostrils and burned her throat.

Then who shall I take? Who shall I make my own, to form the mind of the magic?

There was no hesitation. "Take Thirk!" Faia yelled.

Through the smoke, through the waves of heat that distorted her vision, she saw Thirk as he hung above the mob, suddenly bathed in radiance—and then her tormentor, her would-be killer, Thirk Huddsonne, vanished.

And the magic surged through her body again.

She drew the power to her, and with it blew out the flames that burned Bytoris and threatened to engulf

Edrouss—and that licked at her flesh and left blisters and terrible pain.

She pulled in even more magic, and healed her wounds and the wounds of her loved ones. Then she walked free of the pillar and the still-smoking pyre, and beside her, Edrouss and Bytoris stepped out of their bonds. Their eyes were full of wonder—and their eyes were mirror images of the eyes of the mob, the silent mob, the mob that had seen their priest taken from them, and that saw those that priest had denounced set free.

Faia knew what she had to say—words that would heal, words that would set the people free.

"People of Bonton," she shouted. "Thirk Huddsonne lied to you—about us, about the One God, about everything. The rules he gave you, the demands he made on you— they were all wrong, all evil. He was an evil man—but the god in whose name he worked has wearied of his evil and has taken him. That god—the Dreaming God, whose name is Sorrow—will change him and heal him and over time will make him whole again.

"That same god has set us free. And now that Thirk is gone, you must turn away from his lies, and the evil he demanded. You must go back to your lives. Go back to being the people you were before. Give the First Folk back their dead, and make peace. Rebuild your city, mend your walls and your families, worship the gods you choose to worship."

"You could lead us," someone shouted. "The One True God freed you. You must be his chosen one."

Other people shouted agreement, and the roar of the mob grew again.

Faia winced. She raised her hands and shouted for silence, and they quieted. She shouted, "No one can lead you but you. Look inside yourself for your god. Don't look to me—don't look to anyone else. No path is right for every person."

"You could show us Truth!" someone insisted.

"I don't know Truth," Faia told him. "I know only what is true for me, and I can speak only for myself."

Faia shoved her hands into the pockets of her leather breeches and stared out at the milling horde of humanity. She would not make herself into their intercessor with Sorrow, nor would she tell them how they ought to live their lives. Shepherds were for sheep, not for people.

She turned away as the mob broke up and wandered toward its many homes; when the square was once again silent, she conjured three wingmounts—calling them from wherever they might have been. They answered her summons as quickly as they could; within minutes, three pale grey horses with wings and legs and manes tipped black appeared over the housetops, flying across the sky to her. They landed jarringly on the platform, and stood waiting.

Faia remembered the first time she'd ridden one—when Medwind Song came from Ariss to the little town of Willowlake to fetch Faia back to the University. Faia had been a child then, with everything to learn.

It's been a long, hard, lonely road, she thought. She smiled to herself and looked at Edrouss, and thought of Kirtha. Even lonely roads could lead to happy destinations.

She turned her attention to the wingmounts. None of them wore bridles or saddles—or even halters. They were rough rides even with those amenities—she had no inclination to ride them bareback, guiding them by hope and good thoughts. She closed her eyes and created three hackamores and three light saddles, already in place on the wingmounts.

Then she turned to her brother.

"Good-bye, Bytoris. Hug Renina and your children for me, and thank them for all their care and kindness." She gave him a sad smile. "Have a good life, and be happy with your family."

"Won't you come home with me—at least for a while?"

"I've been away from my family and friends too long. Arhel's magic is back, and Kirtha will be waiting for me." She hugged him briefly. "And I need to check on Medwind. But I'm glad we met. I feel a little better, knowing I have a brother."

"Good-bye, then, sister. For all the disasters that meeting you brought me, I'm still glad I know you."

They hugged again, and Bytoris eyed the wingmount warily. He shook his head. "But, though I thank you for your consideration, I'll walk home," he said. "I don't like the look of that thing."

Faia smiled a wry little smile. "The ride is nice—though sometimes it can be exciting."

He arched an eyebrow. "I've had enough excitement for a while." Then he turned and strode away, and within moments was lost to sight behind the tight-packed buildings of Bonton. Faia urged the extra wingmount forward, to send it back home. It launched itself off the platform, careened down at the stragglers who remained in the square below, and only built up enough speed to pull up at the last instant before it smashed into several fleeing people.

Faia winced, and Edrouss Delmuirie paled.

"You want me to ride one of those?" he asked.

"It isn't as bad as it looks," she lied. To herself she thought, *It's worse.*

"Well," he said, "I suppose I can try it this once." He swung into the saddle and grasped the reins.

Faia slipped onto her own mount's back, finding the placement of the wings as awkward as she ever had. She clicked her tongue, and urged her horse forward, and Edrouss did the same.

They swooped into the empty square—even the stragglers, having seen the first wingmount's less-than-graceful exit, had decided it was time to go home. Her heart lurched into her throat, and behind her, she heard Edrouss howl. Flight would allay the terror of the takeoff—actually flying on a wingmount was a sensation of freedom unlike anything else she had ever known. He would love it.

She decided not to mention to him until the last possible minute, however, that landings were always worse than takeoffs.

Chapter 40

Red light from the firepit illuminated the ancient mosaics in the First Folk dome, its flickering giving them a lifelike appearance that the presence of the two Klaue sitting beneath them only increased. The cat Hrogner—renamed Disaster—curled on the shoulder of the largest of the First Folk, purring; Kirgen had kindly fetched him from Omwimmee Trade to the ruins, where he had discovered he had the undivided attention of the Klaue, who had never seen anything like him.

Medwind, sitting cross-legged beside the fire, said, "Kirgen has definite confirmation that most of the lesser gods have returned."

Faia shivered. "What about—" She whispered her next word. "Hrogner?"

"His worshipers have been to his shrines regularly, taking the usual offerings. I don't know if he's returned, but from all reports, there is as much havoc across Arhel as there ever was. So he's probably back, too."

"Where did they go?" Faia thought of her Lady; she hoped both Lady and Lord had returned safely from wherever they had been.

"Kirgen has a theory—heretical, but it does make sense." Medwind put another log on the fire and rearranged the embers so that it burned higher. Even though summer had returned to Arhel, nights in the mountains remained cold. "He suggests that all gods but the Dreaming God are the manifestations of human desire mingling with the Dreaming God's magic. Kirgen argues that this would explain why—" She lowered her voice. "—*Hrogner*— vanished when you angered Sorrow and he dissolved his emeshest. All the other gods in Arhel vanished at the same time."

"He thinks *we* created our gods?" Faia had to agree with Medwind's assessment. The idea was heretical.

"His theory is that, once the Delmuirie Barrier went up, worshiping Arhelans unknowingly used the magic when they prayed, and created the gods they thought they were worshiping."

Faia raised an eyebrow. "So we gave ourselves the gods we deserved."

Medwind chuckled. "That's one way of looking at it. His theory would also explain why the gods didn't manifest physically until Arhel's magic ran wild. They didn't have enough available power to do it until then."

Faia considered it. "It's an interesting theory. I don't like it very much . . . but I'll think about it."

Medwind stretched until her joints cracked, then laughed. "It doesn't really matter, now. The magic is back, and so are the gods. I never paid much attention to them anyway— except sometimes to Etyt and Thiena. What really matters to me is that I'm young again. If I could manage it, I would be young forever. But since I can't make that happen, I'll take this second chance and enjoy it."

Faia smiled. "Will you be staying here?"

"Cooped up in these ruins reading about the dead past, while the world goes on without me and I grow old for real?" The Hoos woman shook her head. "Choufa wants to see the Hoos plains, and I have a few husbands I would like to look up—and I'm sure there will be plenty of fresh, horny young bucks I could catch if I can't find those. I'll have plenty of time for celibacy once I'm dead—for now, I want to get laid and have fun."

"So you'll go back to headhunting?" Faia asked her, suppressing the shudder she always felt when thinking about her friend's past.

Medwind laughed again. "Oh, no! I have a daughter now—that makes me eligible to sit in Council. I don't need to be a warrior anymore. I made my break with my gods Etyt and Thiena a year ago; I'm thinking about taking up with the god Stempfel and going into clan politics. The Songs have a long history of politicking; it is randy, low-down, and sometimes bloodier than our warrior history. Besides, I got plenty of practice when I was teaching at Daane University, back in Ariss. If I could handle that, I can handle the Hoos. I think a new job and four or five young husbands will be just what I need to make sure I'm appreciating life to the fullest."

Faia watched Edrouss's eyes grow round; she bit her lip to keep from laughing. "That certainly sounds . . . interesting," she said.

Medwind grinned at her. "Interesting. What a tepid word. It's going to be *fantastic*." She sat up and brushed her hair—still luminous, gleaming white—back from her face. "And what about you three? Have you decided where you'll be going next? Back to Omwimmee Trade, perhaps?" The warrior-mage laughed a gravelly laugh. "Or maybe Ariss? I'm sure they'll be delighted to see you there."

Faia sighed. "If they hadn't built the city on a swamp and counted on magic to keep it standing, they would have been fine. As it is, I've heard the mages and sajes will finish raising the last of the buildings from under the water within a year." She shook her head ruefully. "But, no—I don't think we'll be going to Ariss. I had hoped that by fixing Arhel's magic, I could get them to forgive me for the last tragedy I precipitated there. Somehow, I don't think that will happen now."

"Ah . . . no."

Edrouss cleared his throat. "We do have a plan, however."

Faia smiled at him, and he returned her smile.

He told Medwind, "We've been talking to the Klaue. They tell wonderful stories of the world outside of the Delmuirie Barrier, where humans and Klaue have built cities together, different from the separate places they once had. We thought we would travel with them when they return home."

"You're planning on leaving Arhel entirely?" Medwind looked stunned. "How? The Barrier is back."

"It didn't go up by accident this time. Sorrow left a door—well hidden from both directions, but permanent."

"What about Kirgen?"

"He and Roba have the twins, and these ruins, and their work with their universities, and all their goals. But we have different needs." Faia twisted the tip of her braid and stared at Kirtha, sleeping at the feet of the Klaue she had come to adore in the week all of them had been in the ruins. "I have no home here anymore, and neither does Edrouss. Kirtha needs to be away from magic for a while— at least until she learns to control her temper. . . ." Faia shook her head. "But it's more than that. I inherited my father's wanderlust. I want to see the world—and now I have the chance to go places no Arhelan has ever been." She clasped her hands together and leaned forward. The excitement of an unknown, unknowable future burned in her belly like the fire that danced in the firepit.

"Arhel is one tiny continent of a huge world. Outside of the Barrier, there is no magic, but the cities have grown without it. Imagine, Medwind—a whole world of humans and Klaue living side by side. New languages, new customs, wonders no one else in Arhel has ever seen. The Klaue want to go home. Irrarrar has his sister's bones; he wants to take them back to his family. When the Klaue go, we intend to go with them."

Medwind's smile was wistful. "The wonders there will have to be wondrous without me. I can never go outside of the Barrier."

Edrouss slid an arm around Faia's waist, and she moved closer to him. She rested her head on his shoulder and smiled at Medwind. "And yet you will be doing what you want to do, too. Our futures cannot be the same—we aren't the same, and the things that make you happy would not do so for me. But we'll meet again. As long as there is magic in Arhel, I will be able to find you. Someday I'll come back to Arhel with wonderful stories to tell, and you and I will sit beside a fire like this one, and tell our tales."

Medwind laughed. "Fair enough. In the meantime, our tales are waiting for us to live them."

Glossary

Air Tongue (Klaue) One of the four main languages of the ancient First Folk, used to work out ideas and for common conversation. The most flexible but also the most changeable of the Klaue languages, and like the other three, one that exists in both spoken and written form.

See also **Blood Tongue, Stone Tongue, Water Tongue**

Ancient Gekkish The linguistic precursor of modern Hoos in all three of its main forms and dialects.

Annin (Klaue) 1) A pejorative noun for the class of all things ground-bound. 2) The name the ancient First Folk gave to humankind.

antis (prob. Arissonese, ancient) The first meal of the day.

Arhel The small continent in the Southern Hemisphere of Trilling that has been, throughout much of its history, surrounded by the Delmuirie Barrier.

Arissonese Daughter-tongue of Old Arhelan, and if the speakers of all mutually comprehensible dialects are counted, one of the three most common languages in Arhel.

b'dabba (Hoos) The easily-transportable, mostly waterproof, fairly warm goat-felt hut that most Hoos call home. The dwelling adapted equally well to the broad Huong Hoos plains and the rocky, bitter cold fjords and hills of the Stone Teeth Hoos.

backlight lads (Omwimmee Trader) Young, unmarried men who offer themselves for the entertainment of bored Trader women—they seek their companions by going through the alleys looking for backdoor lamps that are lit during the day. While they are sometimes paid a small fee for their companionship, more frequently they are given gifts and if they suit their patrons, can hope for recommendations for regular work as jobs in town come open. Trader women do much of the hiring for the local businesses, and network compulsively.

banim Stately hardwood tree common in the northern and central inland regions of Arhel.

bletch (Old Arhelan) Enormous sea creature, large enough to eat a klaue whole and to attack and sink the largest of Arhelan wooden ships. Vicious, predatory, and fortunately rare within the Delmuirie Barrier, where it has been hunted nearly to extinction.

Blood Tongue (Klaue) The language of war and sex.

bonnechard (Hoos) The leaf of a desert succulent that, when dried and chewed, acts as a strong pain reliever and in most cases a mild soporific. One of its common side effects is a temporary lowering of inhibitions, with the result that some people who take it find themselves saying (and more rarely doing) things they later regret.

Bontonard ideographs (ancient, origin uncertain) Primitive pictographic form of written Arissonese, replaced very early in known history by the **Hortag-Ingesdotte script**. There are fifteen thousand common ideographs and an estimated two-hundred thousand ideographic combinations. The difficulty of the ideographic system has kept the literacy rate among those cultures that still use it (Bontonard, Kareen) low.

Bright Faia Rissedote's birthplace, which now only exists as a glassy spot on the side of a hill.

Caligro Sehchon, god of engineers One of the minor deities of Bonton. Mostly benign.

Celebration of New Souls (Kareen) Festival of the Kareen hill-folk (Faia's birth culture) in which, during the fourteen-day Month of Ghosts and the **Festival of Darkness**, the fertile women attempt to become pregnant, so that the souls of their deceased loved ones, now waiting to be reborn, can find a home among those who already love them.

cherticorn A common grain crop grown for milling into flour and to be made into cereals. Coarse and dry, but hardy and resistant to blight.

chud jerky Jerky made of dried smoked chud fish, an oily fish with an overpowering smell and taste. Because of its high fat content, chud jerky makes a good travel food for adverse conditions.

Daane University (Ariss) Medwind Song's alma màter and at one time the women-only magical university that ruled Mage-Ariss. Still one of the best universities in Arhel, though a bit stuffy.

day-blooming fox-roses Large perennial flowers on tall slender stalks that bloom with the first warm weather. Found in meadows and on hillsides. Commonly pink, fuchsia, and white. Unrelated to cultivated roses.

Delmuirie Barrier The barrier that has, for all of its known human history locked the continent of Arhel behind a wall of impenetrable magic.

Dorrell Province Independent political region that encompasses Bonton and much of the Kareen highlands.

Doweth Ecclesiastic Gate One of the purpose-specific gates built around the wall that protects Bonton. Visitors' ingress and egress are no longer limited to the applicable gate, but in earlier times, the religious went in through the Doweth Ecclesiastic Gate, merchants through **Timnett Merchanter**, and so on. Bonton has sixteen separate gates.

drypress A pale green paper made of pulped and pressed seaweed, algae, and other water plants. The process of its manufacture is complex, and its manufacture is one of the larger industries besides fishing found in seaside towns.

eahnnk gurral (Klaue) Literally 'burning memory'—however, the relationship of the term to a Klaue festival remains mysterious.

ecuvek (Huong Hoos) Literally, 'perverse and unclean.' As used by Medwind Song, it merely demonstrates that she does not share the tastes of some of her fellow Hoos, who don't think goats are **ecuvek** at all.

emeshest (Old Arhelan) 1) Literally, 'the aura of a god.' 2) A powerful field of magic that holds everything within it in stasis.

erda (Kareen) The unattractive all-purpose rectangular overwrap of the Kareen hill-folk. Serves as a poncho, a blanket, and even a tarp. Waterproof, warm and unflattering.

Etyt and Thiena (Huong Hoos) The male and female Huong Hoos gods of war and warriors. Medwind Song's first gods.

Falchus (Ancient) Prehistoric god of unknown aspect. The god most familiar to Edrouss Delmuirie.

Faljon (Kareen) Folk philosopher commonly quoted by the Kareen hill-folk. Though the Kareen tell stories of his life, he may be apocryphal.

Father Dark (Kareen) One aspect of the Lord, consort of the Lady. In this aspect, he is the gatherer and teacher of souls, as well as he who leads them to the Lady's Wheel of Life when their souls prepare to return to human form or move on other planes of existence.

Festival of Darkness, see **Celebration of New Souls**

Fetupad (Forst)   Lovely, temperamental God of Beasts, and a favorite in Forst mythology. Nearly every Arhelan animal has a Fetupad story on how it came to be the way it is.

First Folk   The "First Folk" were long thought to be the human ancestors of the current people of Arhel, until an exploratory team discovered a ruined city and the remains of the non-human Klaue who were the true first inhabitants of Arhel. (For further information, read *Bones of the Past.*)

Fisher Province   Far southern province of Arhel notable for its lousy, cold, rainy weather and primitive living conditions.

Flatterland (Kareen)   Mildly pejorative term for anyplace where there aren't lots of hills or mountains.

Forst   Capitol city of Forst Province.

Forst Province   North-eastern province of Arhel, bitter enemy of Dorrell Province and the Bontonards, and home of a people who exhibit markedly isolationist tendencies.

gallens (Klaue)   Huge, movable wooden screens that served the First Folk in place of hinge-hung wooden doors and shutters.

Galtennor   Eight-armed patron deity of the city of Omwimmee Trade. Each of his eight arms represents

MIND OF THE MAGIC   301

a different aspect of the Trader Ethos. Those eight aspects are Justice, Generosity, Profit, Craftsmanship, Mass Appeal, High Sell-Through, Low Returns and Prompt Payment.

Hada and Bnokt Amatory gods of the Celeidighe Fischebede religion. Hada is the God of the Perpetual Iron Rod; Bnokt is also called The Howling Goddess. According to their priests, Hada and Bnokt have not uncoupled since the creation of time itself. Their most ardent followers strive to emulate them.

Hortag-Ingesdotte script, see **Bontonard ideographs**

hovie Generic term for the hot-blooded, scaled, six-limbed fliers (most types have four wings and two legs) that are everywhere in Arhel. The hovie is one of many Arhelan species built on the six-limbed frame—comparative anatomical studies show that although hovies have analogous features with the equally common four-limbed creatures, there are no point-by-point parallels that would indicate a common ancestral heritage at any time in the past.

Hrogner (Ariss) Saje god of mischief.

Huong Hoos The head-hunting, polyandrous plains dwellers of the south-eastern portion of Arhel.

Kedwar the Finder Bontonard god of those who search.

kekkis (Klaue) A succinct translation would be either 'junk,' 'mess,' or 'crap.'

kellink Six-legged pack hunters and scavengers whose saliva is a deadly toxin, and who hunt by biting their prey and waiting for it to die and rot.

Keyu The deadly, magic-storing God Trees of the Wen Tribes who live in the unmapped jungles north of the Wen Tribes Treaty Line.

Klog A pejorative term for the Klaue, or First Folk. While this term was commonly used during Delmuirie's time, it was rarely uttered in the actual presence of the Klaue.

Lady's Gift (Kareen) Common term for magic used by hill folk who find themselves able to control it.

Mocking God One aspect of the god of tricksters, practical jokers and sadists.

nondes (Arissonese) The night meal, generally a light one.

Old Arhelan Precursor language to Arissonese and its many dialects.

oogins (Kareen) The little folk reputed to play pranks and do favors for children and kind adults.

ourzurd (pronounced WOO-zerd) An ancient word of uncertain origin. A mighty user of magic.

Ranchek the Trickster Another aspect of **Hrogner**. See also **Mocking God**.

Remling Tower Bonton's overdone version of City Hall and the county courthouse.

rit The Bontonard base unit of currency.

sixteen blue hells of Fargorn The ancient Bontonard religion of the Five relates the tale of Fargorn, a man who was never able to find anything once he it put down. Five mythology relates that at his death, his body disappeared into the same place where all his belongings had vanished previously, and that he became the ruler of the unhappy land, and took over responsibility for making sure the belongings of other people got lost.

Skeeree (Klaue) Name for the ruined First Folk city discovered by Medwind Song and Nokar the Librarian. (For further information, read *Bones of the Past*.)

Spavvekith Language of the peregrinating Fisher folk whose origins are in the cold and primitive Fisher Province.

Stone Tongue (Klaue) The language of irrevocable contracts and law. Anything said or written in stone tongue is binding to the writer and to the one for whom the writing is done.

taada kaneddu (Hoos) A god-desert or a taboo place. A place from which all magic has fled.

Temple of Horse-Dancers Gold-topped temple just north of Bonton belonging to an ancient cult that worships horses. Only a few of the Horse Dancers remain, and because their rites are secret, little is known of them.

Terrfaire Septoriim Terrfaire was the poet laureate of Bonton in the Age of Gold. His stories, songs, and poems evoke the long-past beauty and grandeur of the Age of Gold while foreshadowing the sentiment and romanticism of the Humanic Age that followed. His greatest works are widely considered to be the epic fifteen-poem **Maradian Bell Cycle**, the stark **Three Lies and the Maiden**, and the sweet, yet sad **Trees of Unterlei.**

Thessi Ravi Spear-breasted, unreasonable, fiery-tempered female god of war to the Celeidighe Fischebede, most of whose believers reside in Omwimmee Trade and the surrounding region.

Timnett Merchanter The famous merchants' gate in Bonton.

vigonia A popular, easily-cultivate healing herb that also makes an attractive ground cover.

wajeros The paid magic-users of Bonton. Considered by the Bontonards to be the only real professional magic users in the world.

Water Tongue (Klaue) The Klaue spiritual language.

wingmounts The experimental flying horses first developed by the Mottemage of Daane University, and further developed after her death to become one of the most commercial of the properties of that university. (For further information, read *Fire in the Mist*.)